SECRET ISAAC

JEROME CHARYN

 A BARD BOOK/PUBLISHED BY AVON BOOKS

AVON BOOKS
A division of
The Hearst Corporation
959 Eighth Avenue
New York, New York 10019

First Bard Printing, November, 1980

BARD IS A TRADEMARK OF THE HEARST CORPORATION
AND IS REGISTERED IN MANY COUNTRIES AROUND THE WORLD,
MARCA REGISTRADA, HECHO EN U.S.A.

Printed in the U.S.A.

SECRET ISAAC

PART
ONE

ONE

Who's the lad that barks at us and bites our cheeks? Tiger John, Tiger John. They sang that in the hall when he wasn't around, those Irishers from the Commissioner's office. They laughed at him and feared him too. You couldn't tell where his rage would fall. He was a crisp little man with gray hair that had lost its shine and turned a bitter yellow. It was like straw, that crop of dead yellow hair, but it didn't ruin his looks. He was sixty-one years old, and he had the energies and the eager face of a slightly dumb boy.

The Irishers couldn't remember if he'd been a captain in the Bronx, or a shoofly for the Chief Inspector. You didn't talk about his past. John had lived in deep winter a long, long time. He was attached to a little Irish club on First Avenue for decrepit and alcoholic cops until he came out of retirement with the Honorable Sammy Dunne. They were brothers of a sort, the Mayor and his Commissioner of Police.

The PC would closet himself for an hour and comb his dead yellow hair. At the old Headquarters John had a fireplace and a private balcony and his own elevator car. He could ride up and down as often as he liked. No one but his First Deputy could use that car. Now he didn't even have a First Deputy to comfort him. His First Dep was gone. Disappeared into the dust. The famous Isaac Sidel. This Isaac was always on some idiotic mission.

John had a sudden thirst for tea. He didn't have to yell for his chauffeur. Chinatown was across the street. He chose a small dirty cafe, the China Pot, where he wouldn't be recognized as the "Commish." Policemen didn't come here. It was a hole in the wall on Baxter Street.

You couldn't see Tiger John from the window. He sat at a table that was obscured by the counter, a crooked shelf, and the coffee urn, and he drank green tea. He had chicken buns and a cookie made of almond paste. John felt a sudden wind in the cafe. He looked up from his tea and buns. "Jesus, is that Jamey O'Toole?" he said to the man at the next table. The man was six feet seven, and his legs took up half the China Pot. It wasn't his impossible size that disturbed Tiger John. He could live with such prodigious things. But *two* Irishmen in the same cafe, that was a bad idea.

Jamey flipped a bankbook into the Commissioner's lap. "A present for you . . . from the king." John cupped the little book in his hands and opened it under the table. The amount was six thousand dollars and twenty-three cents. The name was *Nosey Flynn*.

"Boyo," he said in a whisper, "how am I going to create the signature of Mr. Nosey Flynn?"

Jamey told him to use his left fist.

John had a pile of these bankbooks. He held them together with a rubber band. They arrived from O'Toole with different names in them. The names were always Irish. *Simon Dedalus. Paddy Dignam. Gertrude Mac-Dowell, Molly and/or Leopold Bloom . . .*

Who the hell was this king of Jamey's? An Irish thug with an Ivy League education. He removed himself to Dublin, because the freeze was on. The Special State Prosecutor, Dennis Mangen, had begun to ride herd over the City. It was Mangen who made life so miserable for Tiger John. Mangen ate up Police Commissioners.

"Jamey, don't come down here anymore."

"Why not?"

"Because I don't want Mangen to catch your ass in Chinatown. He'll wonder why you've been traveling so far."

Jamey smiled. "What's new with the great god Dennis?"

"Shut your mouth," John said. Mangen had a squad of

shooflies, and the shooflies went into every crack. They could have been hiding in the China Pot. "You belong uptown . . . go on."

O'Toole got up from the table. He had to walk with a slanted step. There was no room for his shoulders in the cafe. He stopped near the door and called back to the Commissioner. "How's your First Dep?"

"I haven't seen a hair of him."

"I have," Jamey said. "He mucks around Forty-seventh Street in filthy clothes."

"That's Sheeny Isaac . . . the brains of the Department. He's a bit of a psychopath, if you ask me. Mooning over a dead boy. You remember Manfred Coen?"

"Blue Eyes," Jamey said with a sneer.

"That's the baby. Isaac's daughter put a jinx on Coen."

She was a hungry girl, Marilyn the Wild. The daughter put out for anything in pants. She was the marrying kind. She'd have herself a husband, and shed him in a week. The poor girl went bats in the head. She fell for Isaac's "angel," Blue Eyes Coen. But Isaac wasn't giving Coen away. He tossed him to a family of Bronx pimps, and Blue Eyes got killed. Now Isaac walks around in rags, chasing pimps and lamenting Coen.

"Give him my love, Jamey, if you catch that stinky man on the street."

Both of them hated Sheeny Isaac. O'Toole had been thrown out of the Department, robbed of pension and shield by Isaac the Brave. He had to grovel for the king. He delivered bankbooks to John in a dirty cafe.

John dialed his chauffeur from the China Pot after O'Toole went out the door. "Christie, I'm on Baxter Street . . ." He wouldn't have an Irish chauffeur carry him around. An Irish chauffeur would have sung to him from the driver's seat. John didn't want that much familiarity in his car. Christianson was a Swede, and the Swedes were quiet.

"Cheerio," he said to the Chinese counterman. "So long, boys." His black Mercury was outside the China Pot. He climbed over the curb, and he was gone from Baxter Street, Chinatown, and Police Headquarters. The cushions inside the Mercury were his chief comfort. No one could pester John, or attack him as the PC, when he sat on those high cushions.

A blinking light on the radiotelephone box destroyed

his good cheer. It was the Mayor's light. John picked up the phone. He had to make sure it was Sammy on the line, and not one of those dunderheads from the Mayor's office.

"Your Honor . . . is that you?"

"Himself," the Mayor said.

Sammy had turned remote. He was up for reelection, and he didn't need the Tiger hanging on his tails. *Isaac* was the Mayor's hero. *Isaac* was the grand boy. The newspapers reviled Tiger John. They called him the "Know-Nothing Commish." Isaac could dance in his own shit, and the Police reporters would sniff for gold. They loved whatever sloppy music the First Dep made. It didn't matter to them that Sheeny Isaac had removed himself and gone into the Manhattan wilderness. He was their favorite child.

"I'll be having my bath tonight . . . tell the lads to give it a good scrub. How are you, Johnny?"

"In the pink."

He'd become a buffoon for Mayor Sam, a Commissioner who could be trundled in and out of the closet, depending upon the political climate. These were John's closet days. You never found him at the little parties Sam liked to give. John was keeper of the bath. His club had installed a sauna room for Mayor Sam, so "Hizzoner" would have somewhere to hide. It was John's function to regulate the sauna's heated rocks by spilling cups of water over them. Such were the duties of a Police Commissioner.

The Mayor's light went off. John put the receiver back on the cradle and muttered to himself. *Now that he's in trouble he wants his bath.*

"Take me to the Dingle," John barked.

Tiger John Rathgar was a Dingle Bay boy. The Dingle was *his* club. It began as a kind of temperance league for drunken Irish cops. The Sons of Dingle had the right cure. They would pound that terrible love of "the whiskey" out of any man. John had an added moral obligation. He would visit with the wives, and seduce them if he could. The Dingles had more than temperance on their minds. They were bully boys in the County of Manhattan. They collected bills for local merchants and delivered votes for Democrats who could afford the price. But they'd grown a little obsolete. They couldn't whack men and women

12

outside a polling booth, even with Tiger John as "Commish."

He arrived at a battered storefront on First Avenue: the Dingle Bay. It made no pretense of being a gentleman's club. It was for the hairy Irish. Crossbones were painted on the window, crossbones and a harp. Its sills were crumbling, and its metal awning was eaten with rust. Yet no other society of Hibernian cops could boast a sauna bath.

John sent the Mercury home to Chinatown and made three long knocks on the club's iron door. It was a signal to his mates.

He had to knock again. "It's me . . . John."

The door opened enough to let him through. Jesus, it was dark in there. Those lads didn't believe in sunlight. They had a fetish about covering their freckled pates. Summer and winter, indoors and out, they would wear eight-piece caps of pure Donegal wool. The caps left a deep mark on their foreheads. They were proud of the "Donegal" mark. Others wore black derbies. They were lads from the Retired Sergeants Association who would visit the Dingle from time to time.

John shucked off his suit jacket. He didn't have to play Commissioner at the Dingle. He could go about in his shirtsleeves and not feel compromised.

"Kiddos, the Mayor's coming tonight."

The old men chuckled to themselves. They built a sauna for Mayor Sammy Dunne, but they weren't so fond of Sam.

"Christ, we haven't cleared out the piss from the last time he was here . . . we won't disappoint His Grace. We'll mop up the putrid thing . . . how goes it at the Headquarters, John?"

"The usual shit," he said. "I can't complain."

His Chief Inspector was retiring in another few months. McNeill had a castle in the Old Country. He'd live in it like a duke and fish for salmon in his waters. What would happen to John? He was already shy a First Dep. He'd have to whistle for Isaac.

The old men were in a singing mood. They had their bottles of root beer and Tiger John. It was a temperance society, and they wouldn't keep liquor in the house. They would run next door to sneak Irish whiskey into the root beer.

> We're the Sons of Dingle Bay
> The wild geese who left our home
> Who left our home
> Who left our home
> For Ameriky . . .

It's true, true, Johnny said. *Wild geese. Gone from home.* The Dingles were lucky. They didn't have to preside over Police Headquarters. They could visit the Mother Country, like Coote McNeill and old Tim Snell, and those other lads from the Retired Sergeants Association. Live in Wexford or Dublin half the year. Bring back neckerchiefs, derbies, and a fresh box of Donegal hats.

> We're the Sons of Dingle Bay . . .

The song rid him of Sheeny Isaac. John didn't have to think of Isaac, Chief Inspector McNeill, or the Mayor's bath. He brushed his tongue over a bottle of root beer and began to sing:

> Who left our home
> Who left our home
> For Americky . . .

TWO

THERE was once an old man who had a worm in his gut. The worm liked to wiggle. The old man would clutch at himself, as if to tear out the insides of his body. He lived at a disgusting hotel on West Forty-seventh Street. The hotel didn't even have a name. It was just off Whores' Row. The pimps stayed clear of him. They kept suites at this hotel for all the "brides" they owned, or managed. The "brides" were black girls under nineteen. At least one of them was pregnant. They enjoyed the old man. He wouldn't snarl at them, or look under their summer shirts. A whore's sweaty nipples couldn't surprise him.

So they talked to the old bum, shared orange drinks, confided in him. These "brides" had their own corners. No one could intrude on their rights. If it rained, they worked out of little storefront parlors. It was a rotten year. Five dollars could get you half the world. There was nothing, nothing they wouldn't do for a man. The "brides" were on the street twenty hours a day. The old man could see the rawness in their necks, the hysteria when they would grab at a john and say, "Honey, goin' out?" The seduction was very thin. The black girls were faithful to their pimps. Most of the white whores, who worked the same streets, hated any man who touched them. They were dykes and religious freaks. They'd grown

15

suspicious of the old bum. They wouldn't kiss their girl-friends in front of him. They tried to get their "players" to run him off the street.

The old man had an odd immunity. It had something to do with the worm. He'd been at war with a retarded family of South American pickpockets and thieves. This family had given him the worm. The old man killed one of them, maimed another, and threw the rest of them into some foreign hell. They were groveling in Barcelona, selling parrots with split beaks. And this old man had their worm in his belly, a hookworm that was eating him inch by inch.

Certain men would step out of shiny Buicks and whisper to the old bum. They were much too regal to be members of any vice squad, and they didn't wear the wide trousers of homicide boys. The pimps would wonder to themselves: who is this geek? Their friends at the nearest precinct grew mum when you mentioned the old man with the worm.

He developed a lousy odor. He didn't think much about changing his pants. He wouldn't shave more than once a week. He fed his worm at a Greek dive on Eighth Avenue and Forty-fifth. He would eat salads and whole wheat bread. Then he'd give in to his appetite and crawl to Ninth Avenue for a cappuccino. It was a weakness he had. Strong coffee and steamed milk.

The coffee was bad for his worm. Its thousand little hooks grabbed at the old man's intestines, and he would stumble through the street, saying, "Fuck, God, shit," or whatever madness came into his head. He would avoid the coffee for five or six days. Then he couldn't help himself.

It was after one of these cappuccino fits, when the worm was twisting him half to death, that he saw her on Forty-third Street. It wasn't a good corner for a prostitute. There was always a heavy load of cops that guarded the trucking lanes around the *New York Times* building. The Mayor was scared of the *New York Times*. He had his Police Commissioner, Tiger John, flood Forty-third Street with cops in and out of uniform. So who had stationed this girlie over here? Some forlorn "player," a beginner's pimp who hadn't learned the truths of Times Square? She was no mulatto queen. The old bum watched her in profile. A white whore who didn't have that hard

16

glint of a manhater. She was beautiful. She should have been a rich man's escort, not a bimbo in the street.

The old bum wasn't filled with lecheries. He wouldn't have brought this beauty to his hotel. He had a daughter with the same skinny ankles. The daughter was a sucker for men. She couldn't keep from getting married and divorced. She was on her seventh husband, and she was only twenty-nine. He decided to play the father to this beauty, chase her from Forty-third Street before the Chief Inspector's men picked her up. But he was trembling at the fineness of her nose. Why didn't some Cadillac whisk her off to White Plains? She was a girl to marry, not whore with. Then the old man saw the other side of her face.

It was scarred, wickedly scarred. She had the imprint of what seemed to be a knuckle, as if she'd been gouged with a metal fist. He took a closer look. The letter "D" had been scratched into her face. Christ. A scarlet letter on Forty-third Street.

"Miss, you can't stay here. The cops are fond of this corner. You'd better shove up to Forty-fifth."

"I can't." She smiled, and the gruesome letter wriggled on her cheek. "I don't have a union card. The other girls would bite my ass."

"Who's looking after you?"

"Martin McBride." The smile ended, and the "D" corrected itself.

"Well, this Martin is an idiot. Is he the one who put you in the street?"

The scarred beauty turned agitated.

"Mister, take me somewhere, or go away. Martin doesn't like me talking to strangers."

She didn't have a bimbo's voice, and it confused the old bum. He had no plans to undress her. "What's your name?"

"Annie."

"Annie what?"

"Isn't Annie enough for you?" she said. "It's Annie Powell."

He smuggled her into a French restaurant on Forty-eighth Street, Au Tunnel. The headwaiter was frightened to throw him out. The old bum had twenties in his pocket and a Diners Club card.

Annie Powell laughed. "God, you're crazy."

17

"Who's Martin McBride?"

"Somebody's uncle," she said. "That's all."

The old man pointed to the scar. "Did he do that?"

"No."

They drank a muscatel, had scallops, green beans, trout, and a chocolate mousse.

"Mister, how are you going to make me earn this meal? I might not be kinky enough for you." He hadn't told her his name.

The bum gave her forty dollars. "Do me a favor, Annie Powell. Stay off the street for the rest of the night."

The old man was irritated. He'd gone to his hotel room, but he couldn't sleep. He had visions of Annie being pawed by bull-dykes in some detention cell. "Shit," he said. He put on his clothes, and walked downtown to Centre Street. It was the site of the old, neglected Police Headquarters. Its rooms were abandoned now. The Police had moved to a giant red monolith in Chinatown. Only a few extraneous cops watched the floors of Centre Street, for rats and other vermin. Most of the files were removed. Even the photo unit in the basement was gone. There was a guard at the main desk, but the old man had no trouble getting into the building. He didn't have to flash any identification card. He went up to the third floor, walked through a clutch of rooms, and entered an office with an oak door. The office had a telephone. It was the only phone in the building that worked. He dialed the new Headquarters and shouted into the phone. "I told you," he said. "A cunt named Annie Powell. If she's taken off the street, if she's bothered, if she's touched, I'll flop the whole pussy patrol. And find out who this Martin McBride is. Does he have a nephew with a name that begins with a big D? . . . yes, a *D* . . . like dumb . . . or dim . . . or dead."

He hung up the phone, and managed to fall asleep. He didn't have much of a rest. A boy from the Mayor's office rang him up. His Honor had fled the coop again, walked out of Gracie Mansion in his pajamas on a midnight stroll.

The old bum took a cab uptown. He had the cabbie rake the streets around Carl Schurz Park. Then he got off. His Honor, Mayor Sam, had gone down to Cherokee Place. He didn't seem deprived in striped pajamas and a red silk robe. When he saw the old bum he began to weep.

He was sixty-nine, and he'd turned senile on the Democratic Party over the past two years.

"Laddie, what happened to you?"

"It's nothing, Your Honor," the old bum said. "Just the clothes I'm wearing."

"You gave me a fright," the Mayor said. "We have to fatten you up."

His own aides accused him of being a decrepit fool. He belongs in a nursery, they said. Ancient Sam. But he had no difficulty recognizing the old bum. The Mayor was as lucid as a man in pajamas could ever be. It wasn't a drifting head that brought him out of his mansion. It was a fit of anxiety. All his politics was shrinking around him. Most of his deputies had abandoned Sammy Dunne. He was a Mayor without a Party. He'd become a ghost in the City of New York. You didn't speak of Mayor Sam.

He still wept for the old bum.

"Isaac, I know the enemies you have. They'll eat you alive after I'm gone."

"Let them eat, Your Honor. I've got plenty of hide for them."

"Laddie, what are you talking about? You're skin and bones."

The old bum was thinking of Annie Powell. That scar of hers stuck to him. Annie's "D." He walked the Mayor home to Gracie Mansion and went to his hotel without a name.

THREE

WHY should a whore have turned his head, a bimbo with damaged goods? She couldn't have fared very well with that gash on her face. The worm was biting at him. "Cunt," he told the worm, "are you in love with her too?" He would stroll down to Forty-third to be sure no one molested her. His shuffling with his hands in his pockets didn't please Annie Powell. She couldn't have too many clients with an old bum hanging around. "We're having lunch," he would say. "Come on." It sounded like a threat to her, not an invitation. And she had to leave her corner.

This time he took her to the Cafe des Sports. A bum and a girl in a whore's midriff eating liver pâté. "Annie," he said, "there's going to be a raid at two o'clock. The Commissioner has decided to grab single women off the streets. So you'd better have a long, long lunch."

They had three bottles of wine. "What's your name?" she said, with a drunken growl, "and what the hell do you want from me?"

"Just say I'm Father Isaac."

"A priest," she said, mimicking him, "a priest without a collar . . . is it your hotel or mine, Father Isaac? . . . I perform better in strange hotels."

"Don't bluff me, Annie Powell. You haven't done too

20

many tricks . . . I want to know who put you on the street?"

"Mister," she said, "that's none of your business."

The old bum had to let her go. The worm dug into his bowels when he thought of her going into doorways with other men, getting down on her knees for them. He had to find this Martin McBride and break his Irish toes. But Father Isaac had an appointment today. He washed the dirt off his neck. He shaved the hairs under his nose that might have been construed as a crooked mustache. He bought a half-hour's time of the hotel's single bathtub. You wouldn't have recognized him when he stepped out of the tub. The old bum had shed twenty years. He had a pair of argyle socks in his room. He unwrapped the only suit in his closet. A silk shirt materialized from his drawer. A tie from Bloomingdale's. Underpants that were soft enough for a woman's skin. The ensemble pulled together. A younger man, fifty, fifty-one, emerged from the hotel. He had a sort of handsomeness. The worm had helped redefine the contours of his face. It gave him character and fine hollows in his cheeks.

A cab brought him to a lounge at the New School for Social Research. People shook his hand. He was more despised than worshiped here, but everybody knew him. Isaac Sidel, First Deputy Police Commissioner of New York and mystery cop. He was fond of disappearing, of putting on one disguise after the other. He wouldn't sit at his offices on the thirteenth floor of Police Headquarters. Isaac called the new brick monolith a "coffin house." He did all his paperwork at the old, abandoned Headquarters. You had to search him out at Centre Street, or in some hobo's alley. Isaac was unavailable most of the time. His deputies were loyal to him. They ran his offices without a piece of discord. Isaac could always get a message inside.

The PC, Handsome Johnny Rathgar, couldn't scold him. Isaac was becoming a hero with all the news services. He would walk into a den of crazed Rastafarians and come out with a cache of machine guns. He settled disputes with rival teenaged gangs in the Bronx, parceling out territories to one, taking away bits from the other. Arsonists and child molesters would only surrender themselves to First Deputy Sidel. Isaac had no fear in him. He danced with any lunatic who came up close. You

21

could throw bricks at him off the roofs. Isaac wouldn't duck his head. The First Dep was in great demand. Most organizations in the City wanted to hear him speak. Synagogues, churches, political clubs. Either to heckle him or clap. The Democrats had to live with him for now, because he was close to Sammy Dunne, and it was a little too early to drive "Hizzoner" out of Gracie Mansion. But the Mayor was about to turn seventy, and he couldn't hold a squabbling Party together. The Democrats would lash at Isaac when Sammy vacated City Hall. Republicans were frightened of Isaac's popularity, and the Liberals hated his guts. He was only a cop to them. Isaac despised them all, hacks and politicians who would grab the coat of any winner, and sneer at a Mayor's loss of power. He liked the old Mayor, who was being jettisoned by his Party. The Mayor didn't have a chance in the primaries. He was too dumb, too weak, too old. The *Daily News* had already spoken. New York would have its first Lady Mayor, the honorable Rebecca Karp, who'd come to politics via the beauty line. She was Miss Far Rockaway of 1947. She grabbed votes for Democrats with her bosoms, her bear hugs, and her smiles. She'd been a district leader in Greenwich Village. Now she was Party boss of Manhattan and the Bronx. Rebecca needed *two* boroughs to fight the pols of Brooklyn and save New York from the bumbling political machine of Samuel Dunne.

Isaac was here, at the New School, in liberal territories, to act as the Mayor's dog in debate with Melvin Pears, sachem of the Civil Liberties Union, and a defender of Rebecca Karp. Isaac could have told Rebecca to shit in her hat, but Mayor Sam was in trouble. He hardly went downtown to visit City Hall. His margins were being eaten away. Isaac was the only voice of strength he had.

Pears was seated with the First Dep at a table near the end of the lounge. The Mayor swore that Melvin was romancing Becky Karp, but Isaac didn't always believe Mayor Sam. Melvin came from an aristocratic family, and he had a pretty wife. He was a man of thirty-five, with a fondness for rough clothes: he had workingman's boots at the New School and a cowboy shirt with a button open on his paunch. The boy likes to eat, Isaac observed, thinking of the worm he himself had to nourish. The wife sat next to Melvin. She had unbelievable gray-green eyes that sucked out Isaac with great contempt. He wondered where her shirts came from. The wife wasn't wearing Western clothes. Isaac felt uncomfortable sitting near those boots of Mel's. He shouldn't have arrived in argyle socks. His bum's pants would have held him better in this lounge.

Pears called Isaac a lackey of the Mayor, an instrument of repressive law. Isaac, he said, who drives prostitutes off the street at the Mayor's convenience, without considering the plight of these girls, or their histories. "I'll defend every prostitute you haul in," Pears said. "His Honor always sweeps out before the primaries. You're Sammy's broom."

Isaac growled inside his head. Sammy had enough trouble getting in and out of his pajamas. Isaac couldn't figure what was going on in the street. He had his spies. It wasn't the Civil Liberties Union that was keeping the girls hard at work. You couldn't hold them in a cage for more than half an hour. They had a league of bondsmen holding hands with their "players." The whores multiplied with or without the Police. Inspectors at Isaac's office claimed to know every dude in town. They talked of a mysterious nigger gang that was organizing the pimps into some kind of union. Black Mafia, they said. The "blues" of Sugar Hill. Only you couldn't find any of them. Where were the "blues" of Sugar Hill? It made no sense. Isaac's spies had nothing to sell. They shrugged their shoulders and swore some "heavy shit" was landing in the gutters. That's why Isaac had to go underground, become the old man of Forty-seventh Street. Isaac only trusted what he himself could sniff. And this Melvin Pears was babbling about whores' rights. Every bimbo in Manhattan had more rights and privileges than Rebecca Karp or Pears' green-eyed wife.

Pears had a bald spot, bigger than Isaac's. He was still chopping at the First Dep. "All the glory comes to you," Pears said. "You solve the big number, the big hit, and anonymous old men and women are afraid to go out at night."

Isaac interrupted him. "Would you like us to keep every fourteen-year-old boy in a bullpen after six o'clock?"

Pears leapt on Isaac. "That's the smug answer you can always get from a cop. Arrest *everybody* and crime will go away."

Isaac didn't have Melvin's courtroom wit. He shut his

mouth and let the boy talk. His head drifted to Annie Powell. That "D" on her could sting a man's eyes. That girl's no goddamn hooker. She was being punished for something she did. Annie's sin.

Pears had stopped talking. What was Isaac supposed to do? Defend Mayor Sam? List Police accomplishments? Talk about the new Headquarters and that idiot, Tiger John? Promise an end to sodomy in the women's house of detention? Isaac talked about Oswald Spengler. Pears scratched his head. Rebecca Karp's admirers must have considered him a little cracked. "It's ungovernable," Isaac said. ". . . this terrain. Psychosis is everywhere . . . in your armpit . . . under your shoe. You can smell it in the sweat of this room . . . we're all baby killers, repressed or not . . . how do you measure a man's rage? Either we behave like robots, or we kill. Why do you expect your Police Force to be any less crazy than you?"

There was laughter in the room, some hissing.

Pears shouted at him. "Sidel, you haven't gotten to the point at all. What do I care about your philosophies? Silly contrivances. Glib remarks. We do have a City, and it has to be governed. And the Mayor, *your friend,* is doing an invisible job."

The debate was over. People were congratulating Melvin Pears. He'd gotten around the ignorant carp of a half-educated cop. Isaac only had one semester at Columbia College. He couldn't have told you about the theories of John Locke. He had bits of Nietzsche in him, Spengler, Hegel, and Marx. His readings were savagely curtailed.

Crowds formed close to the lawyer Pears. One old lady came up to Isaac. She was muttering something he couldn't understand. All Isaac could make out was the green in Mrs. Pears' eyes.

One of his own inspectors, Marvin Winch, was waiting for him on the curb. Isaac promised himself that he would manufacture several little talks before he entered another lounge. Pears had cut out Isaac's throat. The First Dep had only a skimpy sense of logic. His ideas came from the worm in his gut. He wasn't a civilized man.

"Well?" Isaac said to Inspector Winch. "Who's Martin McBride?"

"A lowlife. He runs with the nigger pimps."

"Does he have a nephew?"

24

"Yes, a carload of them. Our Martin's got nephews everywhere."

"How many of them have that big *D* I told you about?"

"Only one. Dermott."

"Dermott McBride?"

"No. He took the Irish out of his name. He shortened it to Bride."

"Bring that cocksucker to me. I'd like to have a chat with Dermott Bride. We have a girlfriend in common."

"Isaac, I can't. Nobody knows where Dermott is."

"Then plug into your computer and find him for me."

Oh, they could laugh and call him Sammy's dunce, but Tiger John Rathgar had eyes and ears, like any man, and a mouth to bark with and eat cigarette paper when he was in the mood. A year ago "Hizzoner" had said, "Johnny, the pimps have to live like the rest of us. What's the point of chasing nigger girls off the street? They'll be strolling again in twenty-four hours." So John throttled his pussy patrol, yanked out most of its teeth, and then the bankbooks began coming in. With the Irish names inside. Simon Dedalus, Molly Bloom, and all. John didn't perform one crooked act to earn his *Molly Blooms*. He promised nothing to the pimps of Whores' Row. Could he help it if Jamey O'Toole tossed bankbooks in his lap?

Now it was an election year, and "Hizzoner" wanted the Black Marias out, wagons to hold nigger prostitutes. John had to activate the pussy patrol. But the Mayor warned him, "No white girls. We can't afford a mistake. If your lads pick up a housewife, the papers will crucify us. I'm depending on you, Johnny boy."

John went along with the pussy patrol. His chauffeur, Christianson, put him in front of the Black Marias, which were ancient green wagons with dented roofs. John decided what whores would go into the wagons. He picked the fattest girls, girls with low midriffs and pockmarks on their thighs. The wagons filled up in less than an hour. The girls sat in them and bitched. They couldn't get away from the heat of their own bodies. They tore at their midriffs to cool themselves, and they took long bites of air. John signaled to his chauffeur. "Christie, I've had enough. Come on."

"Where are we going, boss?"

"To the Mayor's house."

Christianson flipped his sirens on and shot across town, ahead of ambulances and fire trucks, and brought the "Commish" to Carl Schurz Park. The policeman came out of his sentry box to salute Tiger John and open the gate for him. John walked under the blue canopy at the side of the house. He loved to visit Gracie Mansion. It was a grand old house with black shutters on the windows and white porch rails. Sam had three bedrooms for himself. He was the first bachelor Mayor to occupy the house.

Through the front door Johnny went, under the fanlight, with Sammy's live-in maid to smile at him and ask about his health. "Thank you, Sarah, I'm tip-top."

"That's good, Commissioner John."

"And how is the Man today?"

"He's bristling," she said. "It's them straw ballots. Everybody's picking Rebecca to win."

"It's meaningless stuff," John said. "He'll pull through."

He walked up the winding stairs on the Mayor's green carpet. It was almost three o'clock, but the Mayor hadn't risen yet. John stood outside the master bedroom and knocked on the door.

"Come in, for God's sake."

Sam was in his underwear. He put pajamas on for his Police Commissioner and returned to bed. He lay under the covers until Sarah arrived with a pot of coffee and sweet rolls for the two bachelor men. He winked at John when Sarah left. An enormous black accounting book poked out of the covers. It was the Mayor's budget for the coming fiscal year. Sam kicked at the book with both his feet. "Becky Karp says I can't add or subtract. But it doesn't take more than ten fingers to know that the City is sinking in shit. Some wizard in the Comptroller's office is always finding a million here and there . . . then he loses it the next day . . . did you run the girlies into the precinct, John?"

"I did."

Sam fell silent and munched on a sweet roll.

Christ, how do you talk to a Mayor? John finished his coffee, taking care not to break the cup. "Ah," he said, "you'll murder Rebecca at the polls."

But the Mayor wasn't listening to him. His jaws churned while he stared into the great mirror alongside his bed. Poor old man. *Hizzoner can't sustain a conversation. His memory is on the blink.*

26

John walked out of the master bedroom as quietly as he could. He said goodbye to Sarah and thanked her for the coffee and the sweet rolls. Christie was parked near the gate. He had an envelope for Tiger John.

"Who gave you this?"

Christianson held out his hands to indicate the overwhelming breadth of a giant. "It was that rogue cop, O'Toole."

"O'Toole? How could he tell I was coming to the Mayor's house?"

Christianson shrugged and pursed his lips.

The PC glared at him, "The Special Prosecutor is on our heels, and you monkey with the whoreboy outside Gracie Mansion? . . . come on. Take me to the Dingle."

He opened the envelope, and a bankbook spilled out. John didn't bother with the sums in the book. Five or six thousand, it was the same to him. They were getting cheeky with the "Commish," these messenger boys. The giant had followed him to Sammy's gate! He shielded the bankbook in his palm, so he could peek at that mother of a name. *Anna Livia Plurabelle.* Go figure out O'Toole and that king of his in Dublin town. John got his bankbooks if he went after whores or not. What in hell were they paying him for? Would bankbooks come faster and faster, the more Black Marias he sent out? *Anna Livia and Molly Bloom.*

"The Dingle," John said, "when do we get to the Dingle?" Then he noticed that the car had stopped.

"Boss, we've been sitting here for five minutes."

"Oh," John said. He got out of the car, knocked three times, muttered his name, and crept inside with the Dingle Bay boys.

FOUR

HE was that bum again, but he didn't have a dirty neck, or so much stubble on his face. His cheeks were lean, and he had the suffering look of a suitor. Annie Powell didn't like it at all. The bum was wearing cologne, an after-shave lotion it was. He would scare anybody away with the dark hollows in his eyes. "Jesus," she said, laughing at him. "How am I going to earn my keep? Buy me for half an hour, but don't feed me another lunch. I can't work on a full stomach."

Isaac stole her from Forty-third Street before she could complain. He had the grip of a large monkey. She couldn't free her hand. The pimps and the young black whores laughed at the image of Annie and Isaac trundling along. You would have thought the bum had himself a wife. They went to the Vinaigrette. Isaac bought her little bottles of champagne. His tactics seemed more aggressive today. Annie preferred white wine and green beans. But those little bottles didn't soften the bum. "I can take you off that corner," he said. "I can make it so you won't have a foot of space to prowl on."

"God, you really are a priest . . . if you'd like to buy a share of me, you'll have to ask Martin McBride."

"Fuck McBride," Isaac said. "I want you to live with me."

28

She didn't laugh at his proposal. Her eyes began to sink into her skull.

"I have a place downtown. On Rivington Street. Don't worry. You can have your men. I won't interfere. I'll mix drinks for them. Go out for bottles of wine. But I don't want you on the damn streets."

"Mister," she said, "I don't need an uncle, thanks. I already have a pimp."

Could he tell Annie Powell that she was torturing him and his rotten worm? That he'd bump any john who went near her corner? He was jealous, stupidly jealous, of a girl he hadn't even slept with. That scar had gotten him crazy.

"Who's McDermott?" he said.

She ate a mouthful of fish.

"I asked you about Dermott Bride."

She got up from the table, put her napkin down, and walked out of the restaurant. Isaac was left with three corks and his little bottles of champagne. He phoned his office. A limousine was outside the Vinaigrette in seven minutes. The waiters at the restaurant saw the bum get into that big car. They were wise men. They understood that strange things existed in this world. The very rich often preferred to dress likes *cloches*. They wouldn't forget this bum with the scarred beauty, the limousine, and the splits of champagne.

Isaac's deputies had located Martin McBride, who lived with a fat wife in eight rooms near Marble Hill. Martin had emphysema. But he had to suffer August in New York. He collected money from the pimps of Manhattan and heard their complaints. He was known in midtown as "Bagman Martin." He'd been a petty crook for over half his life. Poor Martin didn't have much of a record: arrested as a vagrant two or three times. Short spills in the Tombs. But that was twenty years ago. He'd prospered in his old age.

Isaac's men kidnapped him out of his apartment in a three hundred dollar suit. The old bagman was bewildered. Centre Street was completely black. Why was he being shoveled through the halls? He didn't believe Isaac's deputies were cops. But this *was* the old Police Headquarters. They deposited him in a back room on the third floor. The room was dark except for the lamp in his face. Who in Jesus was behind that desk?

"Scumbag, is Annie Powell yours, or not?"

"Sir," the old bagman said, "I don't know who that sweetheart is."

"But she happens to know a lot about you . . . How's Dermott these days?"

"Who, sir?"

Isaac reached over his desk to twist McBride's two ears.

"Ah, the nephew. He's doing fine."

"Could it be that you're working for him, Martin McBride? . . . that the nickles you collect from every whore's purse goes to little McDermott?"

"That's impossible, sir. Dermott's a Yale man, swear to Christ. Helped put him through that college. He was training for the bar . . . but he never got to be a lawyer, sir. The nephew tired of his studies."

"Where is he now?"

"I haven't a clue."

Isaac was tired of twisting ears. He was readying to bang Martin's head against the wall. But Martin suddenly had a coughing fit. It wasn't contrived. Isaac could see the awful blue and yellow of emphysema on him. He had his deputies send Martin home. He learned nothing from the old bagman. He didn't get one bit closer to Dermott Bride.

FIVE

THE pimps wouldn't talk to him. The black whores couldn't even pronounce Dermott's name. Annie would run from him soon as Isaac appeared. She'd have no more lunches or dinners with the old bum. He walked into a pornography shop managed by a friendly Russian Jew. The Jew was smart enough to read under Isaac's disguise. He knew about the legendary First Deputy of New York.

"Sidel, don't play the schmuck with me. Ask me a question, and I'll answer it, but only if I can."

His name was Lazar. And he carried a pistol under his counter, wrapped in a handkerchief.

"The girl with a scar on her face, who is she? She wasn't here a month ago."

"The gorgeous one?" Lazar said, making perfect breasts with his hands. "The knockout? Sidel, lay off of her. She's Dermott's bride."

And he began to titter. Isaac wouldn't smile.

"Who's Dermott?"

"Dermott? Dermott's the king."

He was mum after that. Lazar had to attend to his shop. Isaac was sharp enough not to pull at him. Lazar had told him as much as Lazar cared to tell. Dermott's the king. Now Isaac was beginning to understand why there was peace on Whores' Row. This Dermott had to be the overlord of all the pimping traffic. Uncle Martin was his bagman, the old boy who settled Dermott's accounts. But why didn't some gang of mavericks slit Martin's throat? Was Dermott that much of a king? And how could he hold his little empire together if you couldn't catch sight of him? It all didn't fit. Isaac Sidel shouldn't have been ignorant of the emperor of Times Square.

He had no more time to ruminate in a pornography shop. He was expected at John Jay. Isaac gave lectures twice a week at the School of Criminal Justice. He walked to his hotel, shaved, put on a pair of fresh dungarees. That was Isaac's teaching clothes.

The worm itched when he arrived at John Jay. It was a bad sign for Isaac. The worm was hardly ever wrong. He had a new pupil in his class. Melvin Pears' green-eyed wife. She sat at the back of the room with a notebook in her hands. That notebook inhibited Isaac. He forgot to prance around the classroom. He stood near the window and talked about the futility of criminal justice. "The Bronx is dying," he said to the young firemen and cops in his class. "Street by street. We can't send in artillery. The kids would only burn all our tanks. Soon the edges of Manhattan will go . . . then you'll have towers on the East Side with machine-gunners in the lobby . . . you'll need armed guards to get you in and out of the supermarkets."

One of the firemen raised his hand. "First Deputy Sidel, what can we do about it?"

"Go into the Bronx," Isaac said. "Build over all the rubble. Why can't we have shopping plazas in Crotona Park?"

The cops giggled to themselves. The areas around Crotona Park looked as if they'd been napalmed. There were more arsonists in the Bronx than grocers. These cops would have figured Isaac for a bolshevik if he wasn't the First Dep. They enjoyed jeremiads from a deputy police commissioner. You could light up in class. Isaac didn't care what kind of junk you smoked. But that green-eyed lady worried him. Was she going to use Isaac's words against old Sam in Becky Karp's bid for Mayor? He could watch her scribbling between her legs. That's no place to keep a notebook.

She was there, in the same seat, at his next class. The

32

worm nearly hobbled him. He had to lean against the wall. "Sure," he muttered to himself. "It's not too hard to recognize a traitor. Especially when she has green eyes." But he wouldn't coddle to her, sweeten his own talk. He mentioned Stalinist solutions. "Mobilize. The cops can't do it themselves. Have a goddamn citizens' army. Fight the shits who won't cooperate. Bring back Joe DiMaggio. Get Willie Mays to build a new Polo Grounds . . . behind the Grand Concourse. Where's Durocher now? Take ten percent of everybody's salary . . . a tithe for the Bronx . . . no, make it twenty percent."

The cops laughed, but that green-eyed wife of Pears clutched her notebook. Isaac grew sad. I'm burying Mayor Sam. He ended the class twenty minutes before the bell. He tried to skirt away from Mrs. Pears. She trapped him at the exit. He would have had to crawl under her bubs to get around her. She put a slip of paper in his hand. The specks in her eyes were incredible. They flashed shiny gray dust like small planets about to break apart. He was jealous of Melvin Pears. Isaac also had a wife. Kathleen. A tough Irish lady who had married him before he was twenty. The wife was in real estate. She developed swamps in Florida, had ten suitors and a million in the bank, and she didn't need a cop who liked to go around in bum's pants. He saw her once or twice a year. They made love if Kathleen was in the mood. It was more of a friendly hug than anything else. Now he had to deal with Mrs. Pears.

"I didn't mean to blunder into your class . . . I'm sorry . . . it's just that I was interested in what you had to say . . . can you come to dinner tomorrow night?"

"Your husband's too tough for me, Mrs. Pears."

"I'm Jennifer," she said. "Jenny . . . Mel likes you . . . don't mind his scowls . . . he has to practice making faces to satisfy all the juries . . . he's much nicer at home."

33

SIX

HE expected Rebecca Karp to come out of the closet and eat off his neck with the hors d'oeuvres. It was only a party of three: Pears, his wife, and Isaac Sidel. Jennifer hadn't been wrong. Melvin wasn't the lawyer at home. He offered Isaac sucks from his hash pipe. The First Dep smoked with Mr. and Mrs. Pears. Why not? He was fifty-one. He ought to have a taste of hashish before he died. It didn't offend the worm, and it warmed Isaac's head. But he couldn't let go of the cop in him. "Mel, did you ever hear of an ex-law student named Dermott Bride? . . . went to Yale."

"I don't think so," Pears said, and they all took sucks from the pipe. "I couldn't scribble a brief without some hash in me," he said. "I always work better when I'm stoned."

Isaac didn't see a nudge of affection between husband and wife. Their bodies seemed to exist in some kind of neutral sphere. It's the hash, Isaac figured. They probably fuck three times a day. Mel had the grace not to mention Rebecca Karp. And Isaac didn't talk about the Mayor. A little sleepy boy came out of one of the rooms. He wore fireman's pajamas. He ran to his father. "Alex, say hello to Isaac."

He shook hands with Alexander Pears, who had his father's mouth and his mother's green eyes.

"Isaac's a policeman . . . smarter than Dick Tracy."

Alexander was four and a half. He kissed his father and went to bed. He couldn't stop looking at Isaac. Jennifer was in the kitchen putting whipped cream on a pie. Thank God there had been no politics tonight. Pears didn't say a word about why the Police Commissioner ran prostitutes off the street. Isaac was the one who started to talk about hookers. He was dreaming of Annie Powell. "There are certain pimps. They get their fingers on a girl. And she's owned for life . . . or until she gets ugly and has to be shipped to Nova Scotia, where anything that walks will pass as a woman."

He noticed Jennifer standing over him. "Sorry if that sounds cruel. But it's a fact. You know, if a girl's too beautiful, and her pimp is afraid of losing her, sometimes he'll scar her face. It's a fantasy he has . . . he thinks the scar devalues her in the eyes of other men. But it doesn't always turn out that way. The scar can make her even more desirable. And the pimp will lose her anyway."

They had cognac and chunks of pecan pie. Melvin slumped into his chair and fell asleep. Isaac whispered with some embarrassment to Mrs. Pears. Melvin was snoring hard. Jennifer didn't apologize. She accompanied Isaac to the door. The worm was rising in his gut. The cognac caused his bald spot to twitch. The hash must have been like a love potion to Isaac. He had Mrs. Pears against the door. That's how he found himself. A stumbling man. His tongue was deep in her mouth while he swallowed half her face. He could still hear Melvin snore. That fucking kiss, there was no end to it. The worm didn't keep Isaac's clock. He could have been gnawing at her for an hour. What if the gentleman wakes up? Or the little boy in the red pajamas marches out of his room and sees mama with Dick Tracy's tongue in her mouth? It was Isaac's nervousness that got them apart. He told her about his hotel. "It's too decrepit to have a name. You don't have to meet me there . . ."

He was downstairs, on Madison and Seventy-ninth, outside Melvin's place. What the fuck was it all about? Was it some game plan in Melvin's head to bring him over to Rebecca Karp? Feed the boy some hash, get the wife to kiss him, and he'll fly from Mayor Sam? His tongue was raw as shit. Did Jennifer entertain every guest in a smiliar way? He was so busy kissing her, he hadn't even felt her tits. God, he was dumb about women. His wife Kathleen was right to head for Florida. You couldn't get much companionship from a cop who was married to his own love of mystery and technique. He'd slept with a hundred women, whores and businessmen's wives, and while he probed, stroked, and sucked, his head would grind away at some caper that had been bothering him. The First Dep solved a quarter of his mysteries in bed. Fucking seemed to drive the trivia out of him, to hold his concentration for detail. But that was before the Guzmann family gave him his worm. The worm had idled Isaac's need for sex. That's why this tonguing business with Jennifer was crazy to him. It's the hash, Isaac said. The hash roused a part of him that the worm had laid to rest. He was convinced he wouldn't see Mrs. Pears again. She'd avoid his classes. She'd never come to a shithouse hotel.

Isaac hobbled to West Forty-seventh Street. He changed into his bum's clothes. He had this urge to prowl. Annie wasn't at her corner. So what? Was she sucking off a tie manufacturer from Hoboken? Isaac would murder the son of a bitch. He'd hold every whore in detention, white or black, to ruin Anne's trade. Let no man finger that scar. The First Dep was going mad. He wanted to kiss that "D" Dermott Bride had put on her. To feel the ridges in it with his mouth. He'd keep his tongue in his own face. The tongue was for Mrs. Pears.

She must have given him a bit of luck, Melvin's green-eyed wife. Isaac saw Martin McBride outside Lazar's pornography shop. The bagman wasn't alone. He had Jamey O'Toole with him. Tiny Jim. O'Toole was a renegade cop. Isaac's own investigators, the First Dep's "rat squad," had brought evidence against Tiny Jim. He'd been taking bribes without mercy, "black rent," breaking the heads of local businessmen to further the cause of protection agencies in Brooklyn and the Bronx. Isaac put him out on his ass. O'Toole lost his pension money, but you couldn't hurt a lad who was six feet seven and had a pair of fists on him that could give shorter men a permanent headache. O'Toole was still in business. He'd lent himself out to Dermott and Martin McBride. He was the old bagman's walking shotgun.

36

There weren't too many gangs in New York that would meddle with Jamey O'Toole. You'd need a hatchet to get at him. A bullet would only leave a little nipple in his chest.

But Isaac had a worm to hearten him. He wanted to devil this O'Toole. "Jamey," he said, "I hear your old shield is lying in the property clerk's drawer."

O'Toole had a warm smile for Isaac. "How are you, Chief? It's hard to remember all the different uniforms you own. Isaac, I don't have a grudge, I swear . . . but keep out of the alleys, will you? You could fall and lose one of your eyes on the ground. Have you met my employer, Martin McBride . . . Martin, don't be fooled by the man's stink. It's Isaac himself, the First Deputy of New York."

McBride's fist was soft and wet in Isaac's hand.

"We're already old friends," Isaac said. "Martin visited me . . . at Centre Street."

McBride's fist shot out of Isaac's hand.

"O'Toole, take a message to Dermott, will you, please? Tell him I'm fond of his Annie . . . and I'd like to dig my own initial into his royal Irish face."

Martin scampered behind O'Toole.

Jamey didn't harden to the First Dep. "You'll have to forgive me, Chief. I don't think I'll relay that message. It's a declaration of war, you see. And I might be caught in the middle. You'll have to sing to Dermott yourself."

"I would, if you'd tell me where he is?"

"That's your problem, Chief. Dermott, he doesn't like the notoriety. He's in a bit of retirement now. But you might send him a postcard. If you could get the proper stamps."

O'Toole walked off, taking Martin by the hand.

SEVEN

ISAAC went to brood in his hotel. You needed some Celtic harp to unwind an Irishman's words. Fucking O'Toole. Proper stamps? Retirement? Dermott had to be out of the country. And Martin was doing his trade for him, with O'Toole serving as the muscle. The Italian lads wouldn't soil their fingers with black whores in the street. But not even O'Toole could fight off every nigger gang; there were plenty of "blues" that would have been willing to strangle pimps for nickels and dimes. They were all getting pieces of the pot. That was Dermott's magic. Then why was he in such a shroud?

The bum didn't come out of his room. Knocks on the door couldn't get him off his unmade bed. The worm itched at him and forced him to recognize a face. He had a visitor. Jenny Pears. She wasn't sure it was Isaac until he put on another shirt. He began arranging pillows. She laughed at his pathetic urge to clean up four weeks of filth. She liked Isaac's room.

He tried to explain. "Have to live this way . . . on a heavy case."

"Why are you so skinny," she said.

"Jennifer, I was a fat man until a year ago. Had the thickest neck in Manhattan. But I was trying to hook a gang of thieves. The Guzmanns. I lived with them six

38

months. Had to make them think I'd broken with, the cops. But that was a smart family. I did their chores and they put a worm in my belly. And the worm's been feeding off me ever since."

"Isaac, there are hospitals, you know. Laboratories that can shrink your worm, dissolve it, kill it, prevent it from growing new tails."

"I've had my fill of hospitals. Used to run up to Presbyterian like a religious man. They fluoroscoped me, gave me pills to eat. Nothing happened. And I've been growing fond of my worm."

Isaac begged her to let him wash up. Jennifer refused. Her body gave him the chills. She didn't have a flaw on her back. Her thighs had a strange burnish in Isaac's room. He loved the circles her nipples made, pinkish mounds. What was Melvin's wife doing in his room? Why wasn't Pears with her, his head resting in her groin? Her low, mother's breasts didn't bother him at all. It was amazing to Isaac. He moved in her with a gentleness, a slow, soft rhythm that he'd never had in his possession before. Was the worm bridling him, holding him back? Was it that creature who was making Jennifer Pears, not him? With its own smooth motion, its worm's rocking parts? Do worms have pricks and tongues? Isaac wanted her out of his room.

"Late," he said. "An appointment with the Mayor. Christ, we have to be at this synagogue by six." It was no lie. The little Irish Mayor had to crawl to the Hebrews for votes, run to obscure shuls in the far boroughs. He'd already lost the Irish vote. The Irish loved Rebecca. She was a former beauty queen, and she had a loud voice, wit, humor, and pishogue. She was five feet eight and could tell you a good story. His Honor was nearly a dwarf. Five feet one without his shoes. He was a Party loyalist, a bureaucrat who could barely put two sentences together. He'd had his great rise three and a half years ago. He was chairman of the Potholes Complaint Board, a member of the Landmarks Commission, and an unpaid governor of the Manhattan Shelter for Women. Sam had never finished high school. He seemed perfect for the Mayor's job. The pols liked his mumness, his devotion to their cause. The other candidates, six growling men, were chewing at each other's throat. The Dems turned to Sam. They rewarded him for fifty years of labor. He'd carried milk pails for Party bosses, lit the fires in Democratic clubrooms, slept on his knees in City Hall. But he arrived at Gracie Mansion in the wrong year. "Hizzoner" had a corpse in his arms. The City died on Sammy Dunne. It was fighting bankruptcy and a terrible loss of jobs.

"Hizzoner" wouldn't step out in his own car. He was afraid people would jeer at him. So Isaac sent a limousine to collect the Mayor at Gracie Mansion. Jennifer watched the First Dep get into his synagogue clothes. She had more affection for Isaac the bum. She kissed him good-bye and left him to struggle with his cuffs. The limousine was waiting for Isaac outside the hotel. Mayor Sam was hiding in the back seat. He didn't question Isaac's choice of hotels. He might bully Handsome John Rathgar, the Police Commissioner, but he had absolute faith in Sheeny Isaac.

The car took them to Hollis, Queens. Sam and Isaac had to engage a shul full of retirees, pensioners and their wives who were worried about their own shrinking revenues, crime in their housing projects, and the worth of a Mayor who wouldn't come out of his mansion. They were for Rebecca of the Rockaways. They were indulging Isaac and Sam out of boredom, anger, and frustration. The Mayor had nothing to say. His tongue lolled in his mouth while he whispered to Isaac on the podium. "Jesus God, will you save us now?" Isaac saw the bitterness of their plight. An Irish Mayor and an apostate in a house full of Jews. Isaac had never prayed in a synagogue. But he and Sam had to wear skullcaps over their brains. Isaac became the good policeman for Mayor Sam, but question after question was beginning to break his hump. He had pity for these old men and women. They were stroked at election time, and then forgotten. That was the law of politics. Functionaries ran the City, men and women in gray buildings, who didn't even know there was a synagogue in Hollis, and wouldn't have cared. Rebecca would scream about more golden age clubs, but the same functionaries would rule whether she got in or not. Still, Isaac had to lapse into petty lies. He invented master plans for Mayor Sam Dunne: more cops to walk old women to the bank, patrols to discourage baby thieves, police sergeants to talk about better burglar alarms. The worm was biting him fierce. It had little tolerance for Isaac's shit.

Then the auditorium mellowed. It had no idea of Isaac's apostasy. She synagogue figured it was talking Jew to Jew. One old woman mentioned *their* Nobel laureate. What did Isaac think of Moses Herzog and Saul Bellow? All Isaac could remember about cuckold Moses was that he liked to fornicate belly to belly, face to face. Thoughts of Jennifer Pears crept into him. He had a sudden desire to ravage every inch of her, to lose that gentleness the worm had thrust on him, and eat her out like a crazy Chinaman. His Honor, who was incapable of reading any book, nudged Isaac. "We have them now. Tell them about Herzog's Bellow."

Isaac mouthed some blather about Herzog and the modern Jew, and he and Sam were permitted to go. The worm dug at Isaac in a miserable fashion. He had to keep wrenching from side to side in the limousine. But Sam was happy. "You got them," he said, "you got them with Herzog's Bellow."

Something was drilling in Isaac's skull. "Your Honor, you must know every Irish society in New York . . . does any of them carry a member named Dermott Bride? A rich man, a man who might make contributions here and there."

Sam wasn't listening. He kept singing, "Herzog's Bellow, Herzog's Bellow," and Isaac thought, he'll lose the primary mumbling that song. And Molly would probably get a kiss from Mr. Bellow and throw Isaac to the dogs.

EIGHT

H E wasn't wrong about Jenny. She didn't come to his hotel again. Ah, she's found another primitive guy. Jesus, with a body like that? And those green eyes. He looked for her at John Jay College. There was no green-eyed lady taking down his words. His lectures fell to shit. He stopped caring if the Mayor won or lost. He had only Dermott Bride to consider. His deputies rang him at the hotel. They had no news of Dermott, but Melvin Pears had invited him to a party, a party for Rebecca, at her campaign headquarters in an abandoned Dodge showroom on West Fifty-third. Isaac thought, pish on Becky Karp. He wasn't going to lend himself as a whipping boy to her campaign, appear as the curiosity cop, so Rebecca and her people could get at Mayor Sam through him. But Jennifer might be at the party. Jenny of the flawless back. Isaac arrived at the Dodge showroom in dungarees.

The showroom was packed. All the movie stars had come out for Ms. Rebecca. Streisand; Dustin Hoffman and his wife. The First Dep went unrecognized until Rebecca grabbed him by the shoulders and pulled on him. "Isaac," she said, "Isaac." Even the worm could feel one of Becky's shoulder grips. Isaac was squeezed into her like a bunny rabbit. It was a calculated move on Rebecca's part. She wanted him near enough so she

42

could whisper into his throat. "Cocksucker," she said. This was the Rebecca Isaac enjoyed. "I'll stick your balls in a jar of honey and give them to the rats for a lick . . . Fuckface, why did you marry yourself to a sinking man? You're not supposed to be a fool."

Isaac wiggled out of Rebecca's bear hug and kissed her on the mouth. "Senile he is. There are days Sam can't remember his name . . ."

"Then come over to us," she said.

Isaac smiled, but his lips were narrow, and Rebecca realized she'd just been given a Judas kiss.

"Cunt, he's a better Mayor than you'll ever be."

He would have gone out, tunneled under Streisand's kinky hair on his way to the door, but he discovered Jennifer standing with one of Rebecca's aides, a boy with red eyebrows. They were smiling, talking under their breath. What hotel did *he* live at? Did the boy have red hair on his chest? Would he like to borrow Isaac's worm? Would she fuck him in a doorway? Isaac bullied through a crowd of campaigners, and snatched Jennifer away from the boy. "My savior," she said. "With the iron grip . . . what synagogue do you have on your agenda today? . . . Isaac, my husband's about three feet behind us. *Mel.* Do you remember him?"

"He won't notice," Isaac said. The First Dep was in a burly mood. "He's fixing strategies for Rebecca."

So they walked down to Isaac's hotel. He was into her body before she could get her panties off. It was a kind of friendly rape. He licked her armpits, filled her navel with spit, and sucked between her legs with a brutal energy. He left marks on her thighs, souvenirs for Melvin to look at.

"Isaac, why are you so angry at me?"

"Who knows?"

Was he getting even with the worm, showing it the authentic Isaac, who could take any woman into his bed. He began to eat her nipples like a goddamn baby. She stroked his head, held it there, and the worm had screwed him again. The lust was gone. "Stay with me," he said. "Tonight."

"Isaac, how can I? . . . I have a four-year-old at home . . . and Mel."

"Telephone the kid. Tell him Dick Tracy will play with

43

him tomorrow if he goes to sleep. Mel can take care of himself."

Her green eyes were throwing off that beautiful gray dust again. He put her in a cab. She kissed him thickly, with her fingers in his ear. It wasn't a joke. He was losing his guts to Jennifer Pears. He'd better find himself a bimbo fast, a girl who would let him concentrate on Dermott while he rolled her over and fucked her from behind. He blackened his face with charcoal and got into his bum's clothes. The First Dep was dying for a fight. He'd roam the streets like a crazed animal, slapping pimps, cops, or tourists. You'd have a hard time arresting Isaac, no matter what outfit he wore. The worm could tear at him. Isaac wasn't going to be ruled by a little snake in his belly.

He had the customer he wanted. A man was chatting with Annie Powell, a timid john from the look of him. Was she settling on a price? Isaac could rip the scalp off his ears, give him a beauty treatment he wouldn't forget. But Annie didn't go with the john. Something had scared him off. It wasn't Isaac. His mania couldn't have been obvious from a block away. It was someone else. A horse of a man. Tiny Jim O'Toole. Jamey was bending over her now. Isaac drew close. That horse wasn't making her smile. He had his huge knuckles in the waistband of her whore's shirt.

"O'Toole," Isaac said. "Jamey. You ought to be nicer to King Dermott's bride. If you don't put your hand away, I'll have to chew it off."

It was a ridiculous bluff. O'Toole could have sat Isaac on top of the lamppost and left him there for the fire trucks to bring him down on a ladder. But he took his knuckles out of Annie's shirt.

"Isaac, be kind to the Irish. Don't meddle. Annie, she belongs to another man. Ask her yourself."

Jamey whistled with his knuckles in his pockets, winked at Annie, and stepped into the gutter. Cars stopped for him. No one could be sure how his bumpers would fare against a lad who was six feet seven.

Annie was growling at Isaac. "Who are you? . . . Jesus, can't you play on the next block? And why do you have that black shit on your face? You're comical, you know that . . . with your questions and your little bottles of champagne."

44

She was sobbing now. "Don't I have enough without a pest like you? . . . you're trouble to me . . ."

"Annie, I could help . . . if you'd tell me what it was O'Toole wants."

"Wants?" . . . he has regards to me from somebody I know."

"Dermott?"

But she wouldn't talk to him. And Isaac had to gather up his bum's pants at the waist (he was growing skinnier by the hour), and skunk off to his hotel.

NINE

WAS it a code? *Dermott Bride.* Was Dermott the secret hero of Londonderry? Using his whores' profits to collect money for the "rebels" of Northern Ireland, with Annie the deposed queen of the Provisional IRA? Isaac had his men infiltrate the tough Irish bars around Marble Hill. There was no Dermott Bride or Annie Powell attached to the Irish Republican Army. But Isaac was a stubborn man. He had his agents burrow everywhere. They went into the First Dep's own files. They came up with a memorandum from Ned O'Roarke, the old First Deputy Commissioner, whose death had put Isaac into office. It took them a week to ferret out that pink slip with one sentence written on it eighteen years ago. *"Get Isaac to help little Dermott."* Isaac was horrified. He couldn't mistake the scrawling hand of Ned O'Roarke. O'Roarke had been Isaac's rabbi. He'd sponsored him, brought him into the First Dep's territories, built him up. What did Ned have to do with "little Dermott"? The worm was erasing Isaac's memory, that's it.

He dialed Kathleen in Florida. It was four A.M. The wife had to be in bed with one of her suitors. "Kate," he mumbled, "did *we* ever know a boy named Dermott?"

He had to ask her again. She yawned into the phone. "Isaac, go fuck yourself."

So he was left with a Dermott he might have known, but didn't know now. Ned O'Roarke wouldn't have launched Dermott as a pimp. It couldn't have been Ned who made a "king" of Dermott Bride.

Isaac had Jennifer to console him three days a week. She was the only woman who could drive Dermott out of him. The worm never pinched Isaac when he was with Jennifer Pears.

But he had other pulls on him. "Hizzoner" was growing desperate. The *Daily News* vouched Sam would only get one vote in ten. He was told to remove himself from the primary lists. "Hizzoner" refused. He went on more excursions with Isaac. Then he had a heart attack in Gracie Mansion. He was carried to the hospital across the street. Rebecca sent a full page of condolences to the *New York Times*. People were already calling her Mayor Karp.

Isaac felt sorry for old Sam, but he was glad he didn't have to parrot little lies in churches, shuls, and social clubs. He did more strolling as Isaac the bum. Annie seemed to have fled from her corner. Lazar came out of his pornography shop to chat with Isaac. "Sidel, stop dreaming about that woman . . . I can get you a beauty with poems written on her chest."

"Lazar, you didn't leave your shop to become my pimp . . . what happened to Annie Powell?"

"She's in the hospital . . . Roosevelt. They found her unconscious last night . . . somebody stepped on her face."

Isaac hailed a patrol car. "Get me to Roosevelt Hospital, quick." The cops were ready to laugh at the bum who was giving orders. "Call my office on your radio. I'm First Deputy Sidel."

They ran up to Roosevelt with their sirens on. He found Annie in some rear beggar's ward. The nurses couldn't understand what this bum was doing with two cops. The cops took their eyes off Annie Powell. Her face was one, huge, distorted puff. The lips were split apart. The "D" on her cheek had lost its continuity. Its pith was broken and submerged. Dermott had erased himself from Annie. "Get her out of this fucking hole," Isaac shouted to the resident in charge of the ward. "Put her in a private room."

"Hey," the resident said, trying not to look at Isaac's baggy pants.

"Prick, it's Police business . . . and stop blinking at me. I'll pay for the room."

The patrol car brought him up to Marble Hill. Isaac burst into Martin McBride's eight-room flat. The old bagman was having dinner with a covey of nephews, nieces, and his wife. Isaac lifted him off the floor in front of everybody. The nephews weren't much good. They shrank from the mad bum who was shaking their uncle up and down.

"Martin, you tell me where Dermott is, or I'll squash you into a piece of shit."

"Dublin," Martin said, riding against Isaac's shirt. "The nephew's in Dublin town."

"What's his address?"

"The Shelbourne. St. Stephen's Green."

"Wasn't one scar enough for him? Did he order O'Toole to smash both sides of her face?"

"I don't know, sir. I swear to Christ. Dermott never talks to me . . ."

Isaac didn't return to the hotel. He went down to his monk's corner at Centre Street. He sat in the dark, his fingers rubbing under his nose. The king's in Dublin. Isaac had to murder him. It didn't matter that there was no logic to it. The creature was purring in his belly. That's all the encouragement a man could need. Isaac still had a cop's head. What did Annie Powell mean to him? There were other scarred whores in the world, plenty of them. He hadn't slept with this Annie, hadn't touched her. And she'd mocked his offerings of champagne. But he was already smitten by that letter on her face, Dermott's mark. He could have had his own inspectors swipe O'Toole off the street. Five or ten of Isaac's deputies for each of Jamey's arms. They would have unwired him. But Isaac would fix Jamey himself, when he got back from Dublin. Jamey was only a vassal to that king. It was Dermott Bride who had stepped on Annie's face. He was the lad Isaac wanted. He'd already booked a flight with Aer Lingus, crazy as it was. Isaac was leaving tomorrow.

He wasn't going to Dublin as the great Isaac Sidel. A trusted deputy might have doctored a passport for him.

48

Isaac could have flown under any name. But he didn't want to involve his office. He used a crooked engraver, Duckworth, a thief that Isaac had kept out of jail. He had him smuggled into Centre Street with his bag of tools. The engraver was nervous. He liked thirty-six hours to "make" a passport. And he preferred his own darkroom off Canal Street, where he could exercise his artistry without any pressure from the First Dep.

"Isaac, are you sure there's a camera downstairs?"

"Duckie, why do I have to repeat myself? You've been here before. The photo unit was always in the basement."

"But how do we know what equipment the bastards left behind?"

"That's what we're going to find out."

Isaac grabbed a flashlight and they marched down three flights. Rats scurried around their legs. The smell of rat shit was enough to destroy a man. Isaac kept the engraver on his feet. Duckworth had his camera. The photo unit was intact.

The engraver took half a dozen passports out of his pocket. They were samples of his own work, names he'd invented. All he needed was a photograph of Isaac to go with any one of them. He would legitimize the photograph, fix it to the passport with the State Department seal he carried in his bag. Duckworth rummaged through the passports. "I can give you Larry Fagin O'Neill, Marvin Worth, Ira Goldberg . . . Isaac, they're practically real people. We're just gonna throw one of them your face."

"Keep them for your other clients, Duckie. I have a name. Moses Herzog."

The engraver was heartsore. "Why Moses Herzog? That will triple my work. I'll have to start from scratch. Fagin O'Neill isn't good enough?"

But Isaac was without mercy. Moses Herzog. That's what it would have to be.

PART
TWO

TEN

THE Irish stewardesses were gentle with this businessman philosopher, poet from the City of New York. They fed him coffee and chocolate mints. The worm adored the taste of mint. Moses was asleep when they arrived at Shannon. Passengers disembarked. Then the plane took off for Dublin town.

His baggage was light. He figured on two or three days to dispose of his business with Dermott Bride. They wouldn't miss him at his office. Isaac had disappeared for much longer periods than that.

The cab ride to the Shelbourne cost him nearly three pounds in Irish money. It was a hotel with white pillars, a blue marquee, statuettes holding lanterns over their heads, tall windows, and a white roof. The Shelbourne sat opposite a long, handsome park. St. Stephen's Green. Isaac couldn't see the park from his window. But it still cost him twenty pounds a night. He'd have to kill Dermott and get out of here, or borrow from his pension money to stay alive.

He had no idea what Dermott looked like. Would the king materialize on the staircase and present himself, like a fucking Druid? You couldn't tell what magic Dermott owned in Dublin. But Moses had the rottenest luck. A man latched on to him in the lobby. It was Marshall

Berkowitz, the dean of freshmen at Columbia College and vice-president of the James Joyce Society. Marshall had been Isaac's English prof during his one semester at college. He made a pilgrimage to Dublin every year to walk the streets of Leopold Bloom. How was Isaac supposed to know that Marshall always stopped at the Shelbourne? He had a new, young wife. She had bangs over her eyes, this Sylvia Berkowitz, powerful calves, and a thin, rabbity smile. Something wasn't right with her. Had she taken a graduate course with Marsh, fallen in love with him while they plowed through *Finnegans Wake*? It must have been a devastating courtship. Marshall could capture any man or woman with that purity he had for Joyce. He'd converted Isaac after the first day of class. That was thirty years ago. Isaac had wept at the opening of *A Portrait of the Artist as a Young Man*. Moocows coming down the road. Molly Byrnes and her lemon platt. He was a barbarian from Manhattan and the Bronx. He hadn't known such language could exist. He followed Marshall everywhere, begged him to explain the meaning of this page or that. Isaac walked the campus with a fever in his eye. It couldn't last. Isaac's father deserted his family during Christmas, stole off to Paris in middle age to teach himself how to paint, a fur manufacturer with a craze in his head to become the new Matisse. Isaac had to leave school and help support the family.

He didn't read Joyce after that. He married an Irish woman who worked in real estate, four years older than himself. He became a cop. It was Kathleen who introduced him to First Deputy Commissioner O'Roarke, Kathleen who connected him to all the Irish rabbis who ran the Police Department of New York. It was her Irishness that made him a big cop. Now he had Marshall and Marshall's wife, both of whom had unmasked him on his first day in Dublin.

"Isaac," the dean said. "For God's sake. What's a commissioner like you doing here?"

Isaac had an "agreement" with Marshall Berkowitz. From time to time he would recommend young boys for Columbia College, lads who were the sons or nephews of some cop. Isaac would interview them, and pass on his feelings to Marsh. He had an instinct for who would survive at Columbia and who would not. Marsh always went by Isaac's word.

"Isaac, how the hell are you?"

The First Dep had to shut him up in the Shelbourne lounge. "Marsh, I'm on a caper, please . . . you'll have to call me Moses."

The dean's wife began to laugh. She took those bangs away from her eyes. There were blackish lines around them. Sylvia Berkowitz couldn't have slept a lot.

"Goddamn," Marshall said. "Moses, come with us. You'll do your cop stuff later."

"Where are we going?"

Berkowitz smiled. "To Number Seven Eccles Street."

Thirty years couldn't wipe away *Ulysses*. Isaac knew that book. Number 7 Eccles Street was where Joyce had dropped Leopold Bloom.

"Moses, the Irish are a miserable people. A landmark, a literary property that's impossible to duplicate, and they molest the place. It's a shell of a house . . . but it still exists."

So Isaac borrowed a sweater from the dean, and they went about the city. Moses had his jet lag. He couldn't remember buildings, monuments, and stores except a McDonald's hamburger joint. Trinity College was only an old wall that bent around a street. They crossed the Liffey at O'Connell Bridge. Joyce could have his river and his quays. The currents seemed pissy to Isaac. Then it was O'Connell Street and the Gresham Hotel. "The Gresham's gone down," Marshall said. "They frisked us the last time we went in for tea."

These muttering made no sense to Isaac. His ears were freezing, but he wasn't going to buy a hat in August. It was a turn to the left and up another street, narrower, with a row of gray houses. Then a turn to the right, a high street again with broken signboards and pubs with blue walls that had begun to chip and peel. A jump to the left and they were on Eccles Street, in what had to be a bitten part of town, a much lesser Dublin than Stephen's Green. Marshall led him by the hand to Bloom's house. The roof had been lopped off. The windows were boarded. Weeds showed through the cracks in the wood. The front door was torn out and replaced with ribbons of tin. The cellar was overgrown with harsh, bending flowers that were beginning to stink. The steps had mostly turned to rubble. Marshall swayed in front of Bloom's ravaged house. He was a heavy man, with a thickness behind his ears.

The dean was about to blubber. Isaac heard a dry, hacking sound.

"Poldy," he said. "Poldy Bloom . . . God save us from the Irish and ourselves. We don't deserve James Joyce."

The Irish could destroy Dublin for all Isaac cared, long as they held Dermott Bride. Eccles Street was like portions of the Bronx. Bombed-out territories and a few pubs. Marshall recovered himself. He wanted to drag Moses to a second landmark. A chemist's shop important to Bloom. Sylvia rescued Isaac. "Marsh, why don't you go? I'll take Isaac back to the hotel."

Marshall shrugged and kissed his wife, and he was gone from Eccles Street. Sylvia began to curse her husband. "Did you ever see such a big fat wobbly ass? . . . he was putting on a show for you."

"His crying in front of Bloom's house?"

"That's not it. He *always* cries."

Isaac looked at Mrs. Berkowitz. He was getting used to her sleepless eyes. Moses Herzog muttered to himself. He promised the worm he wouldn't cuckold Dean Berkowitz. Swear on Dermott's life. Sylvia took him on another route. They didn't pass O'Connell Street. They were in a goddamn alley. Isaac couldn't have told you whether they'd crossed the Liffey or not. Sylvia's skirt was up. He had her against the roughened wall of some poorman's lane. He thought they'd get arrested on account of her screams. Sylvia could move against a wall like no other woman. She was wet, wet, wet, but Moses had no feeling in his prick. Was it the worm's doing? He'd have an operation, magical surgery that could cut that bastard out of him. Isaac had a revelation at the wall. He wasn't fucking Sylvia. Her hunger had nothing to do with him. Isaac had a terrible, crazy, killing need for Jennifer Pears. He hadn't even said goodbye to her. Just got on a plane. To avenge a whore with Dermott's mark on her. Bouncing into Sylvia cursed him with visions of Jennifer's body. Was it a kind of punishment? Moses' hell? Why couldn't he keep away from other men's wives?

Marsh was at the Shelbourne, drinking cider with lemon peel, when Sylvia brought him in. The dean should have been in a darker mood. Isaac had Sylvia's smell all over his pants. A school of Dublin orphans could have sensed they'd been out fucking in the streets. But the dean had come back from his landmark, and he wouldn't chastise his wife. "Moses, guess who's living here at the Shelbourne with us?"

"Who?"

"Dermott McBride."

Isaac was prepared to kill. A dean of freshman had more avenues to King Dermott than the First Deputy of New York.

"Marsh, how did you get to know little Dermott?"

"Are you crazy? You're the one who introduced him to me."

"I led you to Dermott?" Isaac said.

"He couldn't have gotten into Columbia without your vote."

"I thought Dermott went to Yale."

"He did. He left us after one semester . . . like you."

Isaac scratched his ear. "I interviewed so many lads for Columbia. I can't remember them all."

"Dermott had a miserable record . . . but you were so fierce about him. And you were right . . . never met a boy who could plunge into *Ulysses* like that. Dermott had the gift. But he's Irish, of course. And now he's a millionaire. Has a whole wing at the hotel, a wing for himself."

"And six bodyguards," Sylvia Berkowitz said.

"Where's that wing of his?" Isaac asked.

"East of the elevator. On the fifth floor."

Isaac excused himself. He strolled up to the fifth floor. The Shelbourne had royal banisters and rugs, with gold leaning posts on the rails. Fuck the costs. He would park at no other hotel in Dublin town. The fifth floor was full of little wings. Isaac couldn't tell east from west. He recognized a man standing behind a closed fire door. It was a retired cop, Timothy Snell, who had once been a sergeant with the Chief Inspector's office. He went up to the old sergeant. Snell didn't open that fire door for Isaac. The First Dep had to mumble through the glass.

"Tim, do me a favor. Tell the king I'd like a word with him."

Old Timothy was playing deaf. "Isaac, what king is that? All the kings I know are dead."

Isaac spoke Dermott's name into the fire door.

57

"Dermott isn't expecting any guests. But if he wants you, we'll knock on your door."

"Timmy, who told him I was staying here?"

"Nobody. We bribed a porter. And we figured Mr. Moses Herzog of New York City had to be Isaac Sidel . . ."

"He knew I was coming, didn't he?"

"Not at all."

Isaac skulked down to his room. He did have a knock on his door. Close to midnight. It was Sylvia Berkowitz, wearing a raincoat with nothing underneath.

"Where's Marsh?"

"Asleep," she said.

"What if he wakes up? He won't think you're with Dermott. He'll come to my room. I don't know how Marsh will take to having three in a bed."

"He'd never notice. And he won't wake up. He likes his dreams too much . . ."

"Does he dream of Number Seven Eccles Street?"

"No," she said. "He dreams of fucking his wife."

The Berkowitzes were too profound for him. It was much easier to lie on his bed with Sylvia. She left her raincoat on. She nibbled Isaac a bit and then climbed on top of him. She writhed with a fury, and Isaac felt like some wooden soldier with a great toy prick that could be sucked on and used as a hilt. She wasn't oblivious of him. She fondled his bald spot, kissed him with devotion, but he couldn't keep up with that hunger she had. He was thinking of his daughter, her many marriages, her wildness for men. And Jennifer Pears? Was her good husband going down on her this minute? Or was Dublin time confusing him? Sylvia's writhing stopped. She fell asleep on Isaac's shoulder. Women, crazy women, were soaking his head. He dreamt of Annie's scar. The scar had moved to her belly in Isaac's dream. She had an "S" on her, for Sidel. The "S" began to wiggle. Isaac woke up, his legs kicking out in some kind of panic. Sylvia wasn't there.

ELEVEN

H E had breakfast with the Berkowitzes in the Shelbourne's Saddle Room. The Dean had kippers, bacon, haddock, eggs, one of Isaac's sausages, most of Sylvia's ham. Sylvia bumped Isaac under the table with both her knees. Isaac had to beg the waiters for toasted whole wheat bread. They weren't impolite. "Sorry, sir, brown bread doesn't toast easily." He was beginning to wonder if the king took his breakfast in his rooms. Then, at half nine, while Marshall was stealing scraps from Sylvia's plate, Dermott came down to eat with his bodyguards. They occupied four tables. You couldn't mistake the king. It was Dermott and six retired New York cops. The calm on Whores' Row began to make sense for Isaac. Dermott had his own rabbis in the Department. He couldn't have kept the nigger gangs from warring with each other over all that revenue unless Dermott had some fat cop in his sleeve.

His vassals ate like pigs around him. Dermott had coffee and white toast. He was a dark and handsome man. He couldn't have been over thirty-five. He had a stronger chin than Isaac. And no bald spot. His hair was black as Moses. It had a lovely sheen in the Saddle Room. But it wasn't marks of physical beauty that bit at Isaac. Dermott was a thinking man. You could see the grooves and gutters in his brow. His eyes had more clarity than those six vassels who ate with him. That was Dermott's power to attract. And he didn't have a worm to give him sunken cheeks.

The First Dep could feel some pressure on his arm.

"Moses, can I have that sausage if you're not going to finish it?"

"Absolutely," Isaac said. "And I'm not Moses anymore. Half of Dublin knows I'm here."

Dermott got up from the table. His vassals had to leave their kippers because of him. He nodded once to Marshall and his wife, but he had nothing for his old sponsor, Isaac Sidel. The First Dep was grateful that the Berkowitzes were going on a trip to the outskirts of Dublin for the morning at least. Howth Castle and Sandycove. Isaac begged to God that Marsh and his wife would lose themselves somewhere. The First Dep needed time to stalk, to fix Dermott's hours in his head, find a schedule, so that he would know when to leap, and he couldn't do anything with Sylvia pulling on his pants.

But he had a hard time looking for weak spots in Dermott. The king kept to his rooms. The vassals had a porter bring up his lunch. About four in the afternoon he went down to eat his tea. The king's party occupied a little nest of chairs in a corner of the lounge that was furthest from the windows. Was someone other than Isaac after the king? At five he went out for a walk in St. Stephen's Green. It wasn't much of a stroll. He kept to the gazebo on the near side of the pond. He was back at the hotel by five-fifteen. At eight he went out again. It was to a little Chinese restaurant on Merrion Row, the Red Ruby, a block and a half from his hotel. He was up in his wing at the Shelbourne before nine. An Irish Cinderella. Did his vassals tuck him in?

Isaac had his first bit of luck. The Berkowitzes were stranded in Sandycove. He could follow Dermott unmolested for a second day. The king's schedule didn't vary very much. Breakfast at the Saddle Room. Lunch upstairs. Tea. A stroll near the pond. Dinner at the Red Ruby. And good night.

How could Isaac get to him, and where? He couldn't make it out of Dublin in less than a week. The Berkowitzes came back. Sylvia would have drifted into Isaac's room without her underpants if the First Dep hadn't taken to the streets on that third day. The girls weren't pretty. They had freckles everywhere and their waists weren't high enough to please him. He was crazy about long-legged girls. The men seemed to have a dumb look around their eyes and a grimness in their cheeks. A nation of halfwits. Isaac wasn't fair. He had mingled with too many American Irish. He couldn't get along with them. His marriage to Kathleen had been twenty years of strife. The marriage were crazy, in Dublin and New York.

He rumbled back to the Shelbourne and sat in the lounge, where he saw an Irish beauty. She must have been a blue-blooded wench. She didn't have much of a brogue. Was she one of the Anglo-Irish who had ruled Dublin for centuries? She was with a perfectly tailored man about Isaac's age. They drank white coffee and muttered things that escaped the First Dep. They could talk without moving their lips, these Anglo-Irish. The woman had a long face and hot green eyes. She never looked at Isaac. The First Dep felt shabby in his clothes. He had no miracle tailor. And it wouldn't have mattered. The best of coats would have wrinkled on his body. The worm was quiet. Isaac trudged upstairs.

He couldn't sleep. He was going to get through that fire door hours before breakfast and squeeze Dermott Bride. Six vassals? Isaac would take them one by one. His only weapon was a hairbrush with a powerful handle and a hard black spine. If he smacked you between the eyes with it, Isaac could put you to sleep. He hid from the porters going up and down the stairs. He got to Dermott's floor. He could tell east from west tonight. He didn't see any vassals behind the fire door fronting Dermott's wing. He smuggled his way in. Six hands must have grabbed at him from different rooms. Isaac was sitting on his ass. Old Tim Snell wasn't laughing at him. "Laddie, it's an odd vacation for you . . . did you come with blessings from Mayor Sam? We hear that dunce is in the hospital. Is it money you want from Dermott? We ain't poor, but tell us why we should give a penny to you?"

"Dermott can keep his whores' gelt. There are enough fingers in the pie. I'd like to ask him about Annie Powell."

Old Tim crouched next to Isaac. "Oh, you're the

world in New York City, Isaac, me dear, but you couldn't sell a fart in Dublin. If you ever say 'Annie' to Dermott, you'll have yourself the grandest Irish funeral. We'll give you something to remember for a long time."

"Thanks, Timmy, but I'm curious why Dermott leaves his signature on a girl's face and then hires a thug to wipe it off."

All six hands grabbed at Isaac and pitched him through the fire door. "Isaac, it would be a pity if we had to throw you out a window . . . we're respected in this hotel. Have your vacation, and don't you bother us."

Sylvia was under Isaac's covers when he returned to his room. He didn't fight her off. Those six hands on Isaac must have livened him. His passion surprised the girl. Isaac licked all her parts. But it was Jennifer's nipples he was feeling in his mouth. The king must have put a spell on him, else the worm was doing its work. Fifty-one years old, and the schmuck was falling in love. Sylvia took his passion, but she wasn't Isaac's fool.

"You're worse than Marsh, do you know that? I come here to punish myself. It's just like a whipping. I'd walk out on that dope, but he'd wear the same underpants for a month if I didn't strip them off his ass. So I have to keep myself happy with the likes of you. Isaac, you're the shittiest lay I've ever had. You know what your cock feels like inside me? . . . a little boy's finger with some jelly on it . . . why are you in Dublin?"

He wasn't going to trifle with her after such appraisals. "I'm here to kill Dermott Bride."

"Moses, you really are a little nuts." But she had softened to him. "Why's it so important to you that Marshall's little scholar be dead?"

"Because the prick happened to torture a woman I like."

"My God," Sylvia said, "you are a human being." And she didn't seem so dark around the eyes. "Moses, who was she . . . this woman of yours?"

"A hooker on Forty-third Street. King Dermott put her there . . ."

Sylvia jumped on top of Isaac. "I'll help you kill the bastard, I swear . . . we won't tell Marsh . . . Marsh's a chickenshit . . . I'll go up to Dermott in my raincoat . . . get him to visit me in your room . . . we'll club him with a

62

pair of lamps . . . hide him under the bed . . . how will we get rid of the body?"

Murder drew her close to Isaac. She was caressing him with wild strokes of her hand. Sylvia discovered a cock on him. The First Dep didn't have a little boy's finger poking out of his groin. Off the wall, Isaac figured to himself, but her comradeship, her willingness to take on Dermott, touched him, and he was much more tender to Marshall's wife.

TWELVE

SYLVIA Berkowitz had become the nightwalker of the Shelbourne Hotel. She traveled abroad, in and out of her husband's room, whenever she pleased. The porters had gotten used to her. She was an American lady. The professor's wife. They would nod to her, taking in the bare knees under her raincoat. *Did you look at the pins on her? Lovely piece, that.* But they weren't disrespectful of Sylvia. "Good night, madam," they would say, each time she pased them in the halls. They knew she was going to her husband from Mr. Moses Herzog's bed. *A ladykiller he is. The man in 411. Mr. Herzog of New York.*

Sylvia was born a Mandel, one of *the* Mandels of Yonkers, Miami, and Hurricane Beach, men's clothiers for thirty-seven years. The Mandels could have found a dentist for Sylvia, a Jewish heart and lung man, a widowed accountant, or the scion of another clothing chain. They had the clout to buy any husband that appealed to them. They wanted something more exotic than a lung specialist. They had to have a scholar in the family, a secular rabbi, a man of words. They grabbed onto Marshall Berkowitz. They didn't worry about his field of interest. James Joyce? A blind Irishman who wrote filthy books.

They could forgive such aberrations in a scholar. Even two earlier wives.

The family would assume Marshall's debts and alimony payments if only Sylvia agreed to marry him. They expected trouble from her. Sylvia had an independent streak. Her full, brazen calves spelled lasciviousness to the Mandels. She'd pick an Arab tuba player to spite them, and they'd have to support a cove of tiny Ishmaels. They were wrong. Sylvia didn't have to be coaxed. Marshall wooed her with maps of Dublin, quotes from a cosmology that he stored in his head. Dublin was a fogtown that sprang out of James Joyce. This man-god could create rivers and streets. The Liffey and Fumbally Lane. Sylvia believed in him.

They were married under a canopy in the chapel of a Yonkers catering hall. A cantor sang the wedding prayers. Marshall wore the *kittel*, a white marriage shroud. Sylvia drank wine under her veil. She had to walk around the groom seven times to show that he was the center of her universe. The rabbi read the articles of their devotion. Sylvia took off the veil. Marshall broke a wine glass under his foot. They kissed. The family pelted them with bits of wheat and straw. They were ushered into a private room. Sylvia had her period. They weren't allowed to make love.

That was her history with Marsh. Menstrual blood and Leopold Bloom. She'd had four years of it. Excursions to Dublin that were holy pilgrimages. Marsh had little energy outside his books. He could raise up a passion for Molly Bloom. But he copulated like a baby boy. Bubbles appeared in his mouth. He would snort after a minute, suck in his belly, and go to sleep.

She couldn't sing to the Mandels. Hadn't she walked around Marsh seven times? They wouldn't listen to the complaints of a wife. God, was she supposed to say, Marshall, Marshall, why won't you chew my tits? She had to take scraps of love wherever she could find them. From Marshall's colleagues. A lonely sculptor at a Beethoven festival. The man from the stationery store. And Isaac.

She was committed to none of them, sculptor, stationery man, or cop. But she did have a feeling for this Moses. Something had eaten the fat out of him. Moses had more character than her other men. There were pieces of chivalry in Isaac Sidel. He didn't peek at women's garters, like Leopold Bloom. Or parade in Nighttown, near the Liffey, with his pants unfurled. He was the kind of man who could kill Dermott Bride for having mistreated a hooker in New York. He wouldn't bawl over a dead house on Eccles Street and shake his big fat ass. Moses had work to do. He was no better than Marsh when it came to chewing her tits. His orgasms seemed to rumble out of him like a bit of dry puke. But she forgave his pathetic courtship. Moses didn't get his Nighttown out of any book. He was in love with a Forty-second Street whore.

So she voyaged through the Shelbourne with a raincoat around her shoulders. Porters were carrying up trays of white coffee and toast. The Irish preferred to rise at six. "Would the madam like her breakfast in bed?"

"Thank you, no."

She might wake the dean, spreading marmalade on her toast. She crept back to Marsh's room, dropped the raincoat on the floor. Marsh was clutching the blanket with his fists. This was the man who wore a shroud at her wedding, who broke a glass under his foot. She opened one fist with gentle pulls on his fingers, got under the covers, closed his fist again, and hugged him around the waist, her Poldy, her Leopold, her Bloohoohoom.

THIRTEEN

ISAAC maundered in Dublin. He had nothing to do.
He couldn't isolate Dermott from his vassals. Killing
the king had become pure whim. Little Dermott was safe
in Dublin town. But Isaac wouldn't go home. His students
at John Jay would have to suffer without his lectures for
a while. He began to follow Dermott's narrow routes, in
order to put himself inside the king's head. So he ate at
the Red Ruby on Merrion Row, an hour before Dermott
was scheduled to arrive. Isaac had his lo mein, a spring
roll, and Chinese chicken soup. He imagined Dermott at
the table, with chopsticks and hot mustard, his vassals
eating with forks. Wasn't there another restaurant in
Dublin that would have the boy? Did Dermott need that
lo mein a block from the hotel? He had peculiar territories for a king.

Isaac would duplicate Dermott's walk in St. Stephen's
park, inhabit Dermott step by step. What did the king
look at from his gazebo? The slow, meticulous paddling
of the ducks? The way they poked their mouths into
the water? Did he notice the scum, leaves, and bottles at the
northern end of the pond? The thick green bowls of the
trees? And did he stare up at the roofs of the Shelbourne
from the park? The iron grilles, the great television aer-
ial, the nude flagpole, dormer windows, the fine white

molding, the four weather vanes? A few hundred yards in front of the Shelbourne. Is that where Dublin ended for Dermott Bride?

Isaac had his room changed. The porters moved him to the front of the hotel. *I want to see what Dermott sees.* He would stare out of his window at St. Stephen's, at the houses near his corner of the park, with their pitched roofs, the traffic, the hills outside Dublin, and then go to the lounge. Funny people were sitting there. Rowdies with broken noses. They drank jars of Guinness and wore helmets that looked like housepainters' hats, only these helmets came with chin straps. Isaac couldn't understand why the porters didn't throw them out. But the lounge seemed to be in awe of them. Men and women came over from the other tables to shake their hands. Isaac was dumbfounded until a porter told him that tomorrow was All-Ireland hurling day. These were the champions. Hurlers from Cork. What the fuck was hurling about? A game with sticks called hurleys and a leather puck. Ireland's national sport. Sixty thousand would rush to the hills of Croke Park for the final game between Wexford and Cork. Rougher than football, the porter said. Break your mouth with one of those hurling sticks. Isaac wished he had a hurley in his hand to come at Dermott's vassals. He'd win for Ireland and the United States. Use Dermott's scalp for a puck. Roll that head in the grass. He's be the master hurler, "man of the match." All the Irish bishops would be at Croke Park. Isaac might get canonized. They'd give him the Rock of Cashel to take home with him to America . . .

The First Dep was out of his skull. These men in their painters' hats wouldn't have served on any team with him. Isaac gave the lounge to them, the champions from Cork. He decided to walk the Liffey. He didn't need *Ulysses* as a primary text. He could have his Dublin without Mr. Joyce. Marshall was the haunted one. Not him. He wasn't going to court the river goddess, Anna Livia. He'd leave that to the Irish. But the river seemed fiercer today, much less of a pissy stream. The sun burnt down on the water, colored it red, like a king's beard.

He'd entered a section of warehouses on the quays. A poorer Dublin again. Dog carts and little grocery stores. Children lunged at his pants. They had dirty faces and torn sleeves. Isaac didn't know what they expected from him. They were trained beggars from some gypsy camp north of Dublin. He gave them all his Irish pennies. They still lunged at him. An old man had to chase them away with a stick, or they would have followed Isaac inside his pants. He was at Sir John Rogerson's Quay. Lime Street and Misery Hill. A huge black sedan was just behind him, trundling at Isaac's pace. Isaac stopped and started again. He wasn't going to give the car an easy time of it. Let the bitches stall on Sir John's Quay. The dog carts could drive them back to O'Connell Street. The car rumbled up close. A door opened for him. The First Dep was hauled in like a stinking fish out of the Liffey. He was sitting on Timothy Snell's lap. "Dumb fuck." There's only two choices, Isaac figured; they'll take me to Dermott, or kill me in an alley off the quays. The car moved into a blind, dead street. Moses the apostate had no prayers to mutter. Would they push him down on his knees? Isaac should have stuck to the Shelbourne, like the king.

He was still a puppet on Timothy's lap. Couldn't they give a man a little more room? Old Tim slapped him on the head. "Dermott is offering twenty thousand . . . he won't go higher than that. You're a nuisance, but he can always dig around you."

Twenty thousand? What were they talking about? Timothy slapped him again. "Isaac, the lad has made you an offer."

Isaac's head was whistling. He didn't mind the slaps, but they must have scared the worm. His gut squeezed horribly tight. He could have fallen off Tim's lap, the way the worm grabbed at him.

"Eat your twenty thousand," Isaac said, swearing his belly would explode and drop his entrails on Timothy's shoe. "Tell the king my trip was all about Annie."

Old Tim pushed him off his lap. Isaac huddled near the door. He realized now that Dermott didn't care to have him dead. They drove him back to the Shelbourne, and kicked him out of the car. The doorman smiled at Tim.

"He's a bit soused," Timothy said. "One jar too many."
The doorman helped Isaac into the hotel.

PART
THREE

FOURTEEN

TIGER John Rathgar became the forgotten man at his club. There were peculiar goings-on inside the Dingle. Irishmen appeared and disappeared without so much as a whisper to the PC. Some of them were lads from the Retired Sergeants Association who had sworn themselves to Chief Inspector McNeill. They wore derbies instead of eight-piece caps. McNeill had swallowed them up. John couldn't get a word out of the boyos. They wouldn't sing in his presence. Those wild geese, retired sergeants and Sons of Dingle Bay, had old boarding passes in their vest pockets. They shuttled between Ireland and Ameriky without telling John.

He was reduced to a ceremonial piece, with his handsome profile and his straw hair. He would arrive at the funeral of a slain cop, hug the widow, give his hellos to the padre. He would hang ribbons on female detectives who had fired their guns at some nigger thief. He would shake his jaw and pronounce statistics of doom at the closing of a precinct.

Otherwise he was at his club, sitting in a corner with bankbooks in his pocket. He knew the names by heart. *Gertrude MacDowell. Nosey Flynn. Molly and/or Leopold Bloom* . . . Where was Jamey O'Toole that would show up at the Mayor's house with a bankbook for

John? Should he cry to Dennis Mangen, the Special State Pros? *Dennis, find me this O'Toole. I'm lonely for the names in a little book.* Why were his brothers at the Dingle so secretive? Were they frightened of the great god Dennis? Couldn't they come to John? He was their headman, the *first* Son, and the Commissioner of Police.

FIFTEEN

MOSES Herzog arrived at Kennedy. He tore his passport to bits. A king and a worm had broken the First Dep. He got out of Dublin with his tail in his ass.

Isaac hid out at his hotel. Phone calls were coming in from his office. Isaac went down to Centre Street, where he could sit in the dark, listen to the scurry of the rats. The cops on duty at the old Headquarters were genuflecting to him. Why? They'd never missed him before. They had a certain terror in their eyes, an awe of him. A miracle passed while Isaac was in Dublin doing futile work. Mayor Sam had won the primary from his hospital bed. He'd smacked Rebecca between the eyes. The Irish came out for Becky Karp, but the "blues" and the Yids went for Mayor Sam. Isaac was lord of the primaries. He'd gathered in the votes for Sam with his talks in the synagogues, his lectures in the clubs. The Dublin idiot, Isaac Sidel, owned New York City.

"Hizzoner" was recuperating inside Gracie Mansion. He'd been asking for Isaac. "Where's the lad?" The First Dep had to rush uptown. It was a madhouse near the old Mayor. The deputies who had deserted Sam months ago crowded the master bedroom. They would have gotten into bed with Sam, under the big chandelier. "Hizzoner" had to drive them away. He was much less senile after the primaries. "Isaac, they laugh at us in

75

Chicago. We deserve a better Commissioner of Police. I'm making you the new PC."

A year ago you couldn't have separated Tiger John and Sam. "Hizzoner" wanted a PC that he could wrap around his thumb. But John had become a hindrance to him. John was an unpopular "Commish." John might lose City Hall for Mayor Sam.

"Your Honor, I won't sit at Headquarters like a loyal mole. Thank you, I'll stay where I am."

"Isaac, you're not a baby anymore. You can't keep wandering around in old suits."

Isaac would avoid Gracie Mansion until winter came. "Hizzoner" had a habit of forgetfulness. The First Dep would creep out of Sam's head in a day or two. Let those rebels who had gone over to Becky find a new Commissioner for Mayor Sam.

Isaac was coming out of his Dublin sloth. He went to Roosevelt Hospital to see Annie Powell. Annie wasn't on the hospital's lists. "What the hell do you mean?" Isaac growled. "She was here two weeks ago with a broken face." The residents, the nurses, and the guards couldn't keep Isaac from going through the hospital. Annie wasn't in the wards. She wasn't in a private bed. "Christ, do sick girls vanish from these fucking rooms?"

A doctor located her discharge slip. "Annie Powell walked out of here."

"When?"

"Last week . . . she got her skirt from the closet and disappeared."

"I suppose that happens all the time," Isaac said. "Losing a girl like that. You didn't have anybody to stop her?"

"We don't run a prison, Commissioner Sidel . . . we can't lock people to their beds."

She was at her whore's station on Forty-third Street, mad-eyed, bruised, with Dermott's mark annihilated from her, that "D" covered over with crisscrossing welts and blue lines. She didn't recognize Isaac without his bum's pants. "Mister, what are you staring at? . . . if you don't like the goods, you can crawl up or down a few more blocks."

"Annie," he said, "I'm Father Isaac."

Those mad eyes whirled in her head. "Keep away from me . . . I don't know any Father Isaac."

76

"Annie . . ."

Her shoulders began to heave with a terrifying rhythm. Isaac had set her off. She was leering at him with froth in her mouth. "The champagne boy . . . wanna buy some pussy?" She pulled her skirt up to her belly. Annie had forgotten her underpants. Tourists and dudes were blinking at her. A plainclothesman ran over from an Irish bar. Isaac kept him from Annie. "Go back to your whiskey house . . . I'm Isaac Sidel. I'll handle the girl."

Annie lowered her skirt the minute Isaac walked away. She muttered to herself. Anybody could have heard the clacking of her teeth. God knows where she would find any johns. Isaac phoned his office from a booth on Ninth Avenue. "Annie Powell," he said. "She's doing the shimmy on Forty-third. I want two kids to watch her day and night . . . hold her hand if they have to . . . she could hurt herself."

He couldn't put on his stinking pants. He wasn't in the mood to be Isaac the bum, with shit on his face. Would Annie show her crotch to the universe every time he came near her corner? Isaac went looking for the king's muscleman, Jamey O'Toole.

O'Toole had stepped on Annie, and somebody had to pay. It wasn't Dublin, where Isaac had to sneak around with a hairbrush as his only weapon. He brought six detectives with him to Jamey's apartment house. O'Toole lived in Chelsea with a thick metal plate on his door to discourage burglars, thieves, and cops like Isaac. It was two in the morning. Issac hadn't come unprepared. His men had shotguns, crowbars, and a sledgehammer.

He didn't knock on Jamey's door. The crowbars bit under the metal plate. The sledgehammer demolished every hinge. The door gave with a scream that nearly sounded human. Isaac wouldn't murder Jamey in his own house, God forbid. But if O'Toole was dumb enough to throw himself at six detectives, Isaac couldn't swear what would happen. A shotgun might go off. And Isaac would have a lot of paperwork. He'd build a good story. Rogue cop, Jamey O'Toole, dies resisting arrest.

Isaac didn't crouch in back of his men. He was the first to climb over Jamey's door.

"O'Toole, come on out . . . it's only Isaac."

Someone was crying in there. It wasn't O'Toole. Isaac

and his men trampled into all the rooms. The sobbing didn't go away. They searched the closets next. Isaac found an old woman sitting behind a pile of brooms. They began to mock her, Isaac's men. "Look at that. Jamey's hiding one of his aunts."

"Shut up," Isaac said.

The men who'd watched that fucking house for Isaac didn't even know Jamey had a mother. Isaac brought her out of the closet. He sat her in the kitchen with a glass of water. He let her drink before he questioned her. He cursed himself for the shotguns and the big hammer. All he'd accomplished was to frighten an old woman. "Mrs. O'Toole, could you help us, please? Where's that son of yours?"

She couldn't say. "He told me the cops was after him."

"Which cops?"

Mrs. O'Toole shrugged at Isaac.

"How long's he been gone?"

She counted on her fingers. "Thirteen days."

What cops could be after Jamey? Isaac's own men hadn't been chasing the big dunce. O'Toole ran from home while Isaac was in Dublin with the king. Why? Irishmen don't abandon their mothers. What kind of trouble was the lad in? It's hard to scare a donkey who's six feet seven.

Isaac left the kitchen. His men got in place behind him. They began to sicken Isaac. O'Toole's neighbors peeked out of cracks of light in their doors. The detectives looked ridiculous lugging shotguns and crowbars in shopping bags. But they had their badges pinned to their chests. "Police," they muttered, "police," and the neighbors closed their doors. It was Isaac who should have calmed the neighbors, if only to cover himself. But those shopping bags tore at Isaac's guts. The creature was stirring again. Isaac's personal "angel," Manfred Coen, used to carry his shotgun inside a shopping bag. He was a blue-eyed detective from the Bronx. Isaac appreciated a sad, beautiful, inarticulate boy around him. Blue Eyes. He was loyal to Isaac, and Isaac got him killed. The First Dep pushed Coen into his war with the Guzmanns. Coen didn't have the cleverness to stay alive. Isaac destroyed the Guzmanns, but his trophies were pretty irregular: a live, live worm and a dead Coen.

78

SIXTEEN

HIS mind must have gone to rot. He didn't understand the street anymore. He lived among pimps and dudes, but couldn't get a word out of them. The "players" had been organizing in the past two years. They weren't so vulnerable to the pussy patrol that Tiger John sent down on them. None of the "brides" would inform on her man. But the "players" were careful not to beat up on a girl. They'd come under the tutelage of Arthur Greer. Sweet Arthur didn't belong to the brotherhood of pimps. He had no need for a wide-brimmed hat. He acted as a kind of magistrate for most Manhattan dudes. If a quarrel developed between pimps, they took it to Arthur. Arthur decided who was right and who was wrong. He was better than a bail bondsman. He always gave you walking money for any "bride" who got into trouble.

What was his real profession? He owned boutiques, nightclubs, massage parlors, grocery stores, and a cab company. Arthur could afford to snub the Taxi Commission. He gave out his own "medallions" to all his gypsy cabs. They had meters and windows in their roofs. The "players" wouldn't ride in any other cabs.

The cops knew all about Sweet Arthur. They decided

to leave him alone. Arthur held tight to his various enterprises and policed them by himself. He was something of a loanshark, but he wouldn't touch any shit. No one bought dope in Arthur's cabs. He warned the pimps to clean their stables of contaminated girls. Junkie whores were cast out of Arthur's zones. They had to operate in the pigsties of Brooklyn.

Arthur had a few comrades under him. It was a family of sorts, a loose confederacy. Killers, bondsmen, pornographers, loansharks, and head pimps. Such were the "blues" of Sugar Hill. But there wasn't much of a Sugar Hill anymore. It was only a name, a manner of describing a certain sweetness among rich black thieves. They lived in co-ops throughout Manhattan and Queens. Arthur had a penthouse near Lincoln Center, whose windows took in half the cliffs of Jersey. Assemblymen showed up for dinner. Judges talked to Arthur at his penthouse. Actresses walked into his boutiques. So it wasn't much of an honor when the First Deputy came to his door.

Isaac had no one else. Whatever black Mafia there was began with Arthur Greer. The pimps hadn't given any of their secrets to Isaac the bum. Black and white hookers shuttled in and out of jail. Money was collected. The king sat in his Dublin hotel. Isaac couldn't put a dent into the traffic on Whores' Row.

Who were the lords of New York City? It was hard to tell. Sam won his primary. But mayors went cheap this year. His own clerks copied his signature behind the Mayor's back. Tiger John Rathgar, Commissioner of Police, prowled the fourteenth floor at Headquarters and bullied cops who got in his way. He could demote you, give you some graveyard for a beat. He terrorized the whole Department, Tiger John. But he couldn't have told you where any of his squads were placed. He didn't have a cop's sense of New York. Arthur Greer probably had more information about Tiger's squads than Tiger did.

"How's my man?" he said to Isaac. Sweet Arthur had a sensitive face. He'd come out of the Bronx, the leader of a notorious gang, the Clay Avenue Devils. You could see the scars along his lips. Who knows how many times he fought with a knife? But he wouldn't take on Isaac, scowl for scowl.

"I hear you've been on the stroll, Mr. Isaac. Wearing funny pants and living at a pimp's hotel. Why'd you wait so long to come to me? I can give you clues about the business. Would you like your own stable of girls? Then you can tell your class at the Police Academy all about the grubby life of a pimp."

"Arthur, your spies are sleeping on you. I teach at John Jay."

"One school's good as another," Arthur said, and he smiled.

"What happened to Jamey O'Toole? His mother says he's hiding from the cops. But I can't figure that one. Jamey doesn't have the smarts to hide from me."

"You can't always believe what a mother says, Mr. Isaac. Maybe he got disgusted swiping pennies from whores and pimps, and he disappeared with a money bag under his arm."

"Not Jamey. He's a loyal son of a bitch."

"Maybe he eloped with Annie Powell."

A rage was gathering in Isaac. He wanted to send Arthur out into the Jersey cliffs.

"What's Annie to you?"

"Nothing. She's out there with all the other dogs. Don't look so sad. I'm tickling you, baby. Everybody knows you're sweet on that girl."

"We were talking about O'Toole."

"That's it, Mr. Isaac. Jamey's sweet on her too."

"Then why did he bang her in the face?"

Arthur laughed. "You ever meet an Irishman who wasn't a litle crazy?"

"And Dermott? Would you call Dermott crazy?"

"Man, he's the craziest of them all."

"Is the king a friend of yours?"

Arthur shook his head in disgust. "No wonder you got stuck in the pig hotel. You must be on the slide. Me and Dermott ran together. We were in the same gang."

Once upon a time Isaac was familiar with every boys' gang in the Bronx. He was the cop who kept the peace. He didn't have to work with the youth patrol. Isaac would walk into any cellar to settle a dispute. The Devils of Clay Avenue owned huge chunks of the Bronx. Their territories took them from Castle Hill to Claremont Park. They were successful because they wouldn't fight along racial lines. Sweet Arthur welcomed Negroes, Italians, Irishers, and Jews into his gang.

"Shit," Isaac said. "You mean Dermott was one of yours?"

"The best I had. My minister of war."

"Then why can't I remember him?"

"Dermott, he didn't like to stick out. He was smart, man. I got most of the glory and the cuts in my cheek. Dermott moved away from us. He went to college without a mark on him."

"Who made Dermott such a king?"

"I did."

"But you said he didn't fight. Dermott doesn't have the scars . . ."

"But he talks like a king. You ever listen to Dermott? He could swipe your beard with five words."

"I don't have a beard," Isaac said.

"So what. He'd make you believe you had one, and then he'd cop it from you. That's why he was minister of war. We battled it out with those other gangs right at the table. They didn't have any crooners on their side. We had Dermott. The king would trade them blind. Maybe I'd back him up with my knife . . . and maybe not. It depended on how much Dermott could steal with his tongue."

"Strange," Isaac said. "I saw the king in Dublin. He didn't open his mouth once. Arthur, what's he doing at the Shelbourne Hotel?"

"Living with his ancestors. The king's got Irish blood."

"What happened between Annie and him?"

"They had a love spat," Arthur said. He couldn't stop smiling at Isaac. The First Dep was forlorn. He'd lost his strength somewhere, dropped it in the street the day he'd met Annie Powell. He'd never shake loose of that girl. He went to kill a man for Annie. He would have done the same to Arthur Greer.

"That mark on her came from a knife, didn't it?"

Isaac was muttering now.

"He put a perfect *D* on her. Dermott loved to croon, you said. A talking man. How did he get to be so handy with a knife?"

"Ask the king. Maybe he did some practicing at college." The smile on Arthur had already turned brittle. ". . . Isaac, I'm getting busy. You'll have to go."

A white maid had come in to dust all the pillows. A boy left with a grocery wagon. Isaac saw a plumber walking on his knees in one of the toilets. Arthur had a functioning army to serve him, but he didn't offer Isaac one small piece of cake.

Isaac had a touch of amnesia. He couldn't remember what his next appointment was. Then his intuition caught hold: he had no more appointments today. He'd grown invisible hiding in that nameless hotel, and it was hard to get his coloring back. He'd thrown himself into too many capers. Now he couldn't solve the riddle of his own existence. Had Annie become Isaac's sphinx? Who was she? Why should Annie's mark have maimed him so?

He went up to Morningside Heights and visited that old school of his, Columbia College. Isaac didn't really have an Alma Mater. Only four months under Marshall Berkowitz. The school year was about to begin. Trunks were being carried into the dormitories. It gave Isaac a scare, reminded him of his own meager education. He shouldn't have stopped reading *Ulysses*.

He didn't wait on line with the other freshmen in the corridors of Hamilton Hall. Isaac crashed into Marshall's office. The dean of freshmen was annoyed with him.

"Isaac, I have a mob of kids outside. Couldn't you telephone?"

"No," Isaac said.

Marshall's desk was littered with folders pierced in every corner with a silver pin. The pins must have represented a kind of system to Marsh. He seemed much skinnier in New York. What had happened to that Dublin rump of his? His ass was gone. Was he still crying over Bloom's dismantled house? Isaac was a pragmatist. He couldn't mourn Number 7 Eccles Street. He had the living to contend with. Specific scars and the king.

"I want that recommendation I wrote for little Dermott."

Marshall trembled over the silver pins. "You see the condition of this place. I couldn't find it in a thousand years."

"Marsh, I'll help you look."

They stood over Marshall's filing cabinets and searched the drawers. Sheets of paper crumbled in Isaac's hand. Folders ripped at the edge. Students were knocking on the door. Marshall wouldn't open up. It took an hour to dig out Isaac's ancient memorandum. It was typed on

Police stationery. Isaac had to glimpse at his own language before he could believe a word.

> . . . Marshall, I know you're going to think this one is a sweetfaced hood. He wears saddlestitched pants. He has sideburns and a duck's ass. He's "Bronx" up to his eyebrows. I could identify the streets he walked on, the rocks he must have thrown into windows. But he has a head on him. The boy can think. It's saved him from those death traps of Southern Boulevard and Boston Road. Forget the shitty grades. High school must have been a bore from beginning to end. I don't know if *Silas Marner* put him to sleep. But talk to him about *Hamlet*. Dermott can tell you about hysteria, idiocy, and revenge. Don't let the kid get away. It would be a shame for Columbia to lose him.

"Isaac, I can Xerox that for you," Marshall said. The search through his files had gentled him.

"Thanks, Marsh, but that's okay. I won't forget it now . . ."

Marshall returned to his desk. He was staring at the walls, surrounded by folders and pins. Isaac came out of his reverie to notice Marsh's fish eyes, that dead, abstracted look.

"What's wrong?"

"Sylvia's left me . . ."

Isaac didn't have to hear why Sylvia Berkowitz fled from *Ulysses* and *Finnegans Wake*. How long can you coexist with James Joyce under the blanket with you? But he couldn't utterly abandon Marsh. "How did it happen?"

"I don't know. She didn't take a thing with her . . . no panties. Not even her books."

It wasn't a hopeless case. Isaac had the resources to track a dean's missing wife. He could descend on 1 Police Plaza, the official home of the First Dep, and organize a search party. Isaac was famous for his ability to climb into the roots of any borough and come up with a handful of runaways.

"Marsh, I'll see what I can do."

The freshmen outside Marshall's office looked surly. Isaac couldn't blame them. They probably had to skip lunch on account of him. Isaac also remembered waiting for Marsh. The freshman with the bull neck. Isaac Sidel. He should have been champion on the wrestling team. Isaac was a devil at a hundred and forty-eight pounds. He'd gone out for wrestling because it was the one sport at college that suited his temperament. Football was for the grubs. You needed stamina, psychology, and strong, slippery arms to wrestle. And Isaac's neck. No one could pin Isaac when his neck was bridged on the mat. He would suck oranges before a match, stare at his opponent, and do warm-ups in his beautiful Columbia leggings. He traveled to Yale with the freshman team. The Yalie he wrestled was disqualified for gouging. It was the first and last Columbia win. He stopped going to practice. He didn't have the time. James Joyce had already bitten Isaac in the ass.

He couldn't get out from under Marshall's influence. He idolized the dean. Wrestling was nothing compared to the music of words. The team dropped Isaac Sidel. He had to give those beautiful leggings back to the college. Language was all. He was jealous of other boys who occupied Marsh. He would catch the dean going in and out of his office. There was always some question to ask. "Why does Joyce say that an Irishman's house is his coffin?"

Had little Dermott behaved like that? Did he follow Marsh around, beg audiences with the dean? Goggle at him over cups of coffee? The romance was shortlived for both of them. Dermott went off to Yale, and Isaac disappeared from college. Were they still votaries of Marsh? Was Dermott writing songs about the Liffey from his hotel room? Is that all his exile meant? A crook returning to scholarship in his middle years? Isaac was the fool of fools. It was business, business, business that was holding the king. And Isaac was a man without a clue. He should have stayed an ordinary Police inspector. He didn't have much resiliency as the First Dep. When a cop falls, he isn't supposed to lie flat.

Marshall must have followed him across South Campus. He ran after Isaac with his tie trailing down the back of his neck. They were like two gaunt, hurt creatures chasing one another. "Isaac," the dean said. "Sylvia told me about you and her . . . she has a habit of con-

85

fessing her love affairs. But she didn't have to tell. It makes sense. You were her Dublin beau."

"I'm sorry, Marsh . . . it happened. We were going downhill from Eccles Street. We landed in a deserted lane and . . ."

"Stop that. She would have gone after Dermott if you hadn't arrived . . . Isaac, please find her for me."

SEVENTEEN

ISAAC thought and thought of Sylvia, and came to Jennifer Pears. He had his men shop for two women at a time. He wouldn't go near that ugly red fortress at 1 Police Plaza. He took a ride to Centre Street and sat in his old rooms. He shouldn't have fucked his mentor's wife. Now he owed Marsh. His deputies were going gray in the head. Who were these two cunts that belonged to Isaac? Sylvia Berkowitz was on the loose. They didn't mind scrambling for her. But why did they have to shadow this Jennifer lady? Isaac demanded all her moves. The First Dep was reluctant to get Mrs. Pears on the phone. She might hang up on a prick like him. Isaac was a terrible suitor. He would snake in and out of a woman's life. No one could stand him for very long. He was an uncivilized boy, fifty-one years old.

His deputies had no "buys" on Sylvia Berkowitz. She must have shrunk into the ground, like that big Irish ape, O'Toole. Not the green-eyed one. Jennifer Pears was a piece of cake. Soon as she said goodbye to her doormen, Isaac's deputies had her under control. These weren't dummy cops. They knew how to fatten a page for Isaac. *Takes her boy to the Little Red Schoolhouse.* (They posed as fire chiefs to follow Jennifer inside.) *Plays with him up on the roof with his kindergarten class. She usu-*

87

ally stays an hour. Then she goes to Fourth Avenue. The lady likes to buy old books . . .

Isaac was religious about reading the reports. It gave him a feeling of power over Jenny. He had her moments at his command. He could intrude upon them whenever he liked. Bookstalls weren't for him. He went to the Little Red Schoolhouse on Christopher Street. He didn't have a fire chief's hat. He had to bluff his way past the bulldog lady who stared at him from a cubicle inside the door. Was she the school's concierge? Isaac had so many bumps in his forehead. He might have been a freak about to paw an innocent child. The concierge would have summoned the janitors to get rid of Isaac. But then he smiled, and the bumps went away.

"I'm Moses," he said. "Moses Herzog Pears. My grandnephew is in your kindergarten. Alexander Pears. I'm supposed to meet his mother on the roof. That's Jennifer, my niece . . ."

Isaac climbed up to the roof. It was a playpen fenced around with wire. It had enough materiel to confuse an army: wagons, sandboxes, tunnels, houses and bridges made of cardboard walls and cinder blocks. He couldn't locate Alex in the muddle of kids. Jennifer stood near the fence. Her green eyes could have sucked in every wagon, tunnel, and bridge. The creep was in love with her. He had crazy knots in his legs. The worm didn't give him any flak. It curled up in Isaac's belly, satisfied with itself.

Jennifer wasn't coy with him. She wouldn't crouch behind a tunnel because the schmuck had disappointed her, gone to Dublin to kill a man without any notice.

"You don't look happy," she said.

He wished her eyes had a more neutral color. Then he could have walked away from that roof without Jennifer Pears. He grunted the word *cappuccino*. Jenny understood. She couldn't leave at Isaac's first grunt. She had responsibilities to the kindergarten. But she met him downstairs in the Cafe Borgia.

Isaac's vocabulary was coming back. "Dublin . . . had to go . . . how's your husband Mel?"

"Isaac, what the fuck do you want from me?"

Sitting next to her terrified him. He licked the coffee with his head between his shoulders, like a snail.

"More sessions at your hotel, is that what you're after? . . . or are you on a culture kick? Isaac, should we

88

take in the Cézanne show at the Modern? . . . do you want to feel me up inside a movie house? What's your pleasure today?"

Couldn't he borrow Dermott's magic tongue? The king would have known how to woo Jennifer Pears.

"I'm pregnant."

The worm beat against the lining of Isaac's gut with its many hooks. His face landed in the cappuccino mug. He came up with milk on his nose, a ridiculous man.

"You're a godsend, Isaac. We've been trying to have another baby for years. A brother or sister for Alex. You know, all that shit about an only child. Nothing happened until you came along . . . would you like a share of the baby? We could form a limited partnership. Put your request in. Would you prefer a girl or a boy? I'm banking on a girl. Should we allow her to pick her own dad? . . . Isaac, do me a favor. Don't visit me at my son's school. It isn't nice."

And she was gone from the Cafe Borgia before Isaac could wipe his nose with a paper napkin. Funny thing, he didn't feel like a patriarch. He had an itch in his testicles. His knees were dead. A worm tore his gut like shavings on a pipe. Was he going to be a daddy every twenty-nine years? He had a daughter who was crazy for men. Marilyn the Wild. She could twist Isaac harder than any worm the Guzmanns had stuck him with. What would Marilyn think of a new half-sister or brother?

Isaac ran out of the cafe. He could have had his men steal Jennifer from the bookstalls of Fourth Avenue, carry her to his hotel, wrapped in a body bag or an old blanket from the horse patrol. He wouldn't have undressed her, no, no, no. I'll take that partnership, he'd say. Half your belly is mine. Whatever lunacy he was into, he still had the eyes of a cop. A man was following him from the next corner. A man with scruffy white hair. Isaac had to laugh. It was a retired captain from precincts in the Bronx. Morton Schapiro. Who would put such a joker on the First Deputy's tail? Isaac led Morton down to Wooster Street and trapped him against the window of a deserted shoe factory. Morton had a Detective Special in his pants. Isaac stole the gun away and tossed it through a crack in the window.

"Morton, who's been hiring you to play Billy the Kid?"

"Nobody."

"Come on. Did Dermott holler in your ear all the way from Dublin?"

"Who's Dermott?" Morton said.

Isaac could have taken him into the factory and pulled on Morton's skull until the old captain lost his beautiful white hair. He'd scalped people before. But he didn't want blood on his fingernails. He was going to be a father again. He grabbed Morton by the collar and jerked his neck. The captain swayed like a large rotting pumpkin. It couldn't have been very serious if Isaac's enemies were hoping to glue Schapiro to him. The captain was no threat. He couldn't hold down a precinct while he was on the Force. The Chief Inspector would ship him from house to house. Schapiro was a "flying" captain, who would take over a precinct for a month and then push on. His lieutenants laughed in his face. The homicide squad wouldn't say hello to him in the hall. There were no parties for Captain Mort when the PC asked him to retire. Whatever job he had now was nothing but charity. Isaac could have choked him to death. But it would have been a bother to round up guests for Morton's Jewish wake.

"Schapiro, talk to me. What pimp are you working for?"

"Arthur Greer."

"That's insane. Why would Arthur send you after me?"

"Dunno . . . he said stick to Isaac. That's all."

"Did he give you a message for me?"

It was a stupid question. Schapiro himself was the message. A fat kite. Isaac wasn't supposed to ask about Dermott anymore. Why? How often could the First Dep trot to Stephen's Green? Dublin wasn't behind the Jersey cliffs. You couldn't reach the Shelbourne by rowboat. The king was jittery about having Isaac in New York.

"Morton, be a good boy. Give Arthur a hug for me. Tell him Isaac doesn't like mysteries. The king can have his exile. But I intend to open him up."

He shoved the captain uptown. He would have liked to pitch him over the roofs of Houston Street, up to Lincoln Center and Arthur Greer. That would have been a sensational kite. No matter. The captain would be in disgrace. He couldn't hold on to Isaac the Pure. Captain Mort

90

should have been out looking for catfish in Eastchester Bay. What was he doing with a gun in his pants? Was there a society of old captains for sale? It didn't make sense. Who was organizing the other Captain Morts? Not Arthur Greer. Arthur didn't have the claws to dig that deep into the Department. Isaac would have known. He had his spies in the Commissioner's office. The First Dep could have broken up any ring of ex-captains that was lending itself out to pimps and crooks. Isaac wasn't asleep. He began to dial his office from a telephone booth. He'd put a fix on Morton Schapiro, find out what the old captain's been doing in the last year or so.

Isaac could have sworn he was in Dublin again. A drunken man and woman were having a mean little fight outside his telephone booth. Their slaps seemed pathetic to Isaac. They maintained a slow dance of arms and legs. Then the man got vicious. He had the woman by her hair. He shook her and shook her as Isaac came out of the booth. It was one of those freak encounters. He recognized the woman beneath the roots of her hair. The drunk was assaulting Marshall's wife. Had Sylvia found a second husband in the streets? Isaac tore the man's fingers out of her hair, dragged him into the booth, and closed the door on him.

"You have terrific friends, Mrs. Berkowitz."

Isaac was pissed at himself. Where was his squad of "angels" that was supposed to prowl for Sylvia? Why should *he* have stumbled upon her after leading Morton Schapiro on a little chase through Soho? Was some miserable tinkering god giving out gifts to Isaac? Or maybe a worm can navigate with its hooks. That punk in his belly had steered him to Sylvia.

He took her into an artists' saloon, treated her to black coffee and cigarettes. The artists at the tables seemed to feel a kinship with Isaac. They must have taken his sunken cheeks as a sign of poverty and powerful, suffering thought. The First Dep had traveled far from Centre Street in his days and nights as a bum. He'd moved beyond some kind of maddening pale. Isaac was less and less a cop.

"Your husband's been bawling for you," he said.

Doses of coffee and cigarettes had revived Sylvia Berkowitz. "Isaac, don't be his mama. Marsh will pick up a

91

new survival kit . . . a Barnard student to scrub his underwear."

"Got any cash on you?"

"No, but I'll sing carols outside a restaurant."

"Sylvia, you're in the wrong season. It isn't Christmas yet. You'll starve. Who was that clown you were with?"

"Nobody special. I met him in a candy store two hours ago."

"Do you have a place . . . a home?"

She didn't have to answer him. Marshall's wife was living among the garbage cans. If she had that much of a need to break away from Marsh, Isaac wasn't going to twist her head around. "Come with me."

The First Dep had a small apartment on Rivington Street. That's where he kept most of his suits. He gave the apartment to Sylvia.

"Isaac, will you stay with me?"

He could remove her filthy blouse, wash her back, and bring her over to his mattress. Who would be the worse for it? Not Sylvia. Not him. And like some magical rabbi, Isaac might be able to soothe her so she'd want to come back to Marsh. But that child he was making in Jennifer Pears got in the way. The old bum was turning chaste. He left her food money and a number where he could be reached. He was down the stairs before Sylvia had the chance to thank him or crawl into his sleeve. She wouldn't have minded raping Isaac the Pure.

EIGHTEEN

SOMETIMES he doubted whether he had an office or not. What was going on at the thirteenth floor of 1 Police Plaza? He demanded independence, a footlooseness, the right to range about the City in dirty pants. And then he wondered why his "angels" should function so well without him. His rat squad would probe underground and surface with a bundle of crooked cops. Isaac had put the squad into motion. He'd trained his men to go for blood.

He had other "angels," other squads that were putting out for him. They couldn't deliver the king's Irish donkey, O'Toole, but they did dredge up morsels on the king himself. They'd gone into New Haven, sought out Dermott's career at Yale. They had his transcripts, his dormitory rooms, and notes from the master of his college, from professors, from New Haven's former Chief of Police. It seems the lad had been thrown out of school in a gentlemanly way. The Yale Corporation invited him never to come back. The reasons weren't clear to Isaac's men. Cops had been on campus looking for Dermott Bride. He was operating a sort of smuggler's ring inside the college. Dermott secured stolen radios, television sets, cameras, fishing rods, and other tripe for Yalies and college groundsmen, dishwashers and cooks. He'd get his supplies from some nigger gang. But no one could tell who that nigger gang was. Isaac smiled to himself: that kid went into business with Arthur Greer. He didn't break with the Devils at all. Arthur's old gang swiped the radios, and brought the merchandise up to Yale.

Isaac looked through the transcripts: it was at Yale that the kid had shortened his name, become Dermott Bride. Isaac could swear that the king never left Arthur's gang. The Clay Avenue Devils were running Whores' Row.

But Isaac's men couldn't pick up on Dermott after he got out of Yale. What happened to those sixteen years between New Haven and the Shelbourne Hotel? How did Dermott groom himself with so much mystery and finesse? Isaac's mind was knocking. He decided to rest. He used the morning to invade the Little Red School-house. Jennifer wouldn't have a cappuccino with him. He had to propose to her from the doorway that led to the playground on the roof.

"You'll divorce that schmuck," he said.

Her eyes burned a green that was so fierce, Isaac had to grab the wall. "What schmuck are you talking about?"

"Your husband. You'll divorce Mel and marry me."

Isaac already had a wife, Kathleen, who was becoming the empress of Florida with all the condominiums she had built in the swamps around Miami. Kathleen couldn't stand Isaac, but she liked being Mrs. Sidel. She didn't need a penny from the boy, and he'd have to strangle Kathleen to get a divorce out of her. Isaac wasn't think-ing of practicalities. He'd fight the laws of Miami and New York, grow into a bigamist, if Jennifer would allow him to be the father of her child.

"Isaac, you must be sick. Eight or nine meetings in a hotel room don't make a marriage. I was fond of you before you ran away to Ireland . . . that worm of yours appealed to me. I liked your crazy room . . . your filthy pants . . . the way you talked. But that doesn't mean I'd ever leave Mel."

"Try me," Isaac said. "I'm as good a father as that schmuck."

"Isaac, if you come here again to annoy me, to talk of marriage proposals, I'll scream downstairs for the cops. I don't give a damn what kind of commissioner you are. I'll have somebody arrest your ass."

Isaac disappeared from the Little Red Schoolhouse.

All those infants in their classrooms began to disturb him. He thought of their moms and dads. So many mothers and fathers living settled lives. Isaac had stations where he could come and go, an office, a room, an apartment to store his clothes, but he was like an animal who existed on the streets. The patriarch was longing for a proper home.

He cruised uptown, ignoring traffic signals. Colors blinked at him. Isaac didn't care. Nothing could break his stride. Cars and trucks had better watch out. You'd have to pay a stiff fine if you ran over the First Deputy of New York.

Annie wasn't at her corner, and Isaac despaired. She was *his* family, even if she revealed her crotch at the sight of him to drive Isaac away. And Dermott? Dermott was family too, though Isaac couldn't explain the connection there. He'd bound himself to the king and his "bride." He'd become lonely at fifty-one, the self-sufficient Isaac, the *brain* of the City Police, who was used to shoving men around like waxed pieces on a board. Chess was too complicated for his dead "angel," Manfred Coen. Isaac loved to play checkers with Blue Eyes. But the First Dep was weary of games. He'd squash the secret rumblings on Whores' Row, the complicated, mysterious shit, and then demand a leave of absence. Sam was snug in the Mayor's house. "Hizzoner" could survive without Isaac Sidel.

He saw Annie totter out of an Irish bar near his hotel. Her face was beginning to heal. But she still had the shadow of a "D" on her. Property of Dermott Bride. She didn't snarl at Isaac, or raise her skirt. She'd passed the morning drinking stout, and she was looking for an early customer, a john who'd pay for her necessities: tampax, lipstick, and beer. That was the only diet Annie could remember. She had enough stout in her not to feel hostile to a nosy, digging cop. "Father Isaac."

"Annie, I . . ."

"If you say anything, one word about a French restaurant, I'll squat right here and piss on the sidewalk. Can't you take a girl to a human place . . . without waiters in black coats who bow at you and want to kiss you on the back?"

She lured him into a Greek dive where Isaac himself liked to go when he was wearing his bum's pants. The restaurant had its own rationale. The waiters weren't Greek. They were Syrian, gruff, sloppy, and lecherous. They uncorked bottles of retsina with their powerful tongues. Annie loved resin-flavored wine. She drank with Father Isaac. He didn't question her about the king. She would flee from the table, and Isaac would have to drink retsina alone.

"Annie, I have a daughter who's a lot like you."

"Mister, keep your daughters to yourself . . . if you give me twenty bucks, I'll wiggle my ass . . ."

That whorish mumble pained the First Dep. She was a madwoman who went down for men in the street. No pimp had taught her to smile. Arthur Greer might have exploited Annie's invisible mark. Disheveled, bitten, she was still the greatest beauty on Whores' Row. It didn't help her much. Even if there had been a school for prostitutes, Annie couldn't matriculate. She'd scream, stick out her tongue, tear off her bra at the wrong moment. If Isaac hadn't put two of his "angels" on her, she wouldn't be alive. They were so expert at their jobs, Isaac had his troubles spotting them: two blondish lads at a far table. They must have arrived at the First Deputy's office after he'd gone to live in his bum's hotel. He couldn't recollect their names.

Isaac wasn't concerned about the sense of diaspora in his own platoons. His "angels" could disperse wherever they liked, so long as they were loyal to him. He had Annie to consider, and the girl confounded Isaac. She was a hooker who didn't know how to bait a man. Her clumsy whore's life belonged to some ritual that was outside Isaac's ken. What weird dream was she acting out? Annie taking vengeance on herself? The retsina came to Isaac's help. It was better than splits of champagne. All that resin in the wine must have loosened the girl. She sang to Isaac.

> Who's the Rose of Connemara?
> The Queen of Cashel Hill?
> Derm had a lady
> And the lady aint no more.

She couldn't carry a tune. The lines slurred out of her. Isaac wished she'd go on singing for him.

"Castledermott," she said.

"What?"

"You need a license to fish, you dope."

He'd play to her, tell her what she expected to hear, and then he'd stitch his own tune out of what she said.

"Where can I get this license?"

"From the Fisherman . . . he'll break your balls if you steal trout from his pond. Poachers can get killed. It's happened before. But it's Dermott's castle. He fries the bread."

Isaac didn't have the faculties to compose a tune. Castles? Fisherman? Trout? "Annie, how do you find Castledermott?"

"Put your hand under my skirt . . . that's where it is. You'll reach the right fish."

He'd have to ignore the gibberish about her genital parts. "Was that castle inside a hotel?"

"Prick," she said, "who's the Rose of Connemara? Me or you?"

He felt ugly gorging her with wine. But he couldn't break her riddles unless she drank some more.

"Did the Fisherman try to hurt you?" he said.

"You crazy? An old gent like that. Father Isaac, you ask funny things."

A waiter sneaked up to them with two of those long retisina bottles. "Get out of here," Isaac muttered. He didn't need a waiter's tongue to open his wine. Isaac bit into the cork and pulled.

"Mister, see my boots?"

Isaac looked. Annie was wearing sandals today.

"I only buy boots at Switzer's. None of your shitty stores. My man won't let me touch Irish paper money. It's got germs. Bulges in your pocket. It's indecent for a lady to carry so much cash. But how can you pay for an ice cream cone with a banker's check? Unless you bring the donkey."

"Is that O'Toole? Was Jamey your protector? Then why did he turn on you."

"The donkey doesn't turn. He's too big."

"Annie, did you live in that hotel with the king? Were you up in the Shelbourne? Was Jamey there too?"

He was beginning to grow frantic in his need for clarity. Why didn't he pursue smaller things, go for the nibble, like that Fisherman, whoever he was.

"I don't like yellow drapes," she told him. "And they

always say, *madam* this, and *madam* that. Why do I have to eat with seven forks? A fork for salmon. A fork for lettuce. A fork for soup. It's only silverware. You think he was happy being like that? I know Derm. He likes to stick his finger in the fish. He didn't care if I had my period . . ."

Could he talk about the scar now, the magical *D*?

"Annie, who . . ."

"Show me a barman who can pull a good pint, and I'll give you some of my kish . . . my man is particular. Don't you ruin the cream line on his Irish coffee. The donkey will have to drink a bad glass."

She got up from the table. But she made Isaac sit where he was. "Annie, I could walk you home . . ."

"Mister, don't think of following me. I'm wise to what you're after. The fish stays in my pants. So forget it . . ."

The girl had fish on the brain. Was it some lovetalk between Annie and the king? She hobbled out of the restaurant, the Syrians peeking at the folds in her ass, drawing Annie in with faces hard as fish hooks. His "angels" didn't move from the chairs they were in. They wouldn't even acknowledge Isaac. He had to introduce himself to his own fucking men.

"I'm Isaac," he said, feeling like an idiot. They didn't jump, those blond lads of his. "You're supposed to stick with her."

He didn't like the harsh neutrality under their eyes. His "angels" should have been more passionate about Annie Powell.

"Isaac, it takes her half an hour to cross the street. We have plenty of time."

"That's not the point," he said. "You're supposed to make sure she gets across the street."

They were slow in getting off their rumps. He asked them about Jamey O'Toole.

"Isaac, that quiff couldn't be in Manhattan. We would have spotted him ages ago."

They left with toothpicks in their mouths and napkins on the table. He'd have to call his office and push them off the case. He wanted livelier boys on Annie Powell, lads he could trust. But he never called. Annie's obsession with fish had taken hold of Isaac. Was there a trout pond in St. Stephen's Green? Could Dermott fish from a window? The king would have had to concentrate all his magic and all his luck. Isaac was demoralized. His primitiveness had failed him here. Once he was a man who could sense the pedigree of any situation. Isaac had the gift. But he'd crawled into the Guzmann family and come out with a worm. The worm had blunted him.

PART
FOUR

NINETEEN

ROSE, Rose of Connemara. Miss Annie Powell. She had to take an awful leak. Enough wine and beer in her to drown a Dublin pony. Father Isaac. She loved to torture that bum who came to her in clean and dirty pants. She wasn't going to be anybody's daughter. Not his. She was selling pussy. Nothing less. She didn't have to eat French dinners with a guy who wouldn't pull off her clothes. She'd had a thousand dinners with her man. He took her to places a bum couldn't afford to go. Steak tartare. She could read all the menus in the world. He let her swipe towels and doilies from the biggest hotels. She could powder her tits with pure Irish lace. Nobody owned her anymore.

The uncle was waiting for her under a lamppost. Mr. Martin McBride. He didn't look very grand. He's got a disease, they say. His lungs are turning to paper. The uncle was scared of something. He'd threaten Annie, then he'd offer cash. It was a disgrace for Dermott to have his lady working in the streets. She wouldn't accept money from this old knish.

"Jesus," he said, "you'll get us all killed. Woman, can't you see? Everywhere you go there's a cop. It means nothing to pay them off. They're after blood. How many times do they have to kick you in the face?"

"I've been kicked before. By uglier people." She ran a finger over that invisible scar. "How's the man?"

"Are you crazy? Dermott won't talk to me. You can't reach the lad. It takes a month to get a call into Ireland. And Dermott never picks up the phone. I have to talk to one of those bulls he keeps around him. 'Sorry, Mr. McBride. But the king isn't here.' Sending a telegram's no good. How do I know who's going to read it? We're in the dark, woman. I take instructions from that nigger, Artie Greer."

"What does he say about Derm?"

The uncle wrinkled his nose. "Merciful God, how can you trust a nigger gombeen man? He swears Dermott's playing golf in his rooms. Woman, do us a favor, please. Walk out of here. I'll get you an apartment in Forest Hills. You can have your own beagle. Six cats if you like. Move, I'm telling you. Shuffle off. We'll all die if you stay too long."

"Dermott knows where I am. Let him come for me."

"Jesus, don't you learn? The nephew's a dead man if he lays a foot in Manhattan. That's the lousy deal they made."

"I didn't put my name on that pact, Martin McBride, so stop bossing me around."

"But you're *his*. You're Dermott's. That's the way they'll look at it. And they'll reach out for you again and again and again."

Annie smiled for uncle Martin. "Not to worry your head about it. I have me a benefactor. A real live beauty. Tough as they come."

"Who?"

"What's the difference? He buys me champagne. In baby bottles."

"Tell me who it is?"

"That high commissioner. Father Isaac."

A grayness overtook uncle Martin, and he rocked on his heels. "That bandit . . . he's the worst of the lot. Woman, he kidnapped me, swear to God. Brought me to a phony precinct. Isaac. He makes his own police stations. He has killers under him . . ."

"So what? He wants to marry me."

Uncle Martin developed a hacking cough; he hugged the lamppost and tried to catch his breath. Annie had to console him.

"I'm only fooling. He's too big a fox to marry. Me with a husband and all. Though I hear Irish weddings aren't too legal in America."

"Woman, eat your tongue. This Isaac, he's got ears in every window."

He trundled away from Annie, bumping into lampposts to regain his strength. Annie went upstairs. She lived in a rooming house that attracted outcasts like herself: rummies, Army deserters, whores unbridled by any pimp. It was cheaper, lower, more slovenly than Isaac's hotel. But at least it had a name. Lord Byron's Rooms. Most cops wouldn't invade the premises. The stairs might collapse under their feet. They could lose their holsters in a darkened hallway, or their whistles and their memorandum books. Annie felt secure. She was safe from unwanted company.

She wouldn't think of locking her door. The rummies would only have swiped her doorknob together with the lock. They liked openness at the Lord Byron. But they didn't poke in Annie's room for a bottle of milk. A man with tremendous hands and feet was resting on her mattress. Jamey O'Toole. He could have been Robinson Crusoe. He'd stopped shaving at the end of August. Now he had a crooked beard. He wore the same things: pants, shirt, and socks that clung to him like pieces of bark. Jamey sweated under his clothes. He was afraid to come out from Annie's room. She'd hidden this Irish donkey, stuffed him away at the Lord Byron. It was strange to watch such a big man shiver. She couldn't desert Jamey O'Toole. The donkey had been good to her. He'd mothered Annie in Ireland, kept her out of harm, saved her from a tribe of gypsy thieves.

No drunkenness could ruin Annie Powell. Dermott's "bride" had been slippery and shrewd at that Greek restaurant. She shoveled bread and cheese under her skirts while she ate with Isaac. Now Jamey had a meal for himself. He ripped the bread with long fingers and gobbled lumps of cheese. Poor man, he couldn't take a bite without Annie. Bread would drop out of his fists. Most of the cheese landed on her mattress. She wasn't too proud to stoop for the donkey. She had to feed Jamey O'Toole. She was grateful for the teeth in his mouth. He still remembered how to chew.

"Jamey, I've got thirty dollars in my pocket. You could jump on a bus, you know."

"They're watching the buses," he said, with cheese stuck on his tongue.

"I could walk with you. I'll scream if they come around."

"Never mind, Annie girl. We'll sit. They're dumb. You can bless the saints for that. They couldn't figure I'd be in your room."

"Why do they want you so bad?"

"Ah, it's a pitiful story. We had the leverage on them. Then Dermott made the peace. He told himself he could spread the waters and hop over the Irish Sea. I begged him not to go. He's nothing but a prisoner over there, Dermott is. They 'yes' him, they bow to the king. But let him try to disappear."

"Is the Fisherman holding Dermott?"

"Yeah, the Fisherman. And other guys."

"Isaac, is he one of them?"

"Who the fuck knows? You can't trust the commissioners or the cops. Isaac has his blue-eyed boys. They'd shoot my ears off if they could. But it's the other cops that worry me . . . old ladies with white hair they are. Retired sergeants. They work for the big McNeill."

She sat with him on her mattress, a loving girl, putting crumbs in Jamey's mouth. What else could she do? When she brought a john into her room, Jamey had to stand in the hall. Customers were suspicious of Robinson Crusoe. They clutched their wallets before and after they made love to Annie Powell. She didn't care. Business was slow. She'd rather fish for crumbs than go out looking for a john.

Miss Annie was a native of Queens. Monday to Friday she took the BMT. She worked in a jewelry store on Fifty-seventh Street. A display girl she was. She didn't handle the expensive goods. She had a lovely figure, you see, and the manager, a Mr. Giles, stationed her near the window. She was meant to draw the customers in. That's how she met the king.

He had a passion for books, old books, first editions, things like that. Faulkner and Mr. James Joyce. It was an odd habit for a crook. But he hadn't forgotten Columbia College, and he could afford any book he liked. He had several dealers in town. The best of them, Eichenborn, was next door to Annie's window. He was coming out of Eichenborn's with a copy of *Ulysses,* Paris, 1922, when he saw Miss Annie Powell. Giles had told her to blush if a man looked in. But she didn't blush at Dermott. She noticed the sockets of his eyes. He was coatless in February. And he had the blackest hair. He didn't seem like a man who would trifle in a jewelry store and let himself be used by Mr. Giles. Oh, but she had the wish: not in terms of silver and gold. She wasn't Giles' mercenary. If only that dark man would come in and talk to her and forget about the jewels. Giles could scream. No. He would have been timid around such a man.

Dermott didn't knock on the window. He never smiled. But he did visit Annie on his next book-buying trip. He marched out of Eichenborn's scowling hard. The lad had paid a stupendous price for a set of galley sheets that must have been living with the worms. The sheets were from *Solider's Pay*, Faulkner's second book. They were in miserable condition: streaked, with ratty edges and cigarette burns. But Eichenborn knew his man. Dermott had a madness to collect. The dealer had been saving these galleys for months. When the bug bites, the lad will buy. Dermott had to have his *Soldier's Pay*. He could have hired a gimp to murder Eichenborn and get back most of his money. But he didn't mind being swindled by a man who loved books. He stood outside Annie's window with a twisted yellow rose. That was as much courtship as Annie could bear. She was sick of baiting men for Giles. She put on her coat to meet with Dermott. "I'm quitting," she told Giles, who couldn't understand why a single rose should propel Annie out of his store.

She had no idea what to do about Dermott. Say hello or goodbye? He didn't rush her into anything. He had a quietness that Annie liked. They sat in a bistro. He talked of books. She wasn't a complete idiot. Ezra Pound meant something to her. It was a name, wasn't it? And William Faulkner's reputation had come to Queens. He showed her the galley sheets. My luck, she said. I had to fall for a professor with dark hair. There was no monkey business. He brought her home in a taxi cab. He didn't leave her stranded at the door. He had doughnuts with her mother and her two young sisters. Her mother felt a strangeness in the house. "How'd you get out of work so early?"

"Ma," Annie said when she had a minute alone with her mother. "He's Irish, I swear. And a professional man. Dermott Bride. He teaches books." Her mother refused to believe that a dark-haired Irishman could exist. "Anybody can call himself Dermott Bride. He has a Puerto Rican nose. Can't you tell?"

Annie wouldn't look for another job or lose her faith that Dermott was descended from the Irish. "Mama, we all broke out of the same potato. Me, Dermott, and you."

She was ashamed to take money from him, but she did. Mothers and sisters have to eat. And Annie's father was long dead. But it was a slow kind of loving they had. He didn't make a mistress out of Annie Powell. They went to the Rockaways. Walked in freezing sand. They had three-hour lunches in Little Italy. She rolled pasta on a fork. She burped into her napkin and said, "Excuse me." She was always home by six o'clock.

What kind of work did her professor do? Available seven days a week he was. Must be a landlord on the side. Dermott had apartments all over the City. After a month he took off her clothes. They were in a flat on Murray Hill. How many maids did Dermott keep? You couldn't find dust under the chairs. Oh, she'd had other boyfriends. But no one had licked her armpits before. He didn't mutter filth in her ears. Or make idiotic marriage proposals. He could touch a woman's body without coming in his pants. He wasn't like her Canarsie beaus, who went in and out of you so fast, you couldn't tell if you had a man inside, a rabbit, or a rush of wind. He had a delicate body that wasn't brittle or soft. It fit into hers like the cardboard teeth of a Chinese puzzle. And she thought, what does it mean to take your pants off in somebody's car? I've been going out with monkey boys. Dermott had magic everywhere, in all his parts. He could make her come with his finger and his mouth. She would twist around and grab pieces of that black hair. She'd never be able to sleep with a Canarsie boy again.

He loved to swipe her underpants, stuff them in his pocket, and sniff them from time to time. It didn't matter where the panties came from, how cheap they were, how flimsy, how many holes they had. She would have carried his underpants too, but her sisters might have gone through her things, spied on Annie, and snitched to her mother. She could imagine how mama would react. "I've raised a whore in my house. Annie, what are you doing with a man's jockey shorts?"

Then Dermott announced to her in a quiet voice, "I'm going to Ireland? Will you come?"

She spoke up like a good Irish girl. "Dermott, my mother would kill me."

"I'll handle that," he said. And it hurt her a little. Because he had to barter with mama, as if Annie were a cow. Mama cursed every misfortune the saints had thrust upon her and accepted Dermott's five thousand dollars. Annie was embittered. Mama should have cried harder and clutched less. It poisoned Annie's lovemaking for a week. But she figured to herself: I'm nobody's cow. That five thousand has nothing to do with me.

Oh, it was a merry life for a girl with a dead father, living in Dublin on a rat's honeymoon. Because wherever Dermott went, that donkey went too. *They* were the married pair, Dermott and Jamey O'Toole. Like brothers they were. Big and Little. And Annie couldn't snuggle between them to locate her man. But she learned to appreciate O'Toole. He would poke drunken men out of her way, choose a nice path for Dermott and Annie. She was a bit unclear about her own Irishness. Mama had never been to the Old Country. Some granddad of Annie's had arrived starving in America after one of those long potato blights. It could have been a thousand years ago. The girl had no sense of history. Irish she was, but she didn't look like any of the freckles she saw on Grafton Street. God, it was a land of freckle-faced people. Her own complexion was kinder than that. Not lumpy, gray, and red. It scared her. She didn't want to become a boiled potato.

You could see row after row of gray heads on the bus to Dalkey. The buildings were gray, or a bloodless brown. But she adored the street signs that were in Gaelic. It was like a fairy's tongue. FAICHE STIABHNA. Stephen's Green. SRAIDIN MUIRE. Little Mary Street. LANA NUTLEY. Nutley Lane.

The town seemed populated with elves. She ran into a soldier four feet high, with a cap and boots and a green, green shirt. The soldier dipped his cap and said, "What do you think?"

Annie struggled for an answer. "Not very much."

"Same as us all," the soldier said, and he was gone from Annie Powell.

And the damn money they had in this Republic. A ten-pound note was big as a napkin, and it had a goblin's face on the back. She didn't know how to spend such things. Dermott gave her banker's checks to use, with her name and his printed on the bottom. ANNIE POWELL OR DERMOTT BRIDE. It was like have a company together. You couldn't cash them at Woolworth's. You had to take Dermott's checks into the prouder stores. She bought everything at Switzer's and Brown Thomas: underwear, peanuts, pajama tops. Cashiers would hold up the checks with their fingers, smile, and shout "Grand!" at Annie. She didn't need identification, no little card with a signature on it. Dermott's checks were finer than gold. That's some man I have, mother dear. The Bank of Ireland sits on his shoulders.

Where was the money flowing from? Dermott took Jamey and her to dinner and lunch. It was a strange kind of eating, more often than not. Dermott might rent out a whole restaurant. He'd reserve twelve tables from seven to nine. O'Toole would be stationed at the door. Busboys and master waiters would hover over them, while Annie stared at empty tablecloths. "Everything to your satisfaction, madam?"

She chugged her head. A sauceboat would arrive on a flaming tray. "Just a dash for you, madam?"

Dermott wore a velvet suit. But she was too miserable to gloat on his handsomeness. Who buys out every chair at a restaurant?

The waiter was a genius. He could slice smoked salmon in front of your eyes. Her man knew all the fancy waiter talk. "Madam would like a bit of toast." It was like having pet camels in your room to fetch whatever you want. The busboys sidled up to Annie with ten racks of toast. Mercy on the miserable and the poor. Annie could have fed off those racks of toast for a year. But she still couldn't tease out her man's line of work.

"Derm, are we ever going home?"

She must have hit on something, because his sockets turned dark.

"We're gypsies now," he said. "But I'll take you to Connemara in a week."

"Where's that?"

"Near Galway. In the west."

You couldn't talk directions to Annie Powell. West was nowhere to her. West of Dublin? West of what? Ireland was a mystery. An Irish cab took them to Dublin airport, and they got on a plane to Shannon. It was no ordinary rent-a-car that waited for them. Her man had reserved a huge limousine. Jamey did the driving. He sang songs about the Rose of this and the Rose of that. "Yes, she's the Rose of Castlebar . . ."

It was a straight road to Galway, a town with one little square, like a pinch on your behind next to Stephen's Green. The lads didn't stop in Galway. But that square confused them. They couldn't decide which turn to make. Dermott growled under his teeth. "The road to Salthill, you dummy."

Jamey wouldn't bend. "It's Clifden we want. And Oughterard."

"Who's car is this?" Dermott asked.

"You're the king and I'm the driver."

They didn't take the road to Oughterard. They were near the ocean in a minute, in some kind of bay. Geese flew over their heads, wild birds with long skinny bodies and delicate wings. Annie couldn't understand their powers of locomotion. How could such tiny wings carry a bird? She was a city girl. Pigeons are what entered her head, not geese that could caw over the knock of an engine.

They hugged a narrow seawall, and Annie was sure the three of them would drop into the bay. The donkey started teasing her. "Look, Annie girl, you can see Manhattan behind them rocks."

"I'm from Sunnyside," she said, and she wouldn't talk to Jamey. He must have been growing delirious. Because he muttered weird stories that went beyond the girl. He used a rough English tongue, as if he weren't enough of a giant without such a voice. "You hear me, laddies. *Neither O nor Mac shall strut nor swagger through the streets of Galway*. This is British land. *From the ferocious O'Tooles, good Lord, deliver us.*"

Dermott laughed. "Jamey, I didn't know your people were from Galway."

"Ah, it's nothing, man. I learned it all from a catechism book. God pity the Irish, at home and abroad. I'm

111

Jamey O'Toole. My people rose out of some pile of shit an Englishman made in Kildare. Show me an Irishman who can trace his ancestry, and you'll find that same pile of shit."

"Agreed," Dermott said.

But Annie took it as an insult. "My granddad dug potatoes. He was a good working man . . . from Omagh, I think. Or Ballyshannon. So speak for yourselves."

"Yes, they'd all love to have one father," Jamey said. "Finn MacCool. Not potatoes, Annie girl. There's a king in all of us. That's why our bones crack so easy."

There was no use arguing with a donkey like him. Her man didn't say a word to defend the Irish. Who was Jamey to talk of people rising out of shit? Annie couldn't find a tree out here. Miles and miles of stone. Rock walls twisted over Hills that turned into low, harsh mountains. Yellow flowers grew between the rocks. You saw cows in the hills, bands of sheep, and haystacks with rags on top. The sheep looked odd to Annie when they came up close with their curled horns and black feet and blue markings on their rumps, as if an idiot had gone about stamping sheep's asses with color. Jamey honked at the beasts. "Get on. Climb on somebody else's back."

But they had to sit until different gangs of sheep passed along both sides of the car. Jamey was perturbed. He drove too fast around a bend in the road and struck a cow. It was an awful sight for Annie. The cow lay dead, its hooves in the air, blood running from a shoulder.

"Jesus," the donkey muttered. "I thought a rock hit us." He didn't have any mercy for the cow.

"Who's going to move that fucking thing?"

A farmer and his boy appeared in front of the seawall and approached the car.

"An accident," Jamey said. "I swear to Christ . . . I wouldn't bash a cow on purpose. It just stood there, man, and looked me in the eye . . . I couldn't turn . . ."

The farmer and his boy dragged the cow off the road. The boy was crying. Jamey removed a wad of that Irish paper money from his wallet. "We're not villains," he said. "Two hundred quid for a dead cow."

The farmer wouldn't take the money. Jamey bundled it in his fist and tried to give it to the boy. But the boy only stared at him out of freckled cheeks. Jamey threw the money on the ground. Then he drove ahead of the farmer and the cow. He was in a fury. "Did you see the fender that animal put on us? It's lucky we can crawl."

Annie was waiting for her man to slap the donkey on his ear. To murder a cow and then offer money, and not a word of real regret. But Dermott never scolded the donkey.

"Let me out," she said.

"What's that, Annie girl?"

"You heard me, Mr. O'Toole. Stop the car. I'm not riding with cow-killers."

O'Toole banged on the dashboard with a knuckle; the cushions under Annie trembled from the blow.

"Jesus, it's a fine day when your own family is against you. Dermott, you think she'll rat on us? . . . Annie, didn't I lay two hundred on that old gizzard for his cow? It was a worthless animal. Dull in the head. A cow that stands in the middle of the road and hogs your lane! . . . Dermott, ask her to forgive us now. We'll order up a Requiem for that animal at the next church. We'll pay for chanters and all . . . I wouldn't disappoint Annie Powell."

Annie hardened against the donkey and her man. "Have your jokes," she said. "Blaspheme a poor cow that doesn't have a soul and can't defend itself against its murderers. But I won't ride with you."

Jamey pummeled the dashboard again. Dermott wasn't amused. "Let her out," he said. They left Annie on the road to Screeb and Maam Cross. She had her suitcase. She'd strut back to Galway and sleep in that little square, she would. She'd show that donkey and the king. Annie Powell could get along without her man. She had some Irish silver in her bag, coins with a bull on one side and a harp on the other. She'd spend them in Galway, live on coffee and scones, and the lemony biscuits she liked. Maybe she *would* buy a mass for that cow. She'd ask the fathers of Galway if such a thing were possible . . .

Annie brooded and brooded, but she hadn't gone a step. She already missed the king. Why did her man throw her out of the car? She should have listened to her mama and stayed in Sunnyside. Sure, she could close her eyes and whisper that her man was in real estate. But how many realtors would pay five thousand for the right to bring a girl to Dublin? Dermott Bride was a crook. His men liked to murder cows. Here she was, a gangster's lady.

It could have been an hour before the dust shivered up off the road. She saw spots of brown fur and a glue made of blood inside the big hollow on Jamey's fender. She was glad the cow had marked the limousine with its own dying. But she didn't say that to her man. She climbed on Dermott's lap when the door opened. She curled into his neck. She would never have gotten to Galway by herself.

"Wake up, Annie. Be a good girl now."

It was Jamey's hand on her shoulder. She had a blanket under her legs. Her man wasn't in the cushions with her, and her ankles were cold. "Where are we, Jamey O'Toole?"

"Are you blind?" he said. "Look around you, Annie. It's Castledermott."

She poked her head out of the car. Mother Mary, you wouldn't believe this world! They were parked in front of an old gray castle on a yellow lake. It was just the right castle for Dermott and his man. Part of its stones were chewed up. The turrets were going to rubble. Castledermott had an ambiguous roof. It could have rained debris on your head during windy times. The walls had great lapses in them, thick pockets where Annie would have loved to hide. Some of the windows were humped with cardboard. But it did have a sturdy door. Oak, Annie figured, though she couldn't tell you much about wood. It wasn't the kind of door that Jamey could have heaved up on his shoulder, famous as he was for uprooting doors, springing them from their hinges, or smashing their center panels with a fist. She would have bet her last Irish coins that O'Toole couldn't hurl this door into the yellow lake.

"Where did Dermott go?"

"He's inside," Jamey said. "With the Fisherman."

She took her suitcase out of the car, and Jamey went to knock on that big oak door. "It's me, O'Toole . . . and the girl." The door swung open without the cry of a hinge. An old man with a shotgun let them through. The house was full of old men. They were on the stairs, in the kitchen, coming in and out of the dining rooms. They carried shoutguns or pistols in a holster, and they cursed at one another with cigarettes and cigars in their mouths.

Strange folks for an Irish castle on a yellow lake. They were as American as Annie Powell. They didn't seem to care for Jamey, these old men. They spit into their palms when he shuffled between them. "The king's washing-boy," they said. Jamey had a temper. Why didn't he bounce them into the walls? They sneered at Annie. They would move close and sniff her with malice in their eyes. "Does the king get a piece of that?"

But Jamey wouldn't have them belittle her. "I'll get a piece of your skull if you don't watch out."

The old men converged on him with their shotguns. The donkey wouldn't back off. Another old man came out of the parlor. He wore funny boots that went up to his crotch. The boots were like jelly. They wobbled with each step he took. "Will you cut it out, for the love of God. Timothy Snell, curb those hounds of yours. We have guests. Be kind to Jamey."

This was the Fisherman, and these old men were his people. He walked into the parlor with those jelly boots. She had ears on her. Dermott was in the parlor with the old Fisherman. She heard them mutter back and forth. O'Toole could sing and froth on the road, but her man did the talking in Castledermott.

"Coote." There were tremors in his sweet voice. "Jamey sticks with me."

"Not a chance," the old Fisherman said. "The lad goes. He's needed in New York."

"Coote, I can get you bigger brains and better muscle."

"Granted, but he looks the part. That's what counts. We can't have any army busting into the streets to hit at merchants and fools. I've me own hand to protect."

"You know his history. He grows violent when I'm not around."

"We'll soothe the lad. Don't you fret."

Her man said, "Find another boy. Jamey's not for sale."

"Who's been your daddy these eighteen years? Coote McNeill."

"Then it might be time to change dads . . ."

One of the old gunmen shooed Annie away from the parlor. She was led to her room. She walked on stairs that had a wine-colored finish in the wood. Did those gunmen wax the floors? Why did O'Toole say "Castledermott?" The Fisherman owned this house. They put her on the third story. A wind pushed through the halls. She could see out onto the yellow lake from her room. She had glass in her window. Not scummy cardboard. But the room had a narrow bed.

Dermott didn't come to her at night. The Fisherman's people mumbled in the hall. They fed her and made rude noises with their tongues, as if such silly old men could devour her body. She would have thrown them down the stairs, shotguns and all, if they tried to touch Annie Powell. She ate bananas and cream and listened to their chatter. It made no sense.

—A yellow lake means salmon, you twit. A blue lake's for trout.

—If you're so smart, why do salmon crave yellow water?

—Because they're a strange fish. Your salmon's very haughty. Why else would the McNeill bother with them? They won't lay their eggs in an ordinary lake. It's got to be yellow.

—Shit, I didn't come to Ireland to live in a fisherman's retreat.

—He'll turn a pretty penny, Coote will. Making this old box into a proper hotel. An angler's nook, you understand. A sort of paradise. You can't fish here without paying a fee to Coote.

—Is Dermott going to fish with us?

—Shut your mouth. The walls have ears, you idiot.

And the muttering would stop. Coote, Coote the Fisherman and his salmon lake. She thought she'd go crazy in the dark. She couldn't sleep on a narrow bed, without her man. She twisted under the blanket, her toes on fire. What a foolish thing it was to have a body. It turned hot and cold. There was a breeze on that yellow lake. She thought of the salmon swimming under there, putting silver streaks in the water with the drive of their fins. It was beautiful at Castledermott. But she'd rather die than be without her man.

He didn't come to her in the morning to say he was sorry. They let her out of the room. God, someone must have seized the castle. The whole place shook. The Fisherman's people had turned to carpenters overnight. They were hammering and sawing on the stairs. Annie knew what a carpenter was. Coote had picked funny guys to build a hotel. The saws buckled on these old men. Nails went in crooked. It wasn't going to be much of a fisherman's paradise.

They fed her in the kitchen. It was bananas and cream again. Maybe her man had disappeared on her. But she was still a guest. Annie had her own feelings about what she ought to eat. The Fisherman couldn't run a hotel on bananas and cream. She'd have to tell him that. If he didn't vary his menu, the hotel would sink.

The old men had gone back to their carpentering, and Annie was in the kitchen alone. She was humming to herself. She sang idle songs about salmon in the water. She began to cry under the breath of her songs. Mama, she dreamt of Dermott's face in the kitchen window. She wouldn't open her eyes for fear the dream would slip away from her and she'd be left without the face she loved. Black his hair. Purple lips. She didn't need to sing about salmon runs in yellow water. Thank God she had the gift to imagine Dermott's cheeks. She invented a smile on Dermott. Then the window opened, and her man was whispering to her. "Annie darling, get off your lovely ass."

Who would say such things? Was it magic blowing off the lake? Some salmon god Annie had neglected to mention in her songs? "Girl, are you coming or not?"

He had hands to help her out the window. She gathered her skirts in one fist and climbed. She felt a little clumsy with her stomach on the windowsill. He was laughing now, and she was angry and confused. He raised her buttocks off the window and carried her like a fish. Then he put her down.

"Derm, why did you have to play the ghost with me? Wasn't I scared enough? Jesus, you never said good night."

"I couldn't. Not in this house. I didn't want those lads thinking of us under the same blanket."

"Well, why didn't you put Jamey outside my door?"

"I'd be jeopardizing him. The boy has to sleep."

"Are they your enemies, Coote and his old guys?"

"Don't you ever call him Coote. He's the Fisherman, and he's a partner of mine."

"Coote, Coote, everybody calls him Coote."

"That's a dumb habit we have. But you might say

117

'Coote' to the wrong party, and it would do hurt to the old man. He's been good to me."

"Dermott, I'll call him the Fisherman forever and ever, if that's what you like, but why haven't you kissed me yet?"

"It's too close to the house. Come on."

"Where are we going?"

"On a picnic, you dope."

He pointed to the hamper near his legs. A basket it was, for a fisherman's lunch. He picked it up, and he ran with her around the lake. She must have been giggling too hard.

"Shhh," he said. "There's an echo off that fucking water."

"It's not a crime to have an echo."

"Yeah, but we don't have to advertise. If the Fisherman knows about our picnic, he might try to come along."

"I'll stuff his head in the basket if he dares to come."

But she wouldn't disobey her man. Annie didn't giggle anymore. They walked and walked in a kind of brown scrub, her skirts tangling in the midst of low, barren blackberry bushes. It wasn't the season for berries, you know, Annie muttered to herself. She couldn't wait to see what was in the hamper. "Love, is this a picnic or a hike?" she said.

"Both. Come on."

She wished now that Jamey had driven them in the car. But could you drive across rocks and fields? Cows blinked at them. And Annie remembered the dead cow in the road. A bull glared at Dermott. The animal had balls that hung below its knees. Dermott wouldn't curtsy to a bull. He didn't let go of the hamper. "Come on."

He must have dragged her for miles. They reached a wire fence, and Dermott separated the wires for her, so Annie could squeeze through. He gave the hamper to her for half a minute and hopped over the fence. They were at the bottom of a mountain. Annie was convinced of that. She could see the crisp, bottle-green waters of a tiny bay. "Are we still on the Fisherman's land?" she said.

"No. Come on. We'll have our picnic on Cashel Hill."

You couldn't tell how many ridges a mountain had. They'd reach one, then find they weren't any closer to the top. There was always another ridge. It was like a magical game for them. The elves were taking over. But you had to watch your feet. Cashel Hill was crusted with goat droppings. Those hard little pellets were on every single rock. A million sheep, or billy goats, must have shit on Cashel Hill.

Oh, God, the skirts on Annie had begun to rip. But she wouldn't let her man climb without her. And always, always she was tricked into believing the next ridge would be the last, the final one. She had a pair of lungs inherited from her mama. She could breathe in and out, and move into Dermott's tracks. She was the Rose of Connemara, the Queen of Cashel Hill, escaping from the Fisherman's house with her man. He hadn't done more than grab her by the hand. But you couldn't lie down in goat shit.

Her thighs were growing sore. She didn't care how many faces a cliff had. It was better than chewing bananas and cream. She'd crawl behind her man if she had to. The air got thick on the mountain, thick and purple-gray, and she'd lose parts of Dermott's back and shoulders for a second, and she wouldn't have any trail to follow. "What's that?" she said, growling into the purple stuff, thick enough to eat.

"It's fog," Dermott said. "Don't think about it, Anne. You can outrun any fog if you hurry."

Annie appealed to her favorite saint to bring them out of the fog. Jude it was, the protector of travelers, idiots, unmarried girls, and desperate people. What a man Jude had given her! King Dermott, of Dublin and the Bronx. They did climb over the fog, with Jude's help. The mountain didn't have any more faces to mock them with. The elves could jeer. The king had dragged her to the top of Cashel Hill. She didn't think of the cliffs that went down to the sea, or the winding stone walls, the fields, the dots of water that could have been a salmon lake. Her belly was making pitiful grumbling sounds. "Will you give a girl some food, for Christ's sake?"

Dermott crouched on a rock that was relatively free of goat shit and unbuckled the hamper's leather straps. The king understood her hunger. They had a soft red cheese and brown bread and coffee in a great mug. He'd brought milk in a tonic water bottle. Thank God he forgot to bring a banana, or she might have puked. They had oranges, a misshapen yellow pear, biscuits in a wrapper, and Irish fruit cake. Annie looked for napkins and forks from Castledermott. The hamper was empty of that. Dermott packed food like any man. He only brought what came into his head. "How can we spread the cheese, love?"

Dermott reached into his pocket. He had a push-button knife with marvelous ruts in the handle. The blade opened with a noise that could have been the gentle smack of two lips. He cut the humpbacked pear and spread the cheese, and then he honed the blade on the edge of the hamper.

"You have to exercise a knife," he said. "It can decay like a tooth and fall apart in your hand. I've seen that happen."

"Who gave the knife to you?"

"Nobody. I took it from a hobby shop on Tremont Avenue. Ah, it was a long time ago."

He fisted the knife with a loving hold that made Annie nervous. "How come you never showed it to me?"

"Because it likes to stay in my pocket," he said, his mouth suddenly full of teeth.

She burped, but the king didn't mind. His head was in her blouse. He had her unbuttoned to the waist, and he sucked on her nipples. Her man was like no other man in the world. Soon he was under her skirt, and Annie thought she would die. Her panties were wet from the king. She'd have picnics every day of her life, climb in tattered skirts, gobble a pear with warts on it and a swollen back, nibble cheese off a knife, if that's what her man desired.

They fell asleep on the mountain, among the goat droppings, with most of Annie crooked under Dermott's shoulder. Then she opened her eyes. "Jesus, how did it get dark so fast?"

You couldn't see your fingernails. It was the worst blackness she'd ever known. The elves must have put a roof on Cashel Hill. Mercy on her that she could still hear her man breathe, and grope for his chest. The fingers under his shirt had woken him.

"Dermott, this hill has a witch. We must have slept for twenty hours."

"We didn't sleep much at all. The fog crept up on us. And the fucker won't burn off. We'll have to sit and wait."

"Wait for what?" she said.

"Until somebody finds us."

"Who's going to find us on Cashel Hill?"

"Farmers," Dermott said. "They have to be out looking for their herds. They'll stumble into us."

"Not when you murder their cows," Annie said. "They'll leave us here to rot. That way all the farmers will get even with you."

He laughed in the fog, and it terrified Annie. Because there wasn't a mouth or lips to go along with it. "Annie, how did you dream such a farmers' plot? Stop worrying. The Fisherman won't let it happen. I'm too important to him."

That didn't satisfy Annie Powell. She prayed for Jude to intervene, to pull this fog down off Cashel Hill. The king heard her mumble. "What's that noise?"

"I'm praying," she said.

"I thought it was a dead cow mooing at us."

She began to cry. Her saint wouldn't come. Dermott made fun of the dead. Their bodies would shrivel and sink into the mountain. No more Dermott. No more Anne. The sky must have turned upside down. She saw a dozen moons float in the distance, under her feet. Dermott saw them too. He wasn't surprised. "That's our rescue party."

The moons seemed to draw closer and then retreat. They turned into glowing sticks. They're only lanterns, Annie assured herself. No moon could stretch itself into a fiery stick. It's Coote and his old men, with a pack of lanterns. Now she prayed that the Fisherman wouldn't bump into Cashel Hill. She'd rather stay lost with Dermott and die in peace.

The lanterns broke into packs of four. It took half an hour for one pack to edge up close. A voice came up off the fog. "Derrrrmott Bride."

"Ah," Dermott said. "They've also learned to moo." He called back into the fog. "Hello, boys. It's Annie and me."

Then a lantern was in her face. It blinded her until she blinked over the light. She recognized one of the Fisherman's people. Other lanterns approached in a pattern of sways.

Four lanterns looked down on them. "There he is . . . the king and his whore."

A pistol with a fat nose appeared in the haze off the lanterns. "Oh, we'd love to kill you, my dears."

She heard that soft, familiar smack. Dermott had opened his knife. He pushed Annie behind him. "Come for me, pretty boys that you are." He lunged, and the pistol fell.

"God, he cut me . . . he cut me . . ."

The Fisherman arrived out of the fog. He didn't have his jelly boots. "What's this shit?"

The old men grumbled around him. "Coote, Coote, we come to rescue this bastard, and he shoves his blade at us. He cut up poor Johnny Boyle."

"Bitches, cunts," he said. "I heard you threaten him. Get out of here, or I'll send you back to First Avenue where you belong. You can sit in the Dingle with Tiger John." He came up to Annie and kissed her on the cheek. "Are you all right?"

"Yes," she said. "Thank you." She stood near Dermott and the Fisherman and started to climb down Cashel Hill.

Dermott had to remain at the Fisherman's house. Annie went to Dublin with O'Toole. "You're both so smart," she said. "You and my man. That's Coote's house. Castlecoote. So why did you call it Castledermott?"

The donkey was tightmouthed with her. Then he snarled, but the snarl wasn't for Annie. "It's the Fisherman's castle, all right. But he bought it and fixed it up with Dermott's money. Those salmon in the lake didn't jump out of the Fisherman's pants."

What was she supposed to do in Dublin without her man? Wade the River Liffey and grab whatever salmon she could find? It was a dirty stream. Fish couldn't breathe in there.

"When's Derm coming back?"

"Who knows? Him and the Fisherman are playing cards over my body."

"What does that mean?"

"They're deciding what to do with little James. Keep the lad here, or throw him back to Ameriky."

"Dermott wouldn't give you away."

"Business is business," he said.

She wasn't going to listen to a donkey all her life. So

she shopped on Grafton Street, bought colored undies and other useless things with those banker's checks, and walked on O'Connell Bridge. She couldn't keep away from the child beggars who cut a territory for themselves along that bridge. She wanted to take a cloth with her and wash their faces. The beggars stood below her knees. She couldn't believe children could exist so small. She fed them candy from Switzer's to improve their shrunken state. The beggars got used to Annie Powell. "There's the lovely," they would say, with the practiced smiles of bitter old men. "There's the girl." They had shriveled skin for five-year-olds.

Annie would devote an afternoon to watching them beg. The children never harmed her. But there was something sinister in the methods they used. They would attack tourists on the bridge, feel around in your pockets, a slew of beggars that wouldn't let you go. They would grab at gentlemen's trousers and ladies' skirts, paw you with fists that were impossible to shake free, like an army of educated rats, and you'd be pulling them to the south side of the bridge and onto Lower O'Connell Street before you were finished with them. They'd have a few of your coins and maybe your pocketbook. These children labored at all hours.

Annie found them sleeping in plastic bags, huddled against the bridge in harsh weather. It might have been a ploy to gain sympathy from innocent people. But their shivering was real. Annie would have liked to march them into the Shelbourne for tea and sandwiches. The porters wouldn't have allowed it. It was Dublin, dearie, and a decent hotel couldn't have beggars passing through.

But Annie wasn't helpless. Didn't the porters say *madam* to her? She was Dermott's lady, and she occupied a suite at the hotel. The Shelbourne prepared huge mugs of tea that Annie brought out to the bridge. The children drank the hot tea with the same grizzled smile. Then, on her fourth day back in Dublin, they kissed her hand in the rain and led her over the bridge. They winked and touched the shallow part of her skirts. They weren't taking Annie by force. It was an invitation to follow them. She wouldn't desert the children now.

Up Gardiner Street they went, Annie and the beggars, to an old house in an obscure alley, off Mountjoy Square. There was the stink of fish and oily margarine. Did they bring her home to meet mum and dad? Doors shut behind her. She didn't remember climbing stairs. She was in a room that might have been a kitchen or a storage place. It seemed high as a barn to Annie. Jesus, there was a dead chicken on the wall, hanging by its neck. Piles and piles of clothing: shirts and vests and a hundred different trousers. A clothes barn it was, with a dead chicken to watch over it and scare away the wrong customers. She was crazy to come here. She shouldn't have crossed the Liffey with these beggar children.

They whirled around her in a cruel dance, pawed at her, as if she were a tourist lady. "Havin' fun?" they said. Her blouse came apart in their fists. They tore the skirts off her body. They held her bra and underpants. She was naked in front of the children. They tried to feel between her legs. Annie turned on them, became a savage of a girl. She was no dummy in the window that children could poke at and fondle with grime in the webbing of their hands. She threw lots of trousers at them, cursed the tea she had brought to O'Connell Bridge.

She might have won, but a man and woman stepped into the fight. They smacked her down to the floor and let the children have their way with her. Their hands were all over Annie Powell. She screamed for Saint Jude. The man kicked at the children and drove them off. Annie didn't care for his smile. He wore a beautiful vest, but his face was as marked as any beggar child. A runt in man's clothes he was.

"Pretty lady," he said. "You'll fetch us a price. Who owns you now?"

"Dermott Bride."

"Never heard of him."

"He's from America," she said.

"Indeed. What does he do, your Mr. Bride?"

"He bought into a castle," she said. "He works with the Fisherman."

"Explain that to me?"

"They plan to open the Paradise Hotel . . . out of Galway. It's for people who like to hunt for salmon. Hunt and fish."

"Does he have a Dublin address?"

"The Shelbourne, St. Stephen's Green."

"Ah, that's better," he said. "That's good. You'll write him a note explaining the circumstances, that un-

124

less he comes up with a thousand pounds . . . in English money, not Irish . . . he'll see you dead."

Even without her skirts, they couldn't threaten Annie in a clothes barn. She wasn't going to be bullied by a runt in a vest who managed beggar children. "My man's in Connemara," she said.

"Isn't that too bad. You'll have to wait with us until he comes to Stephen's Green." He nodded to the woman. "Ethel, don't bother tying her wrists . . . if she hollers, you can split her head with a grease pan."

Annie wouldn't give up her courage to a hag with a pot in her hands. This hag wore the same kind of vest. Was it Dublin, or another country they had lured her to? Her saint had gotten her out of the fog. Jude wouldn't abandon Annie Powell. The beggars scratched the chicken on the wall. They were happiest when they tweaked its neck. Annie heard a slight rumble outside the barn. The rumble repeated itself. She knew what that meant. Her saint had come in the form of a donkey. O'Toole was knocking over doors to get to her. The rumbles were growing loud. The beggars hid behind sacks of clothes. The man and woman hugged themselves as the door to the barn came down. Jamey hopped over the door with dust on his shoulders. He didn't even look at the man.

"Annie girl, put on some clothes."

Her own things were ruined. They searched for a vest and pants among all the heaps. She walked out with Jamey in a beggar's uniform.

"How did you find me?" she said.

"I figured you were tangled up with the gypsies when you didn't come back to the hotel. They've got competing families, you see. I paid one family to spy on the others."

"Why didn't you go to the police?"

"The gardai are a joke . . . they snore in Dublin Castle. They're as dumb as American cops. I should know. I was a detective until this son of a bitch Sidel threw me into the street."

They smuggled her around porters and clerks at the Shelbourne, with Annie naked under her vest. She wouldn't stop muttering about the beggar children.

"It's not their fault, Jamey O'Toole. Their parents train them to stick their fingers in your pocket."

"I say it's in the blood. They're born with a thief's eye.

Once a gypsy, always a gypsy. Don't you ever go near Mountjoy again. They'll shave the hair off your legs and sell it to the feather merchants. There isn't a piece of you they couldn't barter with."

"You've a low opinion of human nature, Mr. O'Toole. Children can be taught *not* to steal."

"Fair enough. But it's a friendlier world inside this hotel. There'll be no more teas on O'Connell Bridge."

The donkey guarded her until Dermott arrived. He wouldn't snitch to the king about Annie girl. Never once did he mention gypsies, beggars, Mountjoy Square. Her man seemed preoccupied. The king mumbled to himself. He had a blackness under his eyes. He hardly noticed Annie Powell. It went on for days. Then he slapped his pockets and said, "Jamey boy, climb into your darkest suit. We're going to church."

The donkey couldn't believe it.

"What about me?" Annie said.

"Girl, any dress will do."

The king ordered up flowers from the hotel. Roses they were, pink, white, and yellow. The flowers had a perfume that made the donkey sneeze. Dermott was cross with him. "Will you recover from that fit? I need a man in a clean suit."

They took a cab out to Donnybrook, the roses in Annie's lap, and Dermott married her inside the Church of the Sacred Heart, with Jamey as a witness before God, the organist, two ushers, and the wedding priest. Jesus, couldn't you ask a girl if she was in the marrying mood? Dermott gave her a wedding ring that she wasn't supposed to wear. A silver band it was. She had to hide it in her pocketbook. "I don't want the Fisherman to know about us," he said. "It's a secret, understand?"

So Dermott's bride had to stay Annie Powell. It made no difference at the hotel. She was *madam* to the porters, whatever name she carried. They did have a wedding feast. Dermott booked a restaurant around the corner on Molesworth Place. You wouldn't have noticed this restaurant from the street. It didn't have much of a sign. You had to knock on the door to get in. A woman shook your hand in the vestibule. "Mr. Dermott Bride," Jamey said. "Party of three." It wasn't a restaurant where you had to eat on the ground floor, with the dampness sticking to your shoes. Annie climbed a flight of stairs to a

126

dining room with six tables. Her man had reserved them all.

Jamey tinkered with his soup. The light from the candle fluttered on his jaw. There was a darkness between the two men. The donkey's jaw began to move. "Did you settle with the Fisherman?"

"I did."

"Well, am I to be banished or not?"

"Yes and no," her man said. "Our accounts are a disaster, Jamey. You'll go to New York and help my uncle Martin. He blunders when he's on his own . . . then you'll come live with us."

Jamey's eyes seemed to close inside his head. The candle couldn't reach into them. He had already shut himself off from Dermott.

"Ah, it's a grand country New York is. Perfect for little James. After all, murder is me business."

"Have you forgotten?" Dermott asked. "We're at a wedding party."

"Sorry, Derm. I'll finish my soup."

The donkey left in the morning. The porters carrying his luggage were like dwarfs around O'Toole. He had to stoop in the Shelbourne to kiss Annie's forehead goodbye. One lip went into her ear. "I'll wallop you, Annie girl, if you strut on O'Connell Bridge." Her man rode with him to the airport. She wasn't invited to come along.

It was lonely without O'Toole. Two of the Fisherman's people moved in with them. Then another two. Now it was Dermott, Annie, and four old men. They were careful with Dermott. They didn't get in his way. But he couldn't walk Annie through St. Stephen's without these old men. A woman she was, married and all, though she wasn't allowed to say it, and she had chaperones, four, with yellow teeth. It was bad enough living with them when her man was there. Then Dermott had to go to Ameriky for a little trip. "Close a few accounts," he said. "Give me the chance to have a pint with Jamey. A week," he said. "No more."

But he didn't come back in a week, and Annie had to survive with Coote's people surrounding her. Their cigars stank up Dermott's suite. Porters shuffled in and out of the rooms with sandwiches and jars of warm black piss that could have been scooped out from the boiling mud at the bottom of the Liffey. They were proud watchdogs,

127

these old men. They loved to shadow Annie in the streets. It took up half her energies and the slyness in her head to shake the old men. She'd stroll into Gaiety Green, a shopping mall on West Street, try on a pair of boots, crawl behind a rack of dresses, and slip out into an alley near Cuffe Lane. They couldn't catch up with her, for all their yellow teeth. Then she'd turn corners and end up at Bewley's Oriental Cafe. She wouldn't sit downstairs and be served by waitresses who scratched your order on a pad and made you eat lemon tarts when you'd asked for scones. Annie went up a flight to the paupers' station, where you had to serve yourself. Oh, it was crowded in that room, and you were obliged to share your table with companies of strange men: if you didn't hold your elbows tight, you'd have the dregs of Dublin in your lap.

But a man protected her, cleared a space for Annie at the table, so she could chew her scones in peace. An American he was, a college instructor in a tattered raincoat and a crumpled hat, come to Dublin on a small grant. He was doing research on a gentleman called Jonathan Swift.

"Are you interviewing that man Swift?" Annie said.

The instructor laughed. "No, he's long dead. He wrote about a giant in the land of little people, *Gulliver's Travels.*"

"I remember that book," Annie said. "The little people captured him. I would have bashed Gulliver, you know, when he was all wrapped up in thread." Annie grew quiet. Here she was with a wedding ring in her pocket. She didn't want the instructor to think she was a frivolous girl. She lied a bit. "My man's a professor too. He studies Mr. Faulkner and Mr. James Joyce."

"Where does he teach?"

"He's unemployed at the moment . . . but he doesn't really need a job. He's rich. He buys up castles and turns them into hotels."

The instructor's name was Gerald. Gerald Charwin. She saw that hungry look in his eyes. What should Annie do if a man was smitten with her? She could meet him by accident, sit and have her scones, but she wouldn't make an appointment with Gerald. He was waiting for her at Bewley's the next day, around three o'clock. He told her scraps of Irish history. There was a river under Dublin, he said. The Poddle.

"I don't believe it."

His man, Jonathan Swift, used to wade in the Poddle. "Gerald, does the Poddle ever seep up when the weather is bad? Imagine a city drowning in the river under its streets."

But Gerald wouldn't encourage her. "The Poddle doesn't go very far. It follows the line of Little Ship Street. Dublin will never drown in it."

He would have liked to take her walking over the channels where the Poddle still flowed. They could touch the pavements, he said, and listen for the sound of water. It was only a block from where he lived. Annie was dying to *feel* the Poddle, touch an underground river with her feet, but she had to refuse. Suppose the watchdogs found them together on Little Ship Street? What would the old men think?

She stuck to Bewley's Cafe with Gerald Charwin. But she couldn't escape the old men. It took one more sit-down with Gerald to bring them into Bewley's. They hovered over the tables with their yellow teeth, sniffing peas, sausages, and chips. You would have figured they were the quiet type, angels off the street, harmless uncles of Annie Powell, looking for a meal of peas. They wore old men's sweaters and caps. They kept muttering, "Fine day," to people at the tables. "Nice, nice." They slouched behind Gerald, the four of them.

"Would you come downstairs with us, laddie? We'd love to have a word with you."

"He's nothing to me," Annie said. "Just a man in a cafe. We talk about rivers a lot. Leave him alone."

They seized Gerald by the arms, lifted him out of his chair, and banged him from table to table, excusing themselves as they did. "Sorry now . . . eat your peas and don't mind us."

They pushed him down the stairs and carried him out of Bewley's and into the street, with Annie pummeling their old men's backs. "Don't you hurt him," she said. "He's a scholar. He's reviving Mr. Jonathan Swift."

They ignored the girl. The old men stepped on Gerald's hat, punched him in the kidneys and the ribs, dropped him into the gutters of Grafton Street. It was over in a minute. The Fisherman's people knew how and where to

129

punch a man without calling notice to themselves. Annie couldn't help Gerald out of the gutters. The old men caught her by the sleeves and shoved her quietly towards the hotel. "Fancy," they said, mocking her with tongues in the middle of yellow teeth. "The king's girl goes to Irish coffeehouses with a scholar boy. It's footsies under the table for Annie Powell. She's the clever one. She can love a boy without taking off an article of clothes."

"Shut your stupid mouths," she said. "Dermott will make you pay for what you did to Gerald."

They tittered under their old men's caps. "It's Gerald, is it? There's a level of intimacy, if you ask me. Don't torment us, Annie Powell. The king will knock you silly for playing with your Geralds."

They couldn't keep her locked in a hotel. The watchdogs grew dumb when it came to following her in the street. She could snake in and out of an alley before they had the chance to catch their breath. She wouldn't crawl back to Bewley's. Annie was ashamed. How could she tell Gerald that her man was a gangster who happened to love James Joyce and had four old idiots to punch your kidneys out of shape for the crime of having a cup of coffee with Annie Powell?

She disappeared into the pubs of Duke Street. The Bailey, or that other one across the road, with awnings in the windows. It made her laugh. Because the Bailey had stolen the door right out of Mr. Leopold Bloom's house on Eccles Street. It exhibited the door in its own parlor. The door had an Egyptian knocker on it. She could surprise her man. Annie understood a thing or two about Mr. James Joyce. The Bailey, the Bailey, and Leopold Bloom. A tourist attraction it was. Come sip your Irish coffee with Leopold's front door. The pub was deep enough for Annie Powell. She could hide in there, against the sunlight off the windows. Bailey's would get crowded close to five. Young executives from Dame Street would come piling in for their jars and pints and glasses of vodka and pink gin, and they nearly drove Annie off her bench with their smooth bodies and starched cuffs. They were a friendly lot. They would ply her with the best Irish whiskey and stick their hands under her skirts. Annie didn't bother with their names. It could have been Jack or Mick or Frenchy Pete. She would go home with none of them. At half ten Annie said goodbye and hobbled from door to door until she got to her hotel.

That was Dublin without the king. Afternoons at the Bailey, running from Coote's old men, while the lads from Duke Street tickled her thighs with the cuff links they wore. She guzzled Jameson's whiskey, drank herself into a terrible fog. Then, one night, with Mick or Frenchy Pete laying an elbow in her skirts, she looked up, because it was time to go, and she saw her man inside the Bailey. Dermott it was. The king himself. His eyes were dark, and she would have warned Mick or Pete, whoever it was, but the lad was busy solving the different layers of Annie's underwear. The king didn't rush that lad. He had too much dignity to destroy a pub. He waited for Annie to fix her skirts and get up from the bench. He'd never punish her in the Bailey, not her man. She would have liked to point out Leopold's door. Bloom, Bloom at the Bailey, but she was too drunk to raise her arm. "Derm," she muttered into the wall, "why don't you buy that fucking door and take it home with us."

She didn't remember much after that. Dermott must have gotten her to the Shelbourne. She was lying in bed. The king sat next to her. She could feel his shivering leg. She was too embarrassed to stare at him with both her eyes. Her man had shadows on his face, as if the cheeks had been pulled out of him and he was left with hollows under his nose.

Oh, Annie heard the knife, the kiss of an opening blade. She didn't move her head off the pillow when that slash arrived. The strokes were very harsh. They hurt like Jesus, but she wouldn't moan or scream. She bit her tongue from all that pain. She would have tolerated it, *loved* the cut in her cheek, if Dermott had only stayed with her, nursed his wicked Anne. But Dermott went into another room. It was the old men who jumped about with the gauze and the cotton. They looked at her with open mouths. "Mother of God!" That was the comfort she had. Bands of yellow teeth. Coote's old men became her nannies. They dressed and undressed the bandages she had to wear. The king was on another trip.

They fed her soup, the Fisherman's people. They wouldn't let a porter near Annie Powell. When the bandages came off, they stuck a mirror up to her face. Annie knew without any mirror. The king hadn't cut her in a

131

mad, purposeless fit. Drunk she was that night. In a stupor. But she was alive to him. She felt every turn of his wrist. He'd given her his own design. She'd wear Dermott's name on her cheek for the rest of her life.

Snow White she was, with a scar on her to spoil her complexion . . . and four benevolent dwarfs. They swept and did her laundry in the sink. They stood around her bed, waving a funny ticket at her. "You're going to Ameriky."

"Where's my man?"

"Well, the king, he's indisposed. He can't see you off. But he did pay for the ticket."

They took her to the airport, sat with her until it was time to get on the plane. They had their knuckles in their eyes. They were sniffling when they put those knuckles down. They were the same old men who had punched Gerald outside Bewley's. They could be so mean and so nice.

"Forgive us, Annie dear."

"There's nothing to forgive."

"We led the king to Duke Street. We thought he'd slap you a bit. We didn't figure on the knife."

"That's Dermott's way," she said. She kissed the hands and mouths of these old crooks who had mended her, and she went off to Ameriky.

Someone met her on the other side of the ocean. Martin McBride. He winced at the sight of her, but he didn't say a word. They wouldn't let her starve in Manhattan, no, no, no. The uncle had an apartment for her and a cash allowance. "Annie, you'll never have to work again."

She told the uncle to stuff himself. "Dermott can keep that apartment for his next lady. I owe him five thousand dollars and I intend to pay it off. I'm not his personal cow."

Martin shrugged. "Five thousand?"

"That's what he gave to my mother for the privilege of renting me. So long, Mr. McBride."

They didn't love the idea of Annie whoring in the street. She'd make that five thousand on her back, she would, with any man who'd have a scarfaced woman. The uncle tried to threaten her. "I'll get the cops after you, I swear."

But the cops didn't bother her. No one bumped Annie

from her corner. The worst of it was having to see O'Toole. She was fond of that donkey, even if he still worked for her man.

"Do us a small favor now, Annie girl."

"What?"

"Can you pick a less strenuous occupation?"

"No."

"Then have a drink with me, for God's sake."

"I will."

The donkey looked after her, kept the most belligerent whores off her tail. But she didn't need Dermott's muscleman. She had a new benefactor. A bum, a *strange* bum. Father Isaac. He took her to lunches in his smelly clothes, mumbled shit about a daughter he had. Annie didn't want complications. The bum wouldn't pay her to undress. He lectured Annie, told her she wasn't for whoring. She should be somebody's wife. She was tempted to laugh and shout in his ear, *Mister, you're looking at the original Mrs. Bride*, but she couldn't give Dermott's secret away. A bum like that, where did he get the money to buy her champagne? She never asked. He had to be a special magician, because cops and pimps became ostriches around Father Isaac. They dug their heads into their shoulders whenever he passed. But it didn't always work in Annie's favor. The bum would scowl at her johns, and she had to get him to disappear, or she couldn't have made a penny.

It was a life for her, standing in doorways, smiling at idiots from New Jersey. She didn't care. She'd shove that five thousand into the uncle's mouth someday. *This is for Dermott, Mr. Martin McBride. Tell him he can brand a girl, but he can't make Annie into a cow.*

Oh, she was a big talker, she was. She began to see *her* dwarfs around the City. Jesus, it could have been the old men who had bandaged her, you know, washed her panties in the hotel sink, but she wasn't sure. All of the Fisherman's people looked alike.

They would come up to Annie and blow in her face. "Get off the street, little girl." But when she asked them how the king was doing, they ran from her in their brittle, old men's shoes. It was beginning to drive her crazy.

She would go into the Irish bars along Eighth Avenue and drink slugs of Jameson's whiskey, crouching on a

133

stool. The whiskey couldn't help. The old men appeared in the window with their yellow teeth. She might as well have carried them inside her skirts, the way these old men clung to Annie. They followed her home. "Last warning, little girl. Invisibility, that's our advice. A certain gentleman would like to see you shrink a bit."

She should have told Jamey about the dwarfs. She didn't. They trapped her in the doorway the very next night. They struck her with the handles off a broom. It wasn't her body they were after. The dwarfs kept banging her face. She woke up in a fucking hospital. Father Isaac was there. She pretended not to notice him. She didn't want a sermon now. She must have been delirious. When she opened her eyes again, two of the Fisherman's people were standing around her bed. They didn't have their broom handles. They smiled, and then they were gone. She prayed to that saint of hers. Jude gave her the will to crawl off the bed. She went into the closet for her skirts and strolled out of the hospital.

The donkey found her wandering in the streets. He brought Annie up to her room. "Jesus, where the hell were you?"

She had bruises on her lips. It was hard to mumble. Her head was mixed up. "Coote, Coote the Fisherman."

"What's that?"

"He put his salmons in the window . . ."

She lay in bed for a week. The donkey came in and out of her room. "Jamey, who are those old men?"

"Retired cops," he said. "Ancient, hairy sergeants . . . they'll never hit you again. Not with O'Toole around."

"Was it Dermott who sent for them?"

"I doubt it, Annie girl."

She ate her bread and butter, and soon she was strong enough to go downstairs. She wasn't much of a whore anymore. Men would blink at her battered face and avoid Annie Powell. So she took to dancing at the corner as a way of attracting johns. She sang Irish songs. But the words didn't come out right.

> In Dermott's old city
> Where the boys are so pretty
> And the rivers run underground
> I met a fisherman

A sweet, sweet fisherman
Who cried, Cockles and cunts,
Alive, alive all . . .

Oh, she did pull in a few customers with her songs, drunken Irishmen and Swedes, old sailors they were, who didn't seem to mind a bashed-in girl. But she had a bit of a problem at home. Jamey was shivering on her bed. He wouldn't tell Annie what he was hiding from. He grew a beard sitting in the dark so long. And he frightened the old sailors.

She had to learn how to live with Robinson Crusoe. It was an odd braying the king's donkey had. He spoke in grunts. It didn't bother her. She had nothing worth jabbering about. Was she meant to recall Dublin with Jamey O'Toole? Tell stories of Dermott? Coote? Cashel Hill? She was possessed with ideas of money. Five thousand, or she'd remain Dermott's cow. She'd buy her freedom, she would. You couldn't take advantage of Annie Powell.

TWENTY

DID you ever see the man on Grafton Street, the sandwichman who holds a huge signboard near his chest, touting some miserable tourist pub, with his eyes dead to this world? He stands with his jaw in the rain, a giant in a shabby coat. Remember him? The signboard stays perfectly still. He never blinks or scratches his nose. The donkey in Annie's room looked just like that. His face wouldn't twitch for thirty hours. But Robinson Crusoe wasn't dead. He was dreaming of the fire escape behind his mother's house in Chelsea.

It was only twenty blocks from Chelsea to Annie's room at the Lord Byron. But Robinson Crusoe couldn't run or crawl those twenty blocks. How can you find your mother's window with holes in your head?

The Fisherman was watching the streets. He's not in Connemara. The salmon don't bite this time of year. The king should have listened to Jamey O'Toole. But Dermott was always the businessman. *Dermott, he's a rat bastard, he is. Didn't I work for him? He'd dummy up the evidence. Or get his lads to knock you on the ear. He poses as the quiet one. But he's the killer, all right. Don't believe him. If he puts us in two cities, he'll be able to pick us off.*

The king sent little James back to Ameriky. O'Toole

had to help uncle Martin collect the rent. It all turned sour when Annie arrived. No one had to tell him the history of that mark on her face. It was Dermott who gave her the cut. Sweet Jesus, how did he lose his own wife?

Then the Fisherman got into the act. His cronies beat her with their sticks. The donkey went looking for Coote's little old men. He found three of those lads at the Kilkenny Inn on West Twenty-fourth. He shoved their skinny behinds into a booth. "That's lovely what you did to Annie Powell. It's kind of you to go for the face. I'll make you dumb in a hurry if you don't explain to me what it's about? I thought we had a bargain with Coote. Why did he attack the girl?"

"Jamey darlin'," the little people said, squashed inside their booth. "That's ancient history. The king threw her out months ago. Dermott doesn't want her on the street. So what's she to you?"

He pushed their flimsy heads all the way under the booth. "She's a friend of mine. Keep your bats and sticks to yourselves, understand? I'll leave your brains stuck to the wall if Annie has another accident."

"Dermott won't like his donkey boy meddling in Coote's affairs."

"To hell with Dermott, and to hell with you."

He tapped them once on the skull to give the lads something to dream about. Then Jamey walked over to the house where he lived with his mother. Two detectives were hunched in the park across the street. There was a third blue-eyed wonder in the alley at the back of the house. These blue-eyed boys were from the First Deputy's office. They belonged to Isaac the Pure. Was Isaac working for Coote? Jesus, the whole Force was under the Fisherman's net.

Jamey trudged uptown. Detectives followed him in their green cars. Coote's people loitered on every other block. They winked at O'Toole. There's a message in the crackle of an old man's eye. The donkey had been sold out. He was an expendable item to Coote. They would get another boy to collect their black rent. It was silly to run from Manhattan. If Isaac had gone in with Coote, they would have their lads checking for him at all the depots. He could smash one or two of them, but he couldn't beat up the City of New York. Oh, it was a merry Police Department when one commissioner danced with the next. They'd be dancing on Jamey's head soon enough. He didn't have much of a choice. The donkey went to hide in Annie's rooming house, because it was a dark, ratty place where cops didn't like to go.

The donkey's instincts were correct. Isaac and the little people kept away from Annie's room. Jamey had a life of it. He drank wine and ale from bottles in the window. His jaw was gripped with patches of hair. His shirt crumpled on his back. He became Robinson Crusoe in less than a month.

It pained him to watch Annie scuttle into the room with her johns. Such geeky old men, sailors from two or three wars ago, rotting in their winter vests. The donkey was obliged to wait in the hall. He would curse the king on those occasions. *Dermott, you gave my ass to Coote and fucked Annie girl.*

He couldn't last in the dark forever, with the odors of Annie's clientele in his beard. The poor girl was always drunk. Whiskey drunk. The whiskey gave her the fortitude and the soft burn she needed to entertain those crumbling sailors, sing to them and part her legs. The donkey had a rage in him. He wasn't going to shrivel because of Isaac and Coote McNeill. He combed his beard. Robinson Crusoe was getting ready for the street.

Daylight hurt his eyes. He could have been indoors for centuries. He wasn't used to crowds of shuffling men and women. They seemed moronic to Jamey, with their hard, fixed faces and translucent ears. They were staring into some uneasy eternity inside themselves that made him want to pick them up and hurl them into the gutters.

Robinson Crusoe left them alone. His education had come in the dark. The king was dumb, swear to God. He'd allowed Coote to jockey him into a hotel wing that was more a prison than a home. Dermott had his Alcatraz in seven large rooms. Coote provided the jailors. Ancient cops with kidney stones, borrowed from the Retired Sergeants Association. Hearing aids and heart murmurs. But they'd served under good commissioners. They were trained to kick a man to death. Lovely boys. The king had given his guts over to them, when he had his Annie and his O'Toole.

Jamey gritted his teeth. The young dudes were out. They tried to feather him with leaflets from all the mas-

138

sage parlors. He knocked the dudes to the side. He stuck his face in windows. People shrank from him. But the cops couldn't get under his beard. Those blue-eyed wonders who walked in and out of cafes scorned this Robinson Crusoe. They didn't connect him with their image of that strongman O'Toole. The donkey was free to cruise.

He traveled down to the Fisherman's territories inside the Kilkenny Inn and picked a table near the door. The little people, Coote's old men, didn't recognize him. They sat on their stools, looking past Robinson Crusoe. He sneered at them.

"Bring the Fisherman here."

The little sergeants squeezed their eyes. "What's this?"

"Never mind. Just get me that old fart."

They complained to the bartender. "He stinks, this bag of garbage. Who invited him in?"

"I don't need invites. I'm your loving friend. The O'Toole."

They smiled at Robinson Crusoe with cracked lips. "Is it Jamey? In the flesh? What makes you think the Fisherman would ever talk to you?"

"Well, would he rather have me knock on his door at Police Headquarters?"

They got up off their stools and stood near the pay telephone. Jamey whistled "Columbus Was an Irishman" and "Phil the Fluter's Ball." Coote was at his table before he could turn his back.

"It must have been a long ride from Chinatown," Jamey said. "The traffic can get pretty thick in the morning . . . isn't that right?"

"What do you want, O'Toole?"

"Where's your bloodhound, Isaac the Pure?"

"Isaac?" the Fisherman said. He wasn't chasing salmon at the Kilkenny Inn. He came without his hip boots. "Isaac snores with the rats on Centre Street. I haven't said hello to that prick in months."

"Then why are Isaac's lads waiting for me outside my mother's building?"

"Maybe he loves you, who knows? . . . I could send a message up to him and find out."

"Don't bother. I'll ask him myself."

"I wouldn't do that, Jamey boy. It's best to leave Isaac out of it."

"Listen, old man, if you hit Annie Powell again, if your

139

little helpers touch her one more time with their sticks, I'll scream . . . scream to Isaac, and if Isaac doesn't hear, I'll go to the PC himself. Tiger John isn't much, but he'll have to protect his reputation . . . he'll throttle you . . . tell me, how are all the McNeills? Has your clan inherited the earth yet? You might retire a bit too soon, and your ass will get shaved, just like mine . . . you're a fouler cop than I ever was, Coote McNeill."

The Fisherman left the table. He didn't motion to the little people on the stools. He walked out of the Kilkenny and got into his car, a blue Chevrolet. The Fisherman drove himself downtown, while Robinson Crusoe rocked at his table. He ordered whiskey in a bottle. He wasn't going to drink one thimble at a time. The little sergeants frowned at him. So he drank without their blessings. He didn't like his conversation with Coote. He was trying to protect Annie girl, but he hadn't jabbed the Fisherman hard as he should. He couldn't run to Isaac now. The bastards would be crouching in the doorways. Coote had people everywhere. They were too short to reach his head. Their sticks would clatter around his shoulders and break. The donkey would get past Twenty-third Street, all right. He'd have splinters in his back from all the sticks. But he'd go deeper and deeper into Chelsea, crawl on his knuckles to find his mother's house. He banged on the table to get the barman's ear. "Another bottle, you fat son of a bitch. Put it on Coote's bill. I wonder if a cheap old fart like that will give me a decent wake."

The little people began to smile. "We'll bury you fine, Jamey, we will."

"You'll be burying Coote before you bury me. I have a whole other bottle to drink."

PART
FIVE

TWENTY-ONE

FUCKING Isaac.

He was the freak of a Department that had been fed the Irish way: on loyalty, discipline, and devotion to the cause. Isaac had no sense of camaraderie. He was a commissioner who fiddled on his own. He wouldn't move into Headquarters. He sat in that old, dying box on Centre Street, a huge limestone hut that was beginning to crumble and sink into the ground. Give him another year, and the boy will be swimming in mud. No one could pull him out of his corner room. The First Dep was an ally of Mayor Sammy Dunne. "Hizzoner" had split Becky Karp's brains in the primaries, beaten the regular and reform wings of his own Party, and now everybody was paying homage to Sam. You couldn't touch Isaac because of him.

Isaac the Pure kept a blanket in his desk. He would sleep at the old building whenever he liked. The one janitor who serviced the place couldn't throw out the First Dep. Isaac was free to stroll the long marble corridors past midnight. The floors had weakened tiles that would break loose under Isaac's feet. He would trip in the dark and curse the old Police Headquarters. But he loved it, tile for tile, with its dented iron rails, the roof that leaked on his head, its cracked dome and useless clock tower. He'd made his house in these ruins.

But his triumph was small. A desk, a blanket, and marble floors weren't much comfort to Isaac the bum. He had a bad dream in his corner of the building. Three women were chasing him: Sylvia, Annie, and Jennifer Pears. Their faces would intermingle in Isaac's dream, twist into odd amalgams. Annie had Jennifer's green eyes. Sylvia had a mark on her cheek. Jennifer began to look like Isaac's dead angel, Manfred Coen.

He muttered "Blue Eyes" and coughed himself awake. His room seemed clogged with a kind of soft gray smoke. It was dust, moving bands of dust. He poked into the hall. The dust was thick as Moses. Isaac could barely see. He felt his way to the landing. There were plasterers on the ground floor, teams of them. They stood on ladders and knocked through the walls. They wore masks with little nose cones and mouth protectors. They had a woman with them. Isaac recognized her under her mask. It was the fallen mayoral candidate, Rebecca Karp. She motioned to Isaac. They walked out of Headquarters and faced one another on the street. Becky took off her mask. She smiled.

"Cocksucker, I warned you to get with me."

Isaac slapped the dust off his shoulders. "Rebecca, Sam would have destroyed you without my help. This town loves a little man. It never votes for big, ballsy women."

"Isaac, you're such a baby. How did you survive so long? Schmuck, we've taken over this building."

Isaac stopped slapping himself. "Who says?"

"Don't you read the papers? I'm president of the Downtown Restoration Committee. We're turning this shithole into a cultural center. And we're kicking you out."

"The City owns the building," Isaac said.

"I know. We leased it from the Department of Real Estate for a dollar a month. Isaac, you can't win."

Isaac went to Broome Street and dialed the Mayor's Office. He couldn't get Sammy on the phone. "Tell him again . . . Isaac wants to see him."

He had to hike down to City Hall. He could never be anonymous in the Mayor's territories. Reporters sniffed him from "Room Nine," their closet near the main door.

They ran out to grab hold of Isaac and badger him. Why wouldn't he give press conferences any longer? Was Sammy going to make him a super "Commish" in charge of all corruption?

"Children," Isaac said, "this is a private call. Catch me at my office."

They had their spokesman, a boy from the *Daily News.* "Isaac, don't bullshit us, please. You come in and out of your own whirlwind. Who can ever catch you?"

He got around them and entered the Mayor's wing. All that swagger he'd enjoyed with Sam was gone. He had to confront the Mayor's three male secretaries. He couldn't get past the third secretary without snarling and rolling his eyes. The second secretary was less afraid of him. Isaac's jaw burned from gnashing his teeth. "Sonny, I don't make appointments with the Mayor." The first secretary had Isaac by the seat of his pants. "Lay off. We're blood brothers, me and Sam . . ."

The cops outside the Mayor's door laughed at the spectacle of Isaac being chased by three male secretaries. They were a pair of plainclothesmen who had sworn to guard Sammy with their lives. They would have had to club the First Deputy Police Commissioner behind the ear. But Sammy heard the commotion and peeked out of his office. The vision in front of his eyes saddened him. "It's only Isaac," he said. "Let him through."

Isaac got into that office on the heels of Mayor Sam. His Honor wouldn't look at him. He stared out the window at City Hall Park. His aides had bolted the window for him. Sam was frightened of September drafts. He was a different Mayor now. That meek illiterate who took to a hospital bed before the primaries had become the fierce Old Man of City Hall.

"You made up with Becky Karp, didn't you, Sam?"

"Not at all."

"She would have broken your neck, and you're kissy with her. I should have figured that. It's pinky politics. All the Democrats roll out of the same barracks room. It's bite, bite at the primaries, and then you lick each other's navel."

"Don't be so harsh. I hate the bitch."

"Then why did you make her a landlady over me?"

"I did not. You're accusing the wrong man."

"You gave her Centre Street. You leased *my* building to her fucking arts committee."

"Jesus," His Honor muttered. "I only lent her one wing. She can't abuse you, Isaac . . . it's your fault."

"How come?"

"I wanted to get rid of Tiger John and give you the PC's job."

"Give it to Chief Inspector McNeill. He's your best cop."

"McNeill's too old."

"Old? He's younger than you are, Sammy Dunne."

"But McNeill's not the Mayor of New York. The people won't stand for a decrepit Police Commissioner."

"Sam, I won't be your Tiger John."

"Then help us out, for God's sake. Mangen is on our back. What can I do? He's the Special Pros. Come in with me, Isaac. Take one of my chairs."

"Is that some title you're thinking of?"

"*Yes.* An assistant mayor to watch the Police."

"A rat, you mean, a rat working out of your office. Sammy, it's not for me."

The Mayor turned glum and retired to the golden-knobbed desk that Fiorello LaGuardia had used. "Isaac, Isaac, you know that job of yours. The First Dep is always a vulnerable man."

One of his inspectors ran up to Isaac outside City Hall. It was fat Marvin Winch. Marvin was out of breath. "Sir, we've been looking all over for you. Our boys found Jamey O'Toole. Looks like he was kicked in the face by a lot of people."

"Is he still alive?"

"No, sir."

"I hope you didn't bring Jamey to Bellevue? I don't want him in the morgue . . . not yet. Those medical examiners will chop his fingers off and put them in a jar."

"Isaac, he's in a yard behind his mama's place. They tried to stuff him in a garbage can. But he's too big."

Marvin Winch drove him up to Chelsea so Isaac could stand in the carnage around Jamey O'Toole. Broken sticks. Blood. Teeth. Patches of wool. A crushed eyeglass frame. A third of someone's sleeve. Jamey had done a bit of dancing before he died. The bastards had left him in an awkward position. He sat with his rump in a garbage can. Nothing more of him could fit. The donkey must have been punched and kicked a thousand times. His head was swollen with bump upon bump. You couldn't see the man's nose. He'd clutched at them in a blinded state. There were clots of blood where his eyes had been.

Isaac didn't examine the sticks and teeth near O'Toole. The lab boys could squat with their clippers and sensitive gloves and play Sherlock Holmes. Isaac left things to Inspector Winch. "Marvin, they'll accuse us of body snatching if we don't watch out. You'll have to bring Jamey's mother downstairs to identify the son of a bitch. You ride with him to Bellevue, hear? The kids from the ambulance like to steal a dead man's shoes. They think it's good luck."

He strode uptown with ambulances in his head. The logistics of getting Jamey to Bellevue were uncertain at best. It would take more than one attendant and cop to move that corpse. Four detectives, *five*, would have to squeeze him into a body bag. A normal stretcher would collapse under O'Toole. They'd be smart to borrow a dolly from a grocery store and trundle him into the ambulance. Isaac's love of detail had gone macabre ever since he returned from Ireland.

Annie Powell wasn't at her corner. Isaac asked the young dudes about her. "You mean the crazy one who sings without her underpants? She's on Ninth Avenue, with all the bag ladies."

He knew that spot. Three old women had built an enclave of cardboard boxes on Ninth and Forty-first. It was an open-air fort; the old women lived inside the enclave with their belongings stuffed in shopping bags. Isaac would permit no cop to drive them out of their fort.

They were Irish hags from Clonmel, Wicklow, and Dun Laoghaire. Annie was drinking coffee with them. Isaac approached that enclave of boxes. Annie's legs were crossed. Her brow wrinkled up when Isaac's shadow fell on her. The three hags said hello. Annie didn't have to raise her eyes; she could tell from the persistence of his shadow who it was.

"You're standing in my sunlight, Father Isaac. Do me a favor and shove your ass a bit."

The hags had a stove in their fort put together from pieces of tin. They were baking sweet potatoes in the

147

stove, and they offered Isaac one. He couldn't hold the potato. He had to slap it and push the potato from hand to hand. Annie laughed at his clumsy routine. She was beginning to like him all over again. Finally he gobbled the bark off the potato and chewed the inside. It was an inherited trait. His crazy mother also loved sweet potatoes. She had a junk shop downtown, and she slept in it with her Arab boyfriend Abdul. Then a gang of kids beat her up. She lay in a coma for months before she died. Those kids had some wild grievance against Isaac, and they got at him through his mother. He was a dumb prick with a worm in him and a host of scars that stayed soft and wet. He bumbled through the City now like a wounded bear. Who was Isaac? The worm, or the bear that grew around it?

"Jamey's dead. Some people kicked him in an alley."

Annie blinked at Isaac. "How do you know?"

"I could take you to the morgue and let you have a look . . . they didn't leave him much of a face."

"Jamey's killers, were they little people with brooms in their hands? . . . then they work for the Fisherman." She couldn't say Coote, Coote, because she'd promised the king never to utter that name. "He's an old man with high boots. He owns a house on a yellow lake. If you get up early in the morning, you can watch the salmon jump."

"Did they have a falling out, Dermott and the Fisherman? Is that why O'Toole got killed?"

No matter how many times he cut her, she wouldn't give her man's secrets away. She'd mourn for the donkey without telling Isaac. "Don't fuck with the old man," she said. "You'll end up with a salmon in your mouth."

The girl spoke in riddles that Isaac couldn't connect. He'd have drawn her out of that enclave, removed her from the hags, but she might lift those skirts and show her quim to Ninth Avenue. Isaac couldn't risk that.

"Go to Castledermott," she said. "You can visit the yellow lake. If you pee in the water, God forbid. You'll murder all the fish."

He left Annie muttering and said goodbye to the three hags. His "angels" were across the street, watching Annie from the inside deck of a fruit and vegetable market. They were unfamiliar boys. His whole Department

148

was shifting under him. Couldn't he get two fucking "angels" that he could recognize and trust? He'd have to call the *new* Headquarters, demand cops with kinder faces, like Manfred Coen. His "angels" were turning hard on Isaac.

TWENTY-TWO

HE was beginning to shy away from Centre Street. He couldn't think with an army of plasterers droning under his corner room, tearing down walls to build a culture house for Rebecca Karp. They would bury Isaac under a curtain of dust. He'd have to spend his days with a handkerchief over his eyes. Sam was fucking him. But Isaac didn't intend to yodel in front of City Hall. Whatever the Mayor promised, whatever the Mayor swore, Becky Karp and her cultural committee would bump him into the street.

Isaac went to his hotel. The pimps were in a somber mood. They shouted at their black mamas. Younger "brides" were coming in, and most of them weren't black. They were runaways from Sioux City, Bismarck, Pierre, and Great Falls, little snow queens, white girls who couldn't have been more than twelve, though their bodies seemed burnt-out. Isaac had a maddening drive in him to arrest every pimp at the hotel and bash them on the skull. These ancient young girls belonged in an orphanage, not a brothel. They were recruits from the prostitution mills of Minneapolis and St. Paul. But if Isaac revealed himself, if he came down on the pimps like a hammer, he'd lose his status as a bum. He wouldn't be able to wander through the hotel, half invisible, an old crock with black shit on his face and his fly unbuttoned.

Still, it hurt him to be near those girls and do nothing for them. They had the mousy complexions of frightened, wingless bats who couldn't stand the light. They thrived in darker places. The girls wore sunglasses inside the hotel. Isaac could hear them walk the corridors in their platform shoes. Was it Dermott or Sweet Arthur Greer who first made the Minneapolis Connection? Girls with pink eyes, skin that bruised at the touch of a finger. It was a monstrous imprisonment. Arthur and the king had helped transfer Isaac's hotel into a boardinghouse for squirrely twelve-year-olds.

He couldn't get to Dermott, so Isaac would have to try Sweet Arthur again. He jumped on the phone to round up detectives for a raid. He would destroy Arthur's penthouse if the "blues" didn't break that Minneapolis Connection and find a better home for these girls. His deputies had to interrupt him. "Isaac, there isn't an Arthur anymore." The "friend" of all Manhattan pimps had jumped from his penthouse roof.

"When did it happen?"

"This afternoon."

"Was he pushed?"

"Isaac, what do you mean? Arthur was alone. We checked with the doormen. They swear no one came up to the penthouse today."

"Dummies," Isaac said, "who gives a shit what a doorman swears? Doormen can tell lies. Like everybody else."

His own inspectors turned to imbeciles when Isaac wasn't around to stroke their wooden heads. Arthur wasn't the type to kill himself. He loved his penthouse too much. He'd been a hoodlum since the age of nine. He wouldn't have let a stranger close enough to shove him off a roof. He was with a "landsman" when he died. It was a familiar face that killed Arthur Greer.

Isaac wondered about that familiar face. He was being followed in the street. He'd had the same shadow a week ago. It was that ex-cop, Morton Schapiro, who used to fly from precinct to precinct in the Bronx. Captain Mort was supposed to be working for Arthur Greer. Isaac banged him into a doorway and grabbed Schapiro by the throat. "Your boss is dead. Schmuck, did you kill Arthur Greer?"

He seemed indignant, Captain Mort. "Isaac, let go of me. I got nothin' to do with that boogie pimp. Honest to God. I have a kite for you . . . from Mangen."

Dennis Montgomery Mangen was the Special State Pros. The Governor had appointed him to ferret out corruption *everywhere* in New York. But Mangen was on a holy mission to clean up the City Police. The mention of his name could scare any cop.

"Mangen wants to see you."

Isaac still had Schapiro by the throat. "Are you one of Dennis' shoofly boys?"

"Yeah, I work for Mangen."

"Tell him I don't have time for him."

"Isaac, that ain't too smart."

Mangen had his own investigators, his own stool pigeons, his own grand jury. He could slap an indictment on you faster than "Hizzoner" could blow his nose.

"Listen," Isaac said. "I don't like Dennis sending shooflies out to sit in my pants. If he wants to see me, he can come to my hotel."

"You're joking," Schapiro said. "Mangen doesn't go into the shithouses."

Isaac gave Captain Mort an extra squeeze on the throat. Then he threw him out of the doorway and went back to his hotel. Mangen appeared in fifteen minutes. He was much younger than Isaac, but they had things in common: Marshall Berkowitz and Columbia College. Mangen was another one of Marshall's protégés. He came to police work after *Ulysses* and *Finnegans Wake*. He was a tall, pugnacious Irishman who kept his old battered "skeleton keys" to Joyce. He wore a coat with a fur collar in the middle of September. He sat with Isaac on Isaac's bed. The bum had no chairs in his room.

"Isaac, your Department stinks, right from the top."

Isaac smiled.

"I'm not talking about you," Mangen said. "It's Tiger John I want."

"Tiger John? The Tiger's pretty dumb for a Police Commissioner."

"I agree. But he still gets a nickel for every whore that has a pair of legs."

"Dennis, I've been scrounging at this hotel for three

rotten months. I've watched the pimps and their women . . . the porno shops . . . the love parlors . . . and I never sniffed Tiger John."

"He doesn't come uptown to grab his nickels. He can sit at Headquarters. Tiger John owns a piece of the trade. He has nineteen different bank accounts . . . and aliases to go with them. You'd get a kick out of John's aliases. They have a deeper imagination than John himself. The accounts are in small bundles, that's true. But they add up to a hundred and fifteen thou."

"Dennis, if you're so sharp, tell me how much I have lying around . . ."

"You," Mangen said, "you're a poor man. You have nine hundred dollars spread in three accounts."

"I didn't think I owned that much," Isaac said. "I wouldn't care if Tiger John had himself a million . . . how do you connect his nineteen bankbooks with the whoring business?"

"Isaac, I can't give my sources away."

Mangen always had his "sources." He was known for the rats he kept on his payroll. If he couldn't buy information from you, he could bring you in front of his grand jury. A "call" from Mangen was enough to ruin a man's career. He would dishonor judges and cops, and make it difficult for bank managers to survive. But his "sources" were tainted with hysteria. A bank manager would announce whatever Dennis wanted to hear. He ran his two floors at the World Trade Center like a Gestapo jailhouse. Assistant prosecutors would bark behind locked doors, while you stood in the corridors waiting to be let in, with closed-circuit television cameras blinking pictures of your face from inside Mangen's walls.

"Dennis, if you chew off the Tiger's knees, you'll get flak from Sam. They were boys together in some Irish county. Sam's getting popular in his old age. If he gives a cry, you'll feel it. The whole Trade Center could begin to rock."

"Let me worry about Sam," Mangen said. "Just help me out with Tiger John."

"Don't mistake me for one of your shooflies. Me and the Tiger never had much in common. We avoid each other whenever we can . . . why did you hire Captain Mort? He may be a good legman, but he's a lousy cop."

"Morton's all right. He does favors for me from time to time."

"But I don't like to have him in my cuffs."

"Why? I put him there to protect your life."

"Who's trying to kill me?"

"Tiger John. He got to Sweet Arthur, and he'll get to you."

Isaac looked at Mangen with a bum's heavy eyes. The worm was waking up. That creature churned in Isaac's belly. "I thought Arthur jumped off his roof."

"He didn't jump. He was pushed."

Mangen had more sense than Isaac's own blue-eyed boys. But he was a little warped on the subject of Tiger John.

"Dennis, did you ever hear of a guy called the Fisherman?"

Mangen said, "No. Who is he?"

"I'm not sure. He's supposed to be partners with Dermott Bride."

"That one. He's a thug . . . and a police spy. He puts out for every cop in Manhattan and the Bronx."

"That's strange," Isaac said. "He never put out for me."

"The Tiger kept him from you . . . he owns Dermott Bride. And they'll fix you the way they fixed Arthur and Tiny Jim O'Toole."

"O'Toole was Dermott's man," Isaac said.

"That doesn't matter. The cunts know I'm onto their scam . . . they'll try to knock out every trail they left on Whores' Row. Isaac, you're a nuisance for them. They don't like the idea of having a commissioner in their neighborhood, pretending to be some kind of bum. They'd blow you away if I didn't have Mort watching out for your health."

The loose hairs on Isaac's mattress must have gotten to Mangen. "We're an odd lot," he said. "You, me, and Dermott. We all flew out of Dean Berkowitz's skull. The only fathers I had were Marsh and Leopold Bloom. Scan one line of *Ulysses* with Marshall Berkowitz and you can become the best prosecutor in the world . . . his wife ran away. Poor Marsh. It's his third marriage. Did you ever meet Sylvia?"

"Once or twice," Isaac said.

"She's a tart, if you ask me. I promised Marsh to help him find her, but the woman's disappeared."

What could Isaac say? That he was hiding her in his flat on Rivington Street? He was giving Sylvia the chance to reconsider her marriage. The First Dep hadn't humped her since his days at the Shelbourne Hotel. That much was true. Mangen got off Isaac's bed. The fur on his coat stood crookedly around his neck.

"Isaac, whatever happened to that sweetheart of yours? Coen. Manfred Coen."

"He died on me," Isaac said. "Last year."

"He was a nice boy. Mr. Blue Eyes."

Mangen left, and Isaac heard a great clumping of feet on the stairs. The Special Prosecutor hadn't come to Isaac without his army of shooflies. He probably had men like Captain Mort stationed on every landing. Dennis was an "angel" with fur on his shoulders. The schmuck thought he was keeping Isaac alive.

Mangen shouldn't have mentioned Sylvia and Marsh. The worm burrowed with its armored heads, skewering Isaac. He walked out, went around the block to shake off Mangen's shooflies, and took a cab down to Rivington Street.

It was past dinner time on the Lower East Side. The knish stores had begun to close. You couldn't even get fried bananas, or yellow rice. Puerto Ricans, Haitians, and Jews were going home to their television sets. Isaac had no expectations that Sylvia would feed him and the worm. He was just looking in on Marshall's wife.

Issac saw a cop's uniform on his chair. Sylvia was in bed with a patrolman from Elizabeth Street. Isaac had worked that precinct once. All the good, tough cops grew out of Elizabeth Street. You had to mend the little wars between a hundred different societies, gangs, and gambling clubs that surrounded the Elizabeth Street station. It was like being the white father in a cranky piece of Shanghai. Isaac was loved and feared on Elizabeth Street long before he became the First Dep. He wasn't wanton with his knuckles. If Isaac busted your head, it had to be something you deserved. He would protect small shopkeepers from rapacious cops and kids without asking for a free bowl of rice. He was Isaac the Pure. But that was twenty-five years ago.

This patrolman was sleeping off his tour of duty,

"cooping" in Isaac's bed. Sylvia had opened her eyes. She wasn't disturbed at the prospect of a bear in the room. She pointed to the sleeping cop. "That's William."

"I wouldn't want to wake the boy," Isaac said.

"Don't be silly. Stay awhile. William never gets up this early. Isaac, would you like a cup of tea?"

"No thanks," he said, his stomach growling for ham, cheese, lettuce, mustard, sweet Seckel pears.

"Then get out of your clothes, for God's sake."

"Sylvia," Isaac said. "William might not go for that."

"That's William's problem . . . not ours. Isaac, you look pale to me. Don't wait too long . . . you could freeze in your pants."

What the hell? Why couldn't Isaac be hugged near a sleeping cop? He'd had so many disappointments in the past few days. Green-eyed Jenny was having *his* child without him. O'Toole was beaten to death. Whore children were invading his hotel. Rebecca Karp had kissed Mayor Sam and secured a lease to Isaac's building. Annie Powell sat with three Irish witches in a paper fort, and wouldn't even nod to Isaac. Now Mangen pestered him with stories of Tiger John. The stories made no sense. Tiger John was Sam's creation. He didn't have the balls to push around a squad of killers from 1 Police Plaza. It had to be someone else.

The bear undressed and climbed in with Sylvia and the sleeping cop. William moaned from his corner of the bed. The cop was having a nightmare. He muttered, "Mama, mama," and pulled most of the blanket on top of him. Part of his leg was exposed. The skin was bitten down near the shank, and the calf muscles seemed to twist into the bone. The cop must have had rickets as a baby. Isaac entered Sylvia. Three in a bed. Three in a bed. She clutched his back and moaned louder than the cop. Isaac was in the middle of a slow despair. Men were dying around him. The Special Pros had more of a grip on the murders attached to Whores' Row than Isaac could ever have from his stinky hotel.

TWENTY-THREE

THE bear had a troubled time. He couldn't tell where he was. Then he remembered that Sylvia lay between him and William the cop. The bear was still on Rivington Street, hugged by Sylvia Berkowitz in his own bed. Images of Marshall, Mangen, and Manfred Coen crept into Isaac. The worm chewed off lumps of him. His misery was complete.

He dressed without disturbing Sylvia and the cop. He watched the two bodies rub and make a creaky music. He wasn't jealous of the way Sylvia turned from Isaac's empty spot and reached for William in her sleep. Isaac had to get out of there.

He walked to Centre Street. Becky's carpenters wouldn't be biting into walls at two A.M. The culture committee had made enormous progress in a week. The bastards had reshaped the ground floor. They were grooming the old Headquarters for a party that would celebrate the beginning of Becky's lease. The pols admired her. She'd stolen a building from the City of New York and was ready to evict her only tenant, Isaac the Pure. All the big-time Democrats would come out for Becky Karp. Rebecca was contemptuous of Isaac. She sent out invitations for her party to everyone but him.

The phone was ringing in Isaac's office. Son of a bitch. "Hello," Isaac said, "hello, hello." It was one of Sammy's live-in aides. His Honor was missing from Gracie Mansion again. Isaac shouted into the phone. "Get Becky Karp. She owes the City a favor or two. She can grab a nightgown to cover her tits and go looking for Sam."

His bitchiness began to gnaw at him. The Mayor was an old man. He'd had problems with his memory before. He could have an attack of senility and lose his way in the streets. Isaac took a cab up to Cherokee Place, where he'd found His Honor strolling in his pajamas two months ago. But there was no Mayor Sam on Cherokee Place. He wondered if His Honor could have gone to an Irish club in the area. Sammy must have belonged to twenty of them. His favorite was the Sons of Dingle Bay, on First Avenue. The Sons had installed a sauna on the premises, because His Honor loved the idea of a Finnish bath. The club wasn't dead at three in the morning. Isaac saw pecks of light behind the screens in the ground-floor window. He had to knock and shout his name to get in. "Isaac Sidel . . . I'm here for Mayor Sam." A few retired cops were playing poker in the game room. Isaac didn't stall. He plunged into the sauna with all his clothes on. The Mayor sat on the sauna's lower deck with a towel under his bum to protect him from the heat of the wood. He was with his toy commissioner, Tiger John. Two old men in a room built like a large dollhouse with rocks burning on a crib that was placed in the corner. "Laddie," the Mayor said, "you'll sweat like a pig if you don't make yourself a little more naked." The Tiger agreed. Their raw bellies moved up and down. They didn't seem surprised to have Isaac in their room.

Sweat poured down from Isaac's eyes. He could feel a hot blowing in his ears. "Your Honor, you ought to notify a few of your aides when you have long hours at the club. They worry about you, and then they call me on the phone."

"Jesus," the Mayor said, "you can't have a dry bath away from home without disturbing the peace . . . Laddie, you didn't have to come on my account."

"I thought you'd like to know something. Mangen visited me at my hotel."

"Ah, the great god himself. What did he want?"

"He had some crazy tale about whores and cops."

"Whores and cops?" His Honor said. The Tiger's belly continued to heave up and down.

"It wasn't important," Isaac said. "Mangen's on his usual crusade."

The bear had to get out. His coat and pants were boiling on him. He left Sammy Dunne and the PC on their wooden deck, with the rocks burning in the corner. The Dingle Bay boys cursed and flung their poker chips behind Isaac's dripping back. A blue Chevrolet was parked in front of the club. It had a curious chauffeur, Coote McNeill. McNeill shared the fourteenth floor with Tiger John at the new Police Headquarters. He had the longest tenure in the Department. He'd risen out of the youth squad twelve years ago to become Chief Inspector. His underlings called him "the McNeill," because he was supposed to be descended from a famous tribe of kings that controlled the lands of Galway until Oliver Cromwell beheaded the last McNeill. Isaac thought it was a lot of shit, but if the old man wanted to make up his own line of kings, who was Isaac to begrudge him?

The McNeill poked his head out the car window. "Sidel, where did you get such a red face?"

"It's my fault. I was in the bath with Sammy and John. I shouldn't have worn my socks . . . are you waiting for His Honor?"

"Yes," the McNeill said. "Somebody has to take him home. Sam's not the walker he once was. He's forgetful now. He could turn the wrong corner and lose that mansion of his."

"McNeill, did you ever know a boy named Dermott? Mangen swears he's a police spy."

Coote McNeill spit into his palm like any king of Galway. "It's a bit of a scandal, son . . . believing Mangen over us. You should come to Headquarters with your own kind. There's too much dust on Centre Street. Isaac, it's gotten into your eyes."

"The dust will clear," Isaac said. "Fat Becky is throwing me out . . . you'll have me for a neighbor sooner than you think."

Before the cops moved to Chinatown, Isaac was the strongman of the Department. All the unsolvable items, all the mysteries, went to him. His blue-eyed boys flashed in and out of the five boroughs, grabbing for clues. But Isaac had gone to sleep. He crept among rats and mice at the old Headquarters. Now Coote McNeill had sway over Chinatown and 1 Police Plaza. With a fumbling PC like Tiger John and an absent First Dep, McNeill had a house to himself. He owned the new Headquarters. He was a little old man about to retire.

Isaac crawled back to his hotel. Sammy's hot box at the Dingle must have smoothed the worm in Isaac and unstuffed his head. Mangen wasn't daft at all. Some fucking dance was going on with Mayor Sam and the McNeill. Tiger John shuffled between them. The Police Commissioner was an errand boy. That senile old Mayor had been stringing Isaac along, playing him for a goose. Herzog's Bellow, His Honor had muttered at the synagogue in Queens. Herzog's Bellow. Sammy was the shrewdest one of all.

Where did Dermott belong? Was he a silent member of the Dingle Bay club? It was crazy to Isaac. Crazy shit. Should he mount an investigation against the Old Man of City Hall? He couldn't even marshal two good boys to protect Annie Powell. Things were slipping past Isaac the Pure. Was the McNeill Annie's goduncle? It was a happy family that Isaac was trying to bust. What did a few corpses mean? The Mayor had his sauna bath. The world had to be all right.

Annie Powell was lonely without her Robinson Crusoe. He'd been a kind of roommate to her. Jamey O'Toole. He wasn't a nuisance in the end. He didn't have to climb into the hall when a customer arrived. Annie had lost most of her trade. Even the decrepit Irish sailors wouldn't come to her. She ranted at them, cackled songs that didn't remind them of the Old Country. It wasn't Dublin she sang about. It was a fish between her legs for somebody named the king. She was serenading Dermott across an ocean, calling to her man. She didn't believe in weather or the ravages of time. She refused to wear underpants, stockings, and blouses in the fall. She had a coat, a ragged slip, and one of the king's old undershirts to put on.

She was lonely, lonely, lonely without O'Toole. Tiny Jim was her last tie to the king. She could smell Connemara on him, sheep droppings, Castledermott—the house that wasn't Dermott's house—salmon struggling in the water, the smoke of a turf fire, bananas and cream, that dead cow in the road. Jesus, she was a girl in a jewelry store, selling her smile to customers, until Dermott pulled her out of there. But he shouldn't have bought

Annie from her mother though. She didn't like a man to pay for her in cash. She could forgive the mad look in his eye, the twitch of his knife. A man could mark Annie Powell if he loved her enough. The king shouldn't have left her alone.

She sat with the three friendly witches of Ninth Avenue, Margaret, Edna, and Mary Jane. They had whiskey and hot potatoes that the witches chewed without their teeth. Margaret, Edna, and Mary Jane wouldn't live indoors. They hated the contraptions of a kitchen, pots and things, the flush of a toilet, radiators, windows, pipes. They couldn't have tolerated a roof over their heads. They needed the howls that came off the river at night. So they camped in the street. They had their home of boxes, crates, and rags strewn around them in a kind of haphazard open fort.

The girls welcomed Annie Powell. She had all the signs of a rag lady. She was a younger, more beautiful version of themselves, a witch with a damaged cheek. She muttered like the girls. She told obscene stories about the Irish male, who had to tuck in his balls for centuries because he was always on the run. She wore the same misspent articles on her body as they did. Nothing matched. One of her socks might be brown. The other green or yellow. The girls were natives of Clonmel, Wicklow, and Dun Laoghaire. They could accept a witch from Sunnyside. County Queens it was. A patch of the Old Country. She secured whiskey for them. They passed the bottle from mouth to mouth. They were widow women, girls who had lost their husbands forty and fifty years ago. They knew about love. They could remember nights under the quilt. Mother Mary, that's a man inside me sleeping gown! What's he doing in there? Those husbands had died young. When the memory of it shook them, they would raise a horrendous cry on Ninth Avenue. They could stop traffic for twelve blocks with their keening. They looked at Annie Powell and realized that she was a lovesick girl.

Annie didn't keen with Margaret, Edna, and Mary Jane. How can you mourn a live man? Oh, there were deaths aplenty. But her king was in Dublin town, having his sausages and marmalade with the Fisherman's people. What was a girl to do? A car passed near the fortress of boxes, a blue car with an old man hunched behind the wheel. The crook of his back wasn't unfamiliar to Annie Powell. When did Coote the Fisherman get from Castledermott to Ninth Avenue and North Ameriky? She stepped over the boxes in her ragged skirts and called after the blue car, so she could interrogate the Fisherman, ask him about the king. "Coote," she said, "wait for me."

The car paused at the end of the block. Annie the witch went over and stuck her face in the window. "How are you, Mr. Coote?"

The Fisherman smiled. "Fit as a fiddle," he said. "And you, love? Have you been stuck in any fogs lately?"

"It don't fog much in New York," Annie said.

"It's a pity I can't help you the way I did in Connemara. I brought you down from Cashel Hill. Me and those lads of mine. But you shouldn't go on picnics in foul weather . . ."

"Would you like a sweet potato, Mr. Coote? I can ask Edna to bake one up for you."

"Thanks, love, but I've got the indigestion. Sidel must have given me his worm."

"Who's Sidel?"

"You know him. The boy who walks around in bum's clothes."

"Father Isaac," she said.

"Have you been talking to him, love? Did you tell him about Dermott and me?"

"I don't remember."

"He's a nasty fellow, that Father Isaac. Has he made any indecent proposals to you?"

"None. He likes to buy me champagne. He thinks I'm his daughter."

"You mean the famous Marilyn? That girl's been married seven times."

"She must have the itch . . . I wouldn't want seven husbands under my skin . . . how's the king? Does he have a new girl by now?"

The Fisherman said, "No, no. You're his sweetheart. He worries about you, love. He says, 'Why is my Annie on the street?' "

"I owe him money. I have to pay it off."

"What kind of money?"

"He stole me from my mother for five thousand dollars."

"Five thousand? You can borrow that from me."

"What's the use? I'd only push my debt around . . . if he wants his Annie off the street, Mr. Coote, tell him he has to come for me."

"I will," the Fisherman said. And he drove off, leaving Annie with the king awash in her head. She had a sweet potato with the girls. She guzzled Irish whiskey. She thought of Marilyn. How did it feel to be seven times a bride? Annie was only married once, but she was *twice* a bride. Dermott's bride she was. Bride's bride. It was all a hoax. Blame it on the king and his donkey. The donkey had given her away in the cool of an Irish church. She had to take the wedding band off her finger. There was small magic in that church. She was still Annie Powell, the same Annie. Dermott's secret bride.

She drank whiskey with Margaret, Edna, and Mary Jane. The three witches understood the restless agony of knees jumping under Annie's skirts. Like a cow she was, a cow gone wild in the head without its mate. The whiskey had maddened her with a hoarse fever. "Bridey," she muttered. "The bride of Little Bride Street. Ah, she had the hallucinations. She was counting the streets of Dublin in her wild talk. Annie climbed over the barricade. Boxes tore around her feet. Rags spilled out. "Good night," she said, with the sun shining in her hair. Even the girls had enough sense in them to declare the difference between night and day. "Night," she said, "good night," and she shuffled into the gutters. She didn't have a penny in her skirts. She was going to hop from bar to bar singing Irish songs like any street musician and collect pints of whiskey for the girls. But she never got to the south side of Ninth Avenue.

The girls had been watching the traffic for her. Housed in their fort, they'd developed a certain prescience. They could feel most disasters, the witches of Clonmel, Wicklow, and Dun Laoghaire. They would have yelled if the cars grew thick in front of Annie. But a cab scuttled out of nowhere to bump Annie Powell. It hadn't been part of the traffic. A willful, angered machine it was, that could throw a girl over a fender and disappear. The blood whipped from Annie's mouth in long, long strings. She shuddered in the air, rose with the force of that machine, her back nearly ripping into two separate wings as she fell into the gutter, with her thighs pulling loose from her shredded skirts. "Mother of Mercy," the witches shrieked, breaking through their barricade to get near Annie Powell.

PART
SIX

TWENTY-FOUR

HE'D killed the girl, *him*, Isaac, the big chief. He'd trusted Annie to pairs of strange boys from his office. He should have interviewed all the bodyguards he assigned to her. Only the schmuck couldn't even walk into Headquarters. He ran his office from an old dungeon that would soon belong to Rebecca of the Rockaways. He couldn't tell who was working for him anymore. He had to telephone his office to find out every piece of news. His blue-eyed angels should have been the scourge of the City. But these angels were falling down. They would bump into each other on various assignments and quests. They didn't have Isaac to pamper them and coordinate their attacks. They were disarmed without Isaac the Pure.

Their chief had a worm in him. The worm fucked his head. He'd gone into seclusion, lived in a ratty hotel, to lay bare the whore markets of New York. His bum's clothes taught him nothing. The pimps mocked the charcoal on his face. His hotel was a canteen for twelve-year-old prostitutes from the Midwest. The traffic in baby women flourished around Isaac. He couldn't make a dent. He scrounged here and there, and forgot to keep Annie alive.

Isaac grew active once she was dead. He couldn't locate the cab that ran her down, but he got in touch with Annie's mother. Mrs. Powell cursed him on the phone. She wouldn't come to the morgue and look at Annie. "My daughter's in Ireland. She went with a lousy thief. I wish I could say he's a Yid. But he's as Irish as Cardinal Cooke. Dermott Bride has my Annie . . . he has my girl. So don't tell me stories about this corpse you collected. I don't care if you're the commissioner to Saint Patrick. If you bother me again, I'll sue."

She hung up on Isaac. Should he give her daughter a Catholic burial? The worm wiggled no. He had to smuggle some kind of ceremony for Annie Powell. Apostate as he was, he still belonged to the Hands of Esau. This was the brotherhood of Jewish cops. Isaac had buried his Blue Eyes, Manfred Coen, through the Hands of Esau. He also tricked a grave out of them for Annie. "Jewish girl," he said. "Never mind her name . . . I need a good plot."

The Hands of Esau hired righteous men to say the kaddish for Annie Powell. Isaac rode out to Queens in the funeral car. He threw bits of earth on top of Annie's coffin, as if he'd been a father to her. The gravediggers had mercy on Isaac. They offered him a cigarette. The First Dep wouldn't smoke near Annie's grave.

He returned to Manhattan and ended his apostasy for seven days. He camped out on Ninth Avenue with the witches of Clonmel, Wicklow, and Dun Laoghaire. He sat shiva behind their barricade, while the witches shrieked. They frightened merchants and cops with their long cries. When they grew exhausted from their keening, Isaac would stuff potatoes in their mouths. He wouldn't let the witches starve.

Sitting on his box, he stirred only for coffee and the needs of his bladder. He didn't wash. He didn't move his bowels. He didn't feed the worm. His chin darkened from the whiskers that were growing there. He got terribly thin.

After those seven days of mourning he stood up and walked to his hotel. He'd come home in the middle of a crisis. The black whores, girls of nineteen, had begun to rebel. They felt betrayed by their pimps, who were bringing twelve-year-olds into the house, white trash from the barns of Minneapolis and St. Paul. The black whores couldn't scare a gentleman off the street. Their trade had dwindled altogether. No one would take them but freaks. Everybody wanted the little snow queens with baby tits. So the black whores had to turn mean in the halls. They went after the little "whiteys," tore the clothes off their skinny backs. The snow queens couldn't scrounge for men in tattered underwear. They hid five and six to a room, trembling against the wrath of the black whores, who patrolled the hotel with hellish eyes.

It couldn't last. The "players" left their purple Cadillacs when they couldn't find one little "whitey" in the street. They marched into the hotel and finished off the rebellion. They freed the little "whiteys" from their rooms, dressed them in different clothes, and pushed them out like big ravaged dolls to draw the customers in. Then the "players" took their revenge.

They were beating and kicking the black whores just as Isaac entered the hotel. The pimps paid no mind to the old bum who had been sitting shiva for seven days and had dust and dark stubble all over him. Isaac saw bloody mouths everywhere. The black whores gave up most of their teeth. It was as if Isaac had stumbled upon the slaughter of twenty cows. The noise was the same. The moaning was horrible to him. The pimps' assault on the black whores didn't make him think like a cop. He couldn't produce handcuffs for every "player" at the hotel. The moans he heard, that constant cowlike moo, gripped Isaac in the belly and maddened him. Isaac was encouraged by the worm. He trucked through the halls slapping blindly at each pimp he met. He knocked off their hats. He bit them on the ear in a show of fury. He ruined their fifty-dollar vests. The black whores were amazed. They'd never had an avenger like this old bum. Isaac muttered to himself as he threw down one pimp after the other. "Pray to Dermott, you lovely boys . . . I'll close this fucking hotel . . . Annie died because of me and you . . . the king can't protect you now."

The "players," the last of them, the ones who were still on their feet, did the best they could: they called the pimp squad at Midtown Station South. "Bring the cops, man . . . we got a maniac on the grounds. He'll murder people, swear to Moses, he will."

Eight detectives arrived. They were part of the First Deputy's office. Isaac himself had created them, a special squad to keep the pimps of Manhattan from hurting

169

their own women. But the pimp squad suffered without any visibility from their chief. Isaac was only a phantom to them. No one on the squad had ever seen the First Dep. The squad's morale was low. Instead of protecting the whores, the squad became friendly with the pimps.

The eight detectives were appalled by the blood and squalor inside the hotel. They'd been sleeping in their squadroom for the past two days. They despised anything to do with the ugly smells of the street. They were on loan from the burglary squad. Some idiot from Isaac's office had fucked up their lives. They were dangling men, cops on a "telephone message." A phone call from Headquarters had reshuffled them, thrown them in with the pimp squad. No orders had been written up. Another phone call could take them away, parachute them into the Bronx. You couldn't depend on shit when you were doing a "telephone message."

They weren't in the mood to placate an old bum on the rampage. They wanted to get back to their squadroom at Midtown Station South, so they could sleep the rest of the afternoon. They caught Isaac on the second floor, with a pimp's ear in his mouth. It was dumb stuff. They couldn't smooth this out. They'd have to arrest the crazy son of a bitch. Six of them fell on top of Isaac. The other two grabbed his feet. They could either kill him, or handcuff him and bring him along to Midtown South. There were a lot of black whores in the hall. The whores were watching Isaac. Now the detectives would have to go through the entire rigmarole of collaring the bum. Their senior man, a detective-sergeant, shook the "rights" card out of his wallet and began reading it to Isaac.

"Hey, you glom, you're under arrest. You have the right to remain silent and refuse to answer questions. Do ya understand?"

Isaac growled up at him. "Eat your ass," he said.

"What's your name, you?"

"Moses Herzog McBride."

"Listen, McBride, anything you say can be used against you in a court of law. Ya understand?"

"Eat your ass."

Some of the detectives dug their knees into Isaac's groin.

"You have the right to consult your attorney before

170

speaking to the police. And to have an attorney present for any questioning now or in the future. Ya understand?"

"My attorney's Tiger John. Go play with the Tiger."

"A clown," the detective-sergeant said. "And a fuckin' moron . . . you have the right to remain silent until you have the chance to consult with your attorney. So don't give me a hard time. Are you willing to answer our questions or not?"

"Eat your ass."

They dragged Isaac out of the hotel, sat him in one of their cars, and drove him to Midtown South. The pimp squad had autonomy over here. They were specialists, assigned from Headquarters. The precinct commander was nothing to them. They could ignore any cop who existed outside of their squadroom. They whisked Isaac past the desk sergeant and brought him upstairs. The bum refused to undress for a strip search. They punched him and shucked off his clothes. They took Polaroids of Isaac with his prick between his legs. They pulled him over a table, spread his cheeks, and looked up his rectum for suspicious foreign matter. This Moses Herzog McBride could be carrying diamonds or coke up his ass. The bum was clean, but he was riddled with pocks and many scars. You could tabulate the different warfares on Isaac's back and chest. The bum must have been knifed and gouged thirty times. He had a welt under his right nipple, a circular piece of raised skin, that looked like it had come from the plunge of an ice pick. The detectives began to finger Isaac's wondrous scars. "Hey, McBride, were you ever in Korea? . . . did the chinks do a job on you?"

"No," Isaac said, with his ass high on the table. "I got banged up at the Police Academy, wrestling with recruits."

They couldn't get a thing out of the joker. They locked him in the squadroom cage, and wouldn't give him back his clothes. Let the bastard shiver for a while. They would search through their pimp files for faces that resembled the old bum. Maybe he was a psycho with a grudge against pimps. If they could get his MO and his full pedigree, they might make a big score with this bum, and receive a commendation from the mysterious First

Dep, who was everywhere and nowhere at the same time.

The bum began to piss in the cage. The detectives were furious with him. They were going to flip him upside down and use his scalp for a mop when they noticed another old man in the room. The man looked like a detective who'd gone downhill. His coat was shitty and he needed a shave. Isaac recognized him: it was Mangen's shoofly, Captain Mort.

"Hey," the detective-sergeant said, "what the fuck do you want?"

"I want your prisoner," Morton said. "Dress that boy . . . and give him to me."

The pimp squad yelled at Captain Mort. "We haven't booked him yet. This is just a friendly interview. We have to escort him down to Elizabeth Street."

The shoofly glared at them. "I wouldn't book him if I was you . . . you'll embarrass yourselves."

"Schmuck, how did you get into this room?"

"I always follow the pimp squad," Morton said. "That's my specialty."

The detectives' bark wasn't so fierce. "Who are you?"

"Schapiro. I work for Dennis Mangen."

Sleeping in the squadroom morning after morning hadn't dulled their minds. They knew all about the Special State Prosecutor. Mangen. The mention of him was enough to turn your testicles gray. No commissioner could protect you from the great god Dennis. But suppose this Schapiro was telling a lie? Anybody could bluff you with Mangen's name.

"Why do you want this guy so bad?" the detective-sergeant muttered with a little more respect.

"I don't want him," Schapiro said. "He's Mangen's baby."

The detectives peeked inside the cage at Isaac's scars and Isaac's prick. "Who is this fuckin' bum?"

Captain Mort showed his contempt for the pimp squad. He had a disgusting grin that almost swallowed his own two ears. "That's your boss. Isaac the Brave."

The detectives stood frozen in the squadroom. Their mouths were brittle and puffy white.

"Don't listen to him," Isaac shouted from the cage. "Take me to Elizabeth Street. I want to be booked without my clothes."

The pimp squad didn't know what to believe. "We frisked him . . . we didn't find a commissioner's badge."

"You think he's a dummy like you?" Morton said. "The First Dep don't wear a badge when he's on a caper."

The detectives were miserable now. Then the man himself, Dennis Mangen, came into the squadroom. It was the proof they'd been begging for. You couldn't mistake Dennis' fur collar and aristocratic Irish nose. They jockeyed with themselves to open the cage for Isaac.

"Boss," they said, "boss, we're sorry . . . you should have told us . . . we'd help you cripple every pimp in New York."

Isaac stepped into his pants. Who had assigned such sleeping beauties to the pimp squad? Not Isaac. No wonder the pimps and whores walked free on Times Square. Isaac had an awful desire to beat them around the ears and stick them in their own cage. Who would miss them if they were padlocked for a month? Their wives? Their daughters? Their sons? They had frightened, rabbity eyes. Isaac began to pity them. He would leave them in place. Was it because of Isaac's scarcity that they were impotent on the street?

He left Midtown South with Mangen and Schapiro. "Dennis, get rid of the shoofly, will you, please?"

"Isaac, you ought to be nicer to Captain Mort. He's been like a fairy godmother to you."

"Baloney," Isaac said. "You planted a pimp in my hotel, that's all. The pimp got in touch with Morton, and Morton hollered to you."

Dennis motioned to the shoofly with his jaw, and Schapiro scampered down the street.

"Mangen, I wish you'd level with me . . . are you looking for Mayor Sam under the Tiger's long johns?"

Mangen frowned at him. "I'm on good terms with Sammy. The Tiger's my meat."

"What about the McNeill?"

"That old man? He's retiring in two weeks. What would I want with the Chief Inspector when I can have the PC?"

Isaac pushed away from him. "So long, Dennis . . . I don't like having my armpits licked by fancy prosecutors. If you feel like talking, give me a blow."

"Isaac, be careful. Those lads might turn mean on you. The Tiger has his private shotgun patrol."

"Oh, I'll be careful, Dennis. Believe me. I'll scream for Captain Mort when the shotguns start to fire. Goodbye."

TWENTY-FIVE

HE was too fired up to go back to his hotel. He would have ravaged pimps again. Isaac the Brave, who was disturbed by the society he kept. He'd fallen in with a hotel full of whores, become a nanny to them. The black girls could lament their old age at nineteen. The little snow queens could drag their frail bodies in front of him. Damn the City of New York. Isaac was the First Dep. Couldn't he manufacture a holy writ, without judges and special prosecutors? Bite into Dermott's trade by shoving every whore and pimp off the street? It wouldn't be an official arrest. Isaac would store the pimps in some secret house, feed them with the petty cash that the First Dep had at his disposal. The Civil Liberties Union would climb on Isaac's back and wrestle him to the ground. Judges would hurl restraining orders at him. The pimps would have to go free.

Mangen should have left him in the cage. He could have danced with his prick out. It would have been a lovely thing to book the First Deputy Commissioner of New York. They'd have to throw a shirt on him for his arraignment. They don't allow you to go naked before a judge. What kind of bail would they set for Isaac the Pure? The bondsmen would titter at him. They'd call it a travesty. Isaac in handcuffs for attacking pimps in a foul

175

hotel. The *Times* might make a wonder of it. City Hall wouldn't know where to leap. Should the Mayor get behind Isaac or the judges? The bitches would take his badge away. Dennis shouldn't have spoiled his fun.

Isaac decided to camp at his office. Rebecca Karp didn't have the power to lock him out of Centre Street. She'd have to send the City marshals after Isaac. He could stall them for another month.

Centre Street wasn't dark tonight. The lights were on for Rebecca's coming-out party. Bunting flew from the windows and the gates. There were balloons on the old Police Commissioner's terrace. Isaac avoided the hubbub of Becky's people, all the little Democrats who had fastened themselves to her cultural committee. He got in through the Commissioner's private entrance at the rear of the building, and stole up to his office without being caught by Becky's spies. The party emerged around him. He heard the slap of kettledrums under his feet. Tubas came through the walls. Every motherfucker in New York was partying with Rebecca of the Rockaways.

Democrats prowled in the halls. There was lots of giggling. Isaac ground his teeth. The noise in his ears wasn't from the Democrats. The worm was communing with him. The bitch was singing to Isaac. Who can pull sense out of the babble of a worm? Someone drifted into Isaac's office. The First Dep dimmed his lights. He hoped this stray Democrat of Becky's would disappear. Isaac could see him in the shine from his window. It was a blue-eyed boy. A shiver tore through the First Dep. A spook had come to visit him. The boy was Manfred Coen.

Isaac blamed the worm. That piece of shit in his belly could drag out spirits from the dead with a nonsensical song. Isaac wasn't afraid to mutter to a ghost. "Blue Eyes," he said. "Manfred?"

The boy jumped. He hadn't noticed the man in bum's clothes sitting behind the desk. "Excuse me . . . I was looking for the men's room."

"Aren't you Manfred Coen?"

"No," the boy said. "I'm Scamotti, Deputy Mayor for Consumer Affairs."

Isaac bellowed at him. "Get the fuck out of my office." Scamotti ran away. Isaac cursed his fifty-one years. He had a worm to trick his eyes. The bitch could

176

give him glaucoma with those squeezes of the belly. That worm ate from Isaac's blood. It thrived on sugar and other food. He'd lost his angel, Manfred. He had no one to play checkers with. Why couldn't the worm bring back Annie Powell?

The party began to irritate Isaac the Pure. He couldn't sleep with kettledrums and the smell of roast beef. The Democrats were devouring sandwiches in the main hall. Isaac went downstairs to join the party.

Men and women glared at him. The women had waxed their legs and wore jewels between their tits. The men had tiepins and flared cuffs under their dinner jackets. They hadn't come here to mingle with a bum. Isaac went for the sandwiches. The worm had hungered him. He'd have to feed the bitch or go around with a pain in his gut that could bend his knees and cause him to whimper in despair. He put roast beef, ham, and chicken salad into his mouth like any pig of a First Deputy would do. He was standing near Marshall Berkowitz and his wife. Sylvia must have gone back to Marsh. The dean wouldn't smile at Isaac.

"Marsh?" Isaac said. The dean turned away.

Isaac brushed into the Police Commissioner. "Hello, John." Tiger John was supposed to be his boss. But he would hunch up and shiver in Isaac's presence. John was helpless without the Mayor of New York. His turkey sandwich fell apart in his fingers. Mustard dropped on his shoes. Isaac wondered how many bank accounts he had under his sweater. He was a doomed boy. *Run, Johnny, run, before Dennis pounces on you.*

"Did you have your bath this week?"

"What?" John said.

"The sauna at the Dingle . . . have you tasted the dry heat with Sammy again?"

"No," John said.

"That's good. Those bloody rocks make your heart beat fast. It's been known to kill a man . . ."

Isaac left him behind a pillar with his unraveled turkey sandwich and mustard on his shoes. Sylvia Berkowitz took Isaac by the elbow and didn't let him swing very far. She'd gotten away from her husband again. Isaac was trapped between Sylvia and a kettledrum. What kind of fucking music did Rebecca hire? Isaac looked and looked, but no band knit together in front of his eyes. Tubas

177

and drums were placed around the stairs like a scattering of orphans. Each instrument breathed its own crazy line. Rebecca had a party where tubas talked to themselves, tubas and drums. It confounded the First Dep. He couldn't make peace with all those screaming melodies. Marshall's wife became a solace to him. He smiled, wanting to please her.

"I'm glad you went home to Marsh . . ."

But his words only angered Sylvia, who showed him her teeth. "I didn't need you to be my kidnapper," she said. "Two of your bulls ran me out of your apartment. They dropped me on Marshall's lap. You bastard, you could have been more polite."

"Hey, those bulls weren't mine."

"Then where did they come from? How many people knew I was living on your mattress?"

"Mangen . . . it was Mangen. He has his shooflies on my tail. Dennis kidnapped you, not me . . ."

The wife wouldn't believe him. "Don't lay it on Mangen," she said. "He wouldn't climb in with a lady and then desert her like that."

Sylvia went looking for canapés. Issac wished he hadn't come downstairs. But he didn't want to sit with the ghost of Blue Eyes in his office. So he began to circulate. He pecked at different sandwiches. His luck brought him nose to nose with his new landlady, Ms. Rebecca. She didn't cackle at him, or scold him for crashing her party.

"Isaac, I heard a friend of yours died . . . a girl . . . Annie Powell."

"Who told you that?"

"The Special Prosecutor."

Did Mangen have a tube attached to Isaac's worm? It wasn't fair. *The fuck owns me.* Isaac was disgusted with himself. But he remembered to thank the landlady for her interest in Annie Powell.

"Isaac, how did you get so thin?"

"Seven days of mourning," he said. "I didn't have much to eat."

"You sat shiva for a gentile girl?"

"Why not?"

She kissed the First Dep on his cheek. She had wet lips for a landlady.

"Isaac, I didn't think you had a heart under all that

178

fur. A cop who makes his own religion . . . that's a surprise to me."

Isaac had to get away from her, or she'd start waltzing with him to those crazy tubas. He saw that boy Scamotti again, the blue-eyed Deputy Mayor. Isaac shuddered hard. Who was this Scamotti? It had to be Coen. Manfred couldn't lie easy in the ground. He had a "kite" to deliver. *Himself.* He had to pay a visit to his murderer, Isaac Sidel. Isaac had used Coen, fed him to the Guzmann family as a kind of bait. Coen's reward was to get killed. Isaac was going to unwind this Scamotti, prove that he was Manfred Coen.

"You," Isaac said. Half the Democrats in the main hall turned to look at the bum with a scowl on his face. Scamotti hid from him. Isaac ended up with the Mayor and Mr. and Mrs. Pears. Melvin must have patched up his differences with Mayor Sam. The lawyer was chatting freely with His Honor. Democrats of every conceivable color had crawled back under Sam's umbrella at City Hall.

"Mother of God," the Mayor said. "Isaac, what happened to you? You're not the boy who went campaigning with me. Did they trample on your skin somewhere? Laddie, put a little meat on you."

"It's nothing, Your Honor. I'm in mourning, that's all."

"Who died on you?" the Mayor asked.

"No one. Just the girlfriend of an ordinary thief. Annie Powell."

The name didn't seem to register with Sam. Isaac wouldn't pump "Hizzoner" with Mr. and Mrs. Pears around. Jenny's green eyes turned him gloomy. He recalled the live thing growing in her, *his* child. *Lady, I've got a thing in me too, a worm that can twist up into a cannonball, and outgrow any fetus in the world. The bitch can scream and claw like Moses. I'll trade brats with you.*

Jennifer couldn't hear the whistling in his skull. Isaac was attractive to her in his mourning clothes. She didn't enjoy him in cop's pants, swaggering, with the mark of a commissioner on him. She preferred him disheveled and unwired. Suffering and the right kind of stubble brought out the character in his cheeks. He looked younger to her, a boy with thinning hair. She was carrying this man's baby. She had a sudden loathing for Mel. She didn't want to be touched by him. Her husband was spending his afternoons with Rebecca Karp. She wasn't jealous of that. They could smother themselves in bear hugs if they liked. But Isaac shouldn't have come to her with all the fat burned off. Mel became a chubby fool in her eyes, a lawyer in cowboy boots sucking up to an old Irish Mayor who hadn't gotten past kindergarten.

She would have rolled on the floor with Isaac among the Democrats. Politics was a mockery to her. Two months ago this Mayor had to move about the City after dark. His clerks rebelled against him. He was received like an oaf at City Hall. His assistants pirated all his files. New York had a shadow Mayor: Rebecca Karp. Rebecca sat judges, bankers, Mel, and Sam's assistants on her knee. She could rock the City to sleep, or create catastrophes with a howl and a slap of her hand. But the old Mayor was shrewd. He brought Isaac into the synagogues and stole the primary from Rebecca Karp. Now the Democrats had to run and kiss the Mayor's ass. And Melvin had gotten in line to kiss, kiss, kiss.

Only one man was aloof from Mayor Sam. Isaac the bum. A draft must have crept between them. Isaac begged nothing off the Mayor. He barely said hello to *her*. Who was this girl he mourned? Some gangster's moll. He walked away from them, left her with a husband who jostled her into Sam, so "Hizzoner" could peek at her tits.

Isaac was ready to go upstairs. He'd have enough of Democrats in the main hall. He couldn't live around Becky's people. They mumbled like the tubas and the kettledrums. But he was trying to catch Scamotti again. He wanted one last look at Blue Eyes. He got Dean Berkowitz instead. Marshall was without his wife.

"Marsh, I had to take her off the street, for Christ's sake . . . she was sleeping in telephone booths when I found her. I couldn't force her into your bed. What could I do?"

The dean was unforgiving. "Snake, you're nothing but a snake. You consoled me while you were eating my wife . . . and you used my office to get criminals into Columbia College. God knows how many other Dermott Brides I launched for you."

"Marsh, I wasn't Dermott's rabbi. Didn't you tell me

how he took to Joyce? . . . he was your star pupil before he went to Yale."

"You primed him, Isaac, you taught him how to sniff for Leopold Bloom."

"You're crazy. I've forgotten every line in that book. It was burned out of me years ago, that shit."

"Cops don't forget," Marshall screamed. "And you're the biggest cop of them all."

Isaac was the snake of Rebecca's party. Democrats squinted at him. Wives lured their husbands out of his reach. Bread turned to cotton in his fist. He couldn't even chew on a sandwich. The snake was out of luck. He stumbled upon Dennis in a pack of young lawyers. Mangen had come to shake Rebecca's hand and wish her success in Isaac's building. Isaac grabbed him away from the lawyers. The lawyers were aghast. They couldn't believe the Special Pros would allow himself to be pawed by a bum.

Isaac's eyeballs were inflamed. He looked like some Ahab hunting whales in an old, dry buildng. A crease appeared in the middle of his forehead. His seven days of mourning had isolated him from all humankind. The hairs stood on his scalp like an idiot's knot.

"You cunt . . . *you* kidnapped Sylvia Berkowitz."

"I only took back what you stole. Where I come from a man's entitled to his wife."

"Dennis, you've been living with subpoenas too long. You think you can scoop up a body and deliver it anywhere. To the courthouse, to one of your jails. Sylvia's a free agent. She doesn't belong to any dean of Columbia College . . . the next time you bring your shooflies into my apartment, I'll break them off at the neck. You've been collecting skunks and pissy old men. I'm not crazy about that rat's army of yours."

"Isaac, you ought to be. That rat's army has been keeping you alive."

"I'm sick of your fairy tails. God save me from protectors like Morton Schapiro . . . you love to play with history. Tell me again how little Dermott is a police spy."

"Ask the king. He can answer for himself."

"How, when he's sitting in Dublin?"

"Dermott's in New York."

"I haven't seen him," Isaac said.

"You will. He wouldn't leave the country without thanking you. You buried his woman for him."

Mangen disappeared from Isaac to mix with his young lawyers. Isaac's brain began to smolder on him. Why was *he* the last to get the news? Isaac had a mess of stoolies and cops clumping through the City. No one had mentioned Dermott Bride. Scamotti brushed into him. Isaac held on to Blue Eyes. "Manfred, don't fuck with me."

Scamotti laughed.

It was Coen's teeth that he saw. Coen's purple mouth. "If you hate me, Manfred, tell it to my face. I don't like to dance with spooks."

"You're hurting me," Scamotti said. "Leggo."

It was futile work. Manfred wouldn't admit who he was. Isaac would have to survive with a ghost around him. He went away from the Democrats and trudged upstairs.

TWENTY-SIX

THE party boomed under Isaac. Becky's people seemed to exist without a place to sleep. Were the Democrats going to snore against the walls? Isaac heard strange nibbling sounds. Someone was eating the woodwork outside his office. Isaac didn't care. The fucker could attack his closets and his brooms. Isaac fell into a dream about Blue Eyes. Blue Eyes and Annie Powell. They were in Dublin together. It made Isaac whimper to see Blue Eyes and Annie wading with the ducks in Stephen's Green. It must have been summertime. Manfred didn't have a shirt. The blond hairs around his nipples were growing wet. Annie's dress was way above her knees. The ducks were hysterical about the condition of her thighs. They quacked at the scars that ran from her groin to her kneecaps. The impressions were deep, like miraculous birth scars, as if a woman could give birth to any creature through her thighs.

Isaac groaned in his chair. The nibbling sound had gotten closer. The party was asleep. The Democrats must have found somewhere else to go. Isaac could have his peace. He opened one eye and saw two little old men crouching in the dark. They wore derbies in October, and long neckerchiefs that could have been used to hide a man's face. The bits of light coming from the lamps in the

183

street gave them fat shadows that humped up against Isaac's wall. The shadows wobbled because of what the old men were carrying in their arms. It could have been two long-headed babies. They're pros, Isaac muttered to himself. Only a cop or a hired killer would hold a shotgun with such profound gentleness. He ducked behind his chair.

The shotguns blasted pencils and cups off his desk. Wood splintered over Isaac's ears. The explosions could have made a fucking eternity around Isaac. The shotguns kept going and going. It was torture for what Isaac did to Coen. He'd have to live with the crump of two shotguns in his ears. They wouldn't even let the schmuck die.

Then the noises stopped. Isaac heard one of the old men say, "Shit." There was some scuffling. Isaac crawled into the foothole of his desk and came out through the other side. The shotguns were gone. He had no more old men with derbies to shoot pencils off his desk. Morton Schapiro was breaking over him, Captain Mort. "The pricks got away," Morton said. "I couldn't wrestle with both of them."

"Who were those guys?"

"Dunno. They looked like cops to me."

"You were in most of the stationhouses, Mort . . . didn't you recognize them?"

"I couldn't," Morton said. "They kept covering their mouths."

"Funny guys they were . . . with derbies sitting on their brains. Morton, what the hell were you doing on my floor?"

"Mangen told me to stay up here. He said you might have a few visitors tonight."

Dennis was his rabbi, all right. And Isaac had a new "angel," Captain Mort. He couldn't be sure if those two old men were serious with their guns. They damaged a lot of wood. But Isaac's skin was pure as ever. They hadn't even singed his hair. Still, Captain Mort had wrestled with them, faced up to their neckerchiefs and those wicked guns. Isaac had to pay his debt to the shoofly.

Morton was delighted with the stingy thanks he got, the mumble of words out of Isaac's mouth. "Now you can go home," Isaac said.

A gloom crept over Captain Mort. "What if they come again?"

"They won't. Morton, they're afraid of you."

He couldn't do much about the shattered wood. He'd have to work in a sea of splinters until Rebecca threw him out. He picked the shotgunned pencils and cups off the floor. Then he sat behind his desk. He was feeling snug as Moses ever could. The arrival of the two old men had been a preliminary dance. It was a bit of foolishness designed to scare the shit out of Isaac. He knew what would come next. He'd have to wait a little while. The main act would begin when the shotgun dust had settled.

A man appeared at the door. Isaac didn't have to blink. "Dermott," he said. "Don't be shy. Come on in."

The king stepped into Isaac's office. He was small, the way Isaac remembered him. He had a crow's black hair, and peculiar features for an Irishman. How did he get so dark? Were there gypsies in the Bronx that mingled with the shanty Irish of Clay Avenue and Crotona Park North? Or did his blood lines go deeper than that? He could have sprung from a hidden race of dark-skinned Irish, seafarers from the Levantine who had come down the Liffey four hundred years ago to settle in Blackrock. Isaac snapped on the lights. The king's eyebrows bunched on his face. Dermott had the right people to take Isaac apart. But no one seemed willing to murder him.

"That's a pair of lovely boys you lent me. Did you supply them with neckerchiefs and all?"

Those eyes beetled up at Isaac until they covered half the king's head. "Isaac, O'Toole is the only gang I ever had. And he's gone."

"What about the Clay Avenue Devils?"

"Christ, I ran from the Devils before I was eighteen. If you're going to make me spit out my past, Isaac, then at least let a man have his chair."

"Sit," Isaac said, and the king sat down across from Isaac in the room's only other chair. The First Dep didn't have a great need for hospitality. He preferred a barren room.

"Well, if the neckerchiefs didn't belong to you, then what was that joke all about? You're not a blind man, Dermott. You walked on the debris they left. Two old men in derby hats shot up my office twenty minutes ago."

"They're not mine, I said."

"Then why are you here? Did Tiger John send you?

185

Are you supposed to warn me never to go near Mangen again? . . . you know, Dennis says you're a police spy. I told him he was full of shit."

The king laughed. "Since when are you so loyal to me?"

"Don't kid yourself," Isaac muttered. "I have eighteen special squads. I'd have known before now if any cop was carrying you on his lists . . . Dermott, I'm curious about something. It seems I got you into Columbia College. I read the report I wrote for Marshall Berkowitz. But kill me, I can't remember meeting you."

"We met. Many times. We had long talks, me and you, when I was with the Devils."

"I talked to Arthur Greer. He was president of the club."

"But Arthur didn't get into Columbia College."

Isaac still had that shotgun music in his ears. His head was a rubble of bones and blood. Why could he picture Arthur, who was pushed from his roof, and not little Dermott?

"What did we talk about?"

"Immanuel Kant."

The king was telling lies. Bronx thugs with black hair couldn't have gotten into Kant.

"You gave me books to read," Dermott said. "Dostoyevsky . . . Kant . . . James Joyce . . . it wasn't only literature. We talked about the South Bronx . . . the death of Crotona Park."

Isaac had to be in his dotage. Does senility strike at fifty-one? The Guzmanns had ruined him, those pimps of Boston Road. They'd given him a clever dose of venereal disease: a syphilitic worm that was eating away at Isaac's prick and Isaac's brain. He'd brought Kant and Dostoyevsky to little Dermott, and Isaac couldn't recollect a word.

"What other cops did you talk to?"

"Why?"

"Because a memo exists from my dead boss, O'Roarke, asking me to put you into college."

"This O'Roarke never came to our clubhouse. I can promise you that. He didn't meet with the Devils."

"Then who could have told him about you?"

"Anybody . . . we were popular in those days. The Devils policed the Bronx."

"And you, you walked from Columbia to Yale, you said hello to Marshall Berkowitz and goodbye, you learned from Marsh about Shem and Shaun and the powers of the Liffey, and you graduated from Marshall's class to become the overlord of every pimp in Manhattan."

"And what did you learn from Marsh? To rush through the streets slapping heads? Big cop who grovels in the dirt and puts on disguises, so he can land in a crook's underwear. The trouble with you, Isaac, is you don't have some poet to celebrate all your deeds."

"I'm not dying to be famous," Isaac said. He was growing less fond of this dark-haired boy, this gypsy Irishman from Clay Avenue. He had an itch to take the king by his ears and shove him into the wall. "What's your secret, Mr. Bride? How did you stay invisible for seventeen years? A whoremaster without a face. Why didn't we have your pedigree in my files? We had pages and pages on Arthur Greer . . . I could have told you the grooves in his knuckles, or the size of his prick."

"Arthur wasn't happy unless he was at the center of things. He entertained judges and movie tycoons. I was the quiet one. I kept my nose clean."

"A pretty story," Isaac said. "But it's mostly shit. Some cop had to be fronting for you . . . you have bad habits for a king. A king ought to be gracious to his friends. He shouldn't sit still when they die."

"Isaac, what the fuck is in your head?"

"I didn't catch you grieving for Arthur and your man O'Toole."

"It's not your business how I grieve and who I grieve for."

"Your uncle, Bagman McBride. Where the hell is he?"

"He's safe," Dermott said. "The uncle is out of your hands."

"And Annie Powell? Once you discard a mistress, I suppose that's it."

Isaac smiled when Dermott reached into his pocket. He could predict the knife that would come out like a long tooth. The king's elbow made a perfect line. That line never wavered, never broke.

"Are you going to cut my face, sweetheart?"

"No," the king said. "I'm not interested in your face. It's your throat I want."

Isaac didn't move from his chair. He was gambling that little Dermott wasn't ready to stick him with the tooth. "Arthur lied for you the last time I saw him. He said you were the mediator for the Devils, and I believed him. The king made his rep with his tongue. No, no. You were his blade. The quiet boy who could scar you for life. That's how you talked . . . poor Arthur was only president of the club. You were the king."

The tooth disappeared with a snap of the king's wrist. "Where did you bury Anne?"

"Her mother wouldn't take her," Isaac said. "I had to find a plot. She's in a Jewish cemetery near Floral Park. Esau Woods."

Those black eyebrows began to rumple like mad, as if the king were having a fit inside his head, and nothing showed, nothing but the rumples over his eyes. He looked up at Isaac. "You shouldn't have let her stay on the street . . . I tried to get O'Toole to pull her into Brooklyn Heights. Jamey couldn't do it. *You* were around. The big rabbi from Headquarters, Isaac Sidel . . . how come you didn't ask me what I remember about you?"

The king was setting him up. Isaac could feel it in the shiver of his voice. Little Dermott had a harsh vocabulary. His words would lead Isaac into some ugly twist. "I didn't think you remembered very much. You wouldn't even nod to me in Dublin."

"Dublin was something else . . . Isaac, I always hated your guts. You were a pain in the ass from the beginning. You had to reform little Bronx boys. Save us from the wildlands of Crotona Park. How many of us did you ship to Columbia College? Savages who were taught to purr. We could mouth any sort of magic. We had Diderot for breakfast. Molière for lunch. Shitface, who told you to meddle? I'm not your rubber baby . . . why did you have to pick out Anne? Couldn't you reform another girl? Isaac, haven't you guessed? People die wherever you plunge. If you'd kept away from Anne, I wouldn't have to go searching for her in your Esau Woods . . ."

The king was through with him. He'd come to Isaac for the name of a cemetery. He hadn't shared a thing with the First Dep. "Isaac, I should have let those boys rip off your mouth in Dublin, when they had you in their car."

"Why didn't you?"

"I'm not inhuman," the king said. "I wouldn't hurt my old teacher." And he was gone from the room. Isaac was in the same bloody fix. He still couldn't remember the king.

There were dead balloons and slices of rye bread on the stairs. The king walked over the shambles of Rebecca's party. The place stank of Democrats: judges, lawyers, and clubhouse whores, men and women that Dermott had to smear with money. He'd bought the little Mayor and the Chief of Police. God knows, half the City lived off Dermott Bride. Manhattan would disappear without the girls of Whores' Row. The king put a tax on the girls that could carry a whole fucking island. The economy of New York lay with its whores, and what they could earn on their backs. He crushed party cups with both feet on his way out of the building.

The king got into a black Mercury. It was Tiger John's official car. The pimps had their Cadillacs, and the Police Commissioner settled for a black machine that was like a fat upholstered toy. It had gadgets hooked into the seats, telephones that could connect the Tiger with his men in the field. But he rarely used the phones. He was frightened of the buzzing they provoked. He preferred silences when he was in the car. Tiger John liked to think about the bankbooks in his pocket.

Dermott was abrupt with him. He didn't enjoy having to mingle with Sammy's toad. "Where's the Fisherman?"

"Are you daft?" the Tiger said. "McNeill can't be seen with you. Not in this country."

"Explain that, will you, Tiger John? Why you can sit with me, and McNeill can't."

"I'm the PC. I can do whatever I like."

This idiot had thirty thousand cops under his command. He could break a full inspector, knock him down to captain if he chose. Or drop a branch of detectives, decimate a squad. He was as gullible as a monkey in the Bronx Zoo. You fed him bankbooks once a month, like a banana in his mouth, and he was delighted with himself. He banged through Headquarters making mischief in the offices he entered. His rages were an enormous bluff. The PC had nothing to do. McNeill ran the Department for him.

"He's angry with you," the Tiger said, "for coming back to America without asking him first."

"Since when do I need Coote's permission to fly?"

"Boyo, that was the bargain you struck."

The Tiger had a crafty approach for an imbecile. Mayor Sam must have given him lessons in the art of Irish persuasion.

"Coote doesn't have to worry," the king said.

"You'll spoil his retirement if you don't get out of here fast."

"I'll be home in Dublin by tomorrow night."

The Tiger looked at him out of a pair of tiny, nervous eyes. "Boyo, tomorrow could be too late. Sheeny Isaac is crawling around. He followed me and Sam into the sauna room at the Dingle. He didn't have the decency to take off his clothes. All he did was talk about Dennis Mangen."

"He's your First Dep. Can't you quiet him down?"

"Jesus, I'd love to get rid of him. But he's the darling of the press. The newspaper lads bruise their own two feet begging interviews off the boy."

"Was that your shotgun party that Isaac was complaining about?"

"Not mine," the Tiger said. "McNeill's. The Fisherman sent over two retired sergeants to drop a neat kite on Isaac's room. But Mangen had his shooflies in the hall. The sergeants were lucky to get out of there alive."

The king laughed to himself. The cops of New York made a mad, struggling army. Mangen was biting everybody on the ass. Except for Isaac. Isaac was the great survivor. He could rise out of a curtain of shotgun smoke in his stinky pants. The First Dep was so smart and so dumb. Isaac had each point of Dermott's history in his heavy brain, but he couldn't pull them into a straight line. The Devils were a local club. They didn't have the firepower to terrorize a boroughful of gangs. They couldn't have gone out on rampages to enforce the peace without a little help from the cops. McNeill lent his youth squad to the Devils. The gang was a baby wing of the NYPD. Coote wouldn't deal with Arthur Greer. He touched Dermott on the shoulder, made him the king.

"Boyo," the Tiger said, "where are we going now?"

"To a cemetery in Queens."

"At this hour?" Tiger John bristled in his coat.

"The harpies are walking about. Why are we going to a graveyard?"

"To meet a lady of mine."

Isaac had blabbered about a loss of memory. The poor demented boy couldn't picture Dermott's face among the Devils. The king remembered the old gang. They had to use a shack in Claremont Park as a clubhouse, the Devils of Clay Avenue. They didn't have the funds to buy colored jerseys. The Devils were nothing until the cops picked them up. They had to run to the cellars and the trees whenever the Fordham Baldies arrived on Clay Avenue. The shabbiest nigger gang could have destroyed them in an even fight.

The Devils were without a single patch of honor. They were the scavengers of the borough, mocked by other clubs. Only the worst pariahs came over to the Devils' side, outcasts and imbeciles. The Devils lacked the scars of open combat. They would fall upon the isolated members of some gang more craven than themselves. It took twelve of them to beat up one boy. They would whoop and scream, steal a pocket off the boy's shirt, and run back to their clubhouse in the park. They shivered summer and winter long, with the hysterical passion of cowards and invalids. They feared that an enemy might retaliate and burn down their miserable shack. But few gangs would bother with them.

Then McNeill wed his cops to the Devils. It was the only bunch of kids that the youth squad could control. He gave the Devils a bit of fighting blood. His motor pool would taxi them to different parts of the Bronx, so they could hit an unsuspecting gang and disappear. The Devils became known for these lightning attacks. They still couldn't have won if McNeill hadn't dressed his toughest boys in the Devils' jerseys to smack Fordham Baldies over the head. The king began to earn a reputation with his knife. He could slash out and rip a shirt sleeve, shave an enemy's skull, with Coote's boys behind him.

Things went according to McNeill. He could slap any gang in the Bronx through little Dermott and the Devils of Clay Avenue. But the king had ambitions of his own. He wasn't satisfied with his existence as Coote McNeill's knife and stick. He met in secret with the man. They stood outside the Webster Avenue shul, smoking cigarettes. No one would suspect an Irish captain and an

Irish pug to declare new policies in the shadows of a synagogue.

"Ungrateful brat," McNeill said. "Haven't I blessed you enough? I picked you over that jigaboo, Arthur Greer. You're the goddamn lord of the Bronx. The Baldies piss on their toes when the king takes out his knife."

"I want more," Dermott muttered from the side of his mouth.

"That's grand. Should I pin a badge on your chest and call you Sergeant McBride?"

"No. You'd better gimme a college education."

McNeill had a laughing fit on the steps of the old shul. He wiped his eyes with a handkerchief. "They don't let donkeys into college. You're too old. You must be twenty, for God's sake."

"I'm seventeen."

"You never finished high school."

"So what? I want college from you, Captain McNeill. Or find yourself another baby."

They grinned at each other. The kid was bluffing. They both knew that. Little Dermott was stuck in his shack. He had nowhere else to go. But Coote liked the idea of a little gangster in college. The Department could raise up a lovely, educated pigeon. Coote went to see his boss, First Deputy O'Roarke. "Ned, that dark bitch will be useful to us. We'll have ourselves a cutthroat with a college degree." But even the great O'Roarke couldn't convince a college to take him. They had to groom him first. Only one lad in Ned's entire office could jabber about Karl Marx. That was young deputy inspector Sidel. "Ned, will you lend us the brain?"

"You can have him," O'Roarke said.

Isaac was a natural for them. The brain had ties to Columbia College. They could shove the king in that direction. But they didn't tell Isaac about their plan to educate little Dermott. They sent Isaac over to sit with the Devils. He brought Dostoyevsky into the clubhouse. Most of the Devils yawned. They wanted to go on a scalping party. The king took Isaac's prattle in. He had to make up for years of neglect. He memorized every murder in Prince Hamlet of Elsinore, and he got into Columbia College.

"Graveyards," Tiger John smirked into his coat. It

took him and his driver hours to locate the cemetery at Esau Woods. John wouldn't step out of the car. He wasn't going to carouse near the tombstones in a Jewish yard, and let the harpies grab at him from the trees. Why was this Annie Powell buried with the Yids?

"That's an odd priest that would let her lie down in Esau Woods," he said to Dermott.

"The priest was Isaac."

Dermott walked over to the caretaker's shack and knocked on the window. The caretaker wouldn't come out. Dermott crumpled fifty dollars under the door. The caretaker smelled the money and stuck his head in the window. He wore a thick wool cap. "What do you want?"

"A grave," Dermott said.

"For yourself?"

"No. A girl was buried here."

"Under what auspices?" the caretaker asked.

"I don't know. She came with Isaac Sidel."

A sense of recognition grew out from under the cap. The caretaker smiled. "The Christian girl, you mean . . . they can't fool us, those big commissioners. She's in Lot Eleven, Row B . . . you'll find a marker with a red flag."

Dermott moved away from the shack. The caretaker shouted between Dermott's shoulder blades with genuine scorn. "What's the matter with you? You can't go in thee naked! This is holy grrounds."

He gave the king a skullcap to wear. He also put a huge flashlight in Dermott's hands. Half the graveyards in the borough of Queens could have heard those batteries knock. Dermott clumped through Esau Woods with a big, loud metal canister that couldn't light up his shoes: the bulb was nearly dead. He came to that marker on Lot Eleven, Row B. It was a stick on a smudge of earth, with a filthy rag knotted to it. That was all of Annie Powell. The king trembled near that grave. The cold burrowed through him. Why? It wasn't winter yet.

That rag knotted to a stick was the king's sign: a dirty sniveling crook he was, in a silk necktie, who rode out of the Bronx like a cannonball, with police money and police wit, and bribed a judge in Connecticut to shorten his name, so he wouldn't sound like a shanty Irish boy. Dermott Bride. Dermott Bride. Funny coloring for a mick. Dark the hair and dark the eyes. Would you believe it now? They have Irish niggers in the New Country. They live in a land called the Bronx. His dad couldn't explain this complexion of the male McBrides. The old man was a dark-haired janitor. He kept his family outside the Church. He wouldn't have child Dermott beaten by any bald witch of a nun. The boy went to public school. All the other micks in his class were so ruddy. Green-eyed girls. They grew taller than little Dermott. He fought those big Irish mules, boys and girls, biting, scratching, gouging with his thumbs, or he would have been eaten alive. They still wouldn't have much to do with him. He couldn't join the Salters, the Green Bays, the Emerald Knights. He had to go with the Devils, a mangy gang without a clubhouse, that took sheenies in, and had a nigger for a president.

The Devils couldn't smoke out his lineage for him. Dermott went to the history books. How do you look up *Irishman, Dark Hair?* He read about the Gaels, and the rude islands that Caesar bypassed when he conquered the world. An island of savage people with bulls and cows. But where, where was the dark eyes? He read some more. The English conquerors, and the Pale they established around Dublin, where only Englishmen could tread. The Irish kings had to shiver in the booleys, with their cattle and their priests. And then little Dermott discovered his own history in the drowning of the Spanish Armada. A few of the ships were knocked into the coast of Ireland by a storm. It was 1588. Pockets of Anglo-Irish militia stood on the shore with clubs in their hands. The dark-haired sailors were beaten to death, one by one, as they crawled out of their ships. A handful escaped into the interior, and were hidden in some obscure Irish village beyond the Pale. Dermott's true fathers came from such a handful. He was a Spanish mick, an Irisher with eyebrows. He'd solved the obscurity of his line. It made no difference what his dad was doing in the Bronx. The boy was descended from Spanish-Irish pigherders, or something close to that. The McBrides had walked in pigshit for two hundred years. Dermott swore to himself that he'd climb out of the muck.

"Johnny, are you sleeping now?"

The king gave John a fright. The Tiger shut his eyes while little Dermott went creeping in the Jewish graveyard for his Anne, and Holy Mother of God, the lad returns before John could take a blink!

"Did you catch any harpies in the woods?"

"None at all."

"Too bad," the Tiger said. "If they pluck one eyebrow, it's supposed to charm you for a month. But harpies can be dangerous. God help you if they nest in your hair."

"The harpies weren't out tonight."

"It's the warmth," Tiger John said. "They won't come to you in October."

The Commissioner had an idiotic mythology for every beast that stirred in the woods. Let the harpies nest in Dermott's hair. He'd take them into Dublin and tickle them to sleep. Then he'd root them out with his knife.

"Did Isaac provide for the lady?"

"He did. A rag and a stick on a hump of dirt."

"Ah, that's the Hebrew law. You go to lots of Jewish funerals when you're the Commish. We have sheenies in the Department, you know. Thousands of them. It's years and years before they put a stone on a grave. So it has to be a rag for Annie Powell."

"I'll order a stone tomorrow," the king said, sucking with his teeth.

"The Jews won't deliver it. Not for six years."

"I'll hire my own deliverers."

"The rabbis will run them out of the graveyard."

"Then I'll buy rabbis to fight the rabbis of Esau Woods."

The Tiger chuckled to himself. "That will be a sight. Rabbis clawing each other's holy shirt . . . boyo, you don't have the time. No playing with rabbis. Mangen's not a fool. He'll wonder why you're here. You might never get to Dublin with Mangen around. His grand juries are notorious for latching on to boyos like you, so they can't leave the country."

"Dennis won't find me."

"That's good news," the Tiger said. "I'll pray for you."

You're the lad that needs praying for, the king understood. Someone would have to take a fall. It wouldn't be Sam. The bankers might cry over the prospect of a Mayor in jail. It could eat into the worth of municipal paper. But a crooked Police Commissioner wasn't that much of a liability. You could always put another toad in his place.

This one, John the tiger-toad, looked out at Dermott with a strange compassion in his eyes. He winked and blew his nose. "I can calm the rabbis for you. I'm the PC . . . you'll get your stone for Annie Powell."

The king nodded once. The old, dumb Commissioner meant no harm. Whose fault was it that he didn't have Sammy's wit or the Fisherman's brains? He could only bluster through Headquarters doing his Tiger dance. Dermott had already gone way, way into his Spanish skull. The bumping of the Mercury didn't register in his ears. The king despised himself. He was no better than a pimp who marks his woman for some small sin, like holding back five dollars, or daring to talk to one of the dudes at an after-hours club. The pimp would take a wire coat hanger and twist it into his main initial, heat it on the burner of his woman's stove, and stick it in her face. Dermott used a knife.

It was an old Bronx ritual that existed long before the Devils got their start. Girls didn't have an independent status in any gang, no matter how tough or beautiful they were. A girl was property, like an ice pick, or a tamed pigeon. And if she "wounded" you, if she roused your jealousy, if she shamed you in the eyes of the gang, you cut her with a knife, to show her and everyone else in the Bronx where the lines of your property ought to begin and end.

That was a dumb ritual for a king to follow. He'd been away from the Devils for sixteen years. He should have curbed his jealousies. Annie Powell. He'd left her alone in Dublin with those ancient bodyguards, while he sat in Connemara with the Fisherman, and established how many pieces they could get from a whore's pie, and where the pieces would go. What did he expect from Anne? Coote had pulled Jamey out of Ireland. She didn't have the king's donkey to watch over her anymore. It's a brave lad who gives his wife a scar and sends her back to Ameriky. Prick that he was, he should have cut his own face.

A noise blasted through the king. It was Tiger John's radiotelephone. It rang and rang from a niche in the upholstery. "Answer it," the king said. "Go on, Johnny. Scream your hello."

196

Dermott picked up the receiver and clapped it to the left side of John's head. John mumbled, "Yes . . . no . . . yes . . ."

Then he put the receiver into its place. But he didn't offer any information to little Dermott.

"Who was that? . . . Coote?"

"No." Tiger John took to whispering in the rear of his car. "It was Mayor Sam."

"Why didn't he talk to me?"

"Jesus, you're poison to Sam. The Mayor wants you out of the country on the next aeroplane."

"The Mayor can go fuck himself. I'm not leaving until I pay my respects to the mother of O'Toole."

John was certain the king had a draft in his head. "Mangen is closing in, and you can't leave until you kiss the mother of O'Toole? We'll send flowers in your name to that old hag."

"Don't send shit. The Fisherman killed my man."

"Swear to God, Dermott. It was sink or swim. Your man grew a beard and went crazy. He was going to run to Isaac and snitch on us all."

Coote was right about little Dermott. The king had lost his grip. A man with a nose for business wouldn't have come to New York to buy tombstones for an Irish bitch. Where's the value of it? The girl was already in the ground.

"John, are you driving me to the old woman, or not? If I have to walk to Chelsea, I won't be in Dublin until the day after tomorrow."

God forbid. "Hold your horses," the Tiger said. "I didn't say I wasn't driving you, did I now?" He'd have to get himself a castle, just like Coote. Then he could give the Mercury back, and retire to Kerry and Dingle Bay.

TWENTY-SEVEN

THE king had never been a shylock, a *gombeen-man*, like Arthur Greer. He didn't have a countinghouse in Dublin or New York. His bagmen collected a fee from the pimps of Manhattan and the Bronx, and the king took this pimping money and scrubbed it the best way he could. He threw it into restaurants, bowling alleys, limousine services, and rare books. A good portion of it was churned back, so the king could stock a yellow lake with salmon for Coote McNeill, provide a secret pension fund for the Mayor, create bankbooks for Handsome John.

It was smooth and lovely work. The pimps would swagger in their long coats, because Mr. Dermott Bride had arranged a charter of principles for them with the Police. They were shrewd enough not to ask about the details of this charter. The sweetest mack always gave a dumb picture of himself. He had a harem to protect, a stable of "brides," little snow queens, and all his number-one ladies who broke their humps in his behalf. The macks realized that some of their nickels and dimes were going to the Police Commissioner. If Tiger John Rathgar lived off their bounty, what could happen to them?

But the Special Prosecutor arrived on Whores' Row.

Mangen dropped a fucking siege around Headquarters. Cops bit their fingers and ran from him like a galaxy of cockroaches. Mangen had the power to subpoena bishops, whores, mayors, and pimps. The king couldn't peddle charters anymore. He moved to a fancy hotel in Dublin town, and the cops began to pull entire harems off the street. Bail money was getting hard to find. The macks' own gombeen-man, Sweet Arthur Greer, fell off a roof. The king had to hide his old uncle Martin, or the bagman would have been dead. But he couldn't save his Irish bitch . . .

He got to Chelsea in Tiger John's car. Dermott was bringing a packet of money for Mrs. O'Toole, blood money it was, because he'd made a dirty bargain with Chief Inspector McNeill. The king had killed Jamey boy by sending him back to New York. There were no bugaboos in the hall, no cops from the First Deputy's office. *You're a gorgeous man, Dermott McBride, with your black hair and your knife. You can cut your name into a woman, give her your mark for other men to be wary of.* He was the fool of fools. *A thief shouldn't marry. He's like any businessman who has to neglect his wife for the silly bickerings of trade . . . Shouldn't have left her in Dublin with Coote's people . . . Prick that I am, playing Moses the punisher.* It wasn't the absence of her flesh that rankled the king. He could have bought and sold a hundred look-alikes to Annie Powell. Get another doll of a girl. But he loved that dumb banter she had, the way she could mourn a cow. His childy woman.

The mother of O'Toole had a metal plate on her door. It was open. The king walked in. Mrs. O'Toole sat in a rocking chair with a kind of bonnet on her head. She had big ears for an old lady. But the king hadn't come to criticize her looks.

He took out his packet of money, six thousand in hundred-dollar bills. "I'm Dermott Bride," he said. "I used to employ your son."

The old woman was made up like a whore, with lipstick that spread onto her cheeks in an impasto of purple moons. The knuckles in her lap were hairy and thick. Her feet stuck out of the brogans she wore. She had muscular ankles, this mother of O'Toole. Dermott picked the bonnet off her head. It was a curious scalp she had, with short white bristles on top. A Detective Special appeared from under her blouse.

"I'm Captain Schapiro," she said. "Stay where you are, you lousy crook."

The king didn't have to shiver. He had a blade on him that could carve up this beauty in the rocking chair. He heard the voice of a man behind him.

"Dermott, please don't go for the knife . . ."

The man had a coat with a fur collar. He wasn't carrying a weapon, like Mother O'Toole. "I'm the Special Pros." He sent Schapiro into the kitchen, so he could be alone with the king.

"Where's the mother of O'Toole?"

"She's all right," Mangen said. "We figured you wouldn't leave the country without laying some gelt on her. You're not a careless man . . . we put her in a home on Charles Street.

"That's kind of you. Too bad I can't produce Jamey's ghost. He'd give you a shake of the hand for shuffling his ma around . . . Mangen, why did you dress Schapiro in women's clothes? Was it to entertain a Bronx boy like me? You needn't have bothered, you know, I would have liked Schapiro without his bonnet . . ."

"Forget that little trick of mine. I didn't want you to wrestle with an army of cops. You might have scratched them all, and I'd have to pay the bill . . . how could I thank you if we didn't have a talk?"

Dermott stared at this maniac in the fur collar. "Thank me for what?"

"For those names you put in Tiger John's bankbooks."

"Ah, it was nothing. A bit of fun. I was hoping John would enjoy it."

"He did," Mangen said. "And so did I . . . I couldn't have traced his phony signatures without your *Molly Bloom*s and your *Gertrude MacDowell*s. I thought you were trying to tell me something . . . that you were fed up with McNeill and the whole rotten bunch."

"Hey Mangen . . . Molly Bloom wasn't any signal to you. It's a name, that's all."

He had a sad face for a boy millionaire. The king was stuck in two milieus. He was a hoodlum with a love for books. What could money get for him? He didn't belong anywhere. Not with Isaac, not with Marsh, not with Coote McNeill.

"Dermott, you don't have to go to Dublin. I could give you a suite in a good hotel . . . with bodyguards and everything."

"Sure, and then I'd be your canary. Thank you, but I'll take Stephen's Green." He bowed to the Special Pros and held out the packet of money. "You could do me a favor though, and give this bundle to Mrs. O'Toole . . . and my regrets for the life of her son."

Mangen took the six thousand. "I could confiscate this money, tag it, and save it for my property clerk."

"I know," the king said. "But you won't." He went out the door, and Mangen felt like an idiot, holding a bundle of whores' money in his hand. He called to Schapiro in the kitchen.

"You had to shove your Detective Special at him . . . never pull a gun on a man while you're sitting down. He could have chopped your nose off. Will you hurry up, Morton, and wiggle out of that skirt. Wipe the lipstick off, for shit's sake. They'll think we've been smooching on the stairs . . ."

PART
SEVEN

TWENTY-EIGHT

IT was the middle of October, and you couldn't find Sam in the streets. No one was alarmed. His Honor had won the primary. He didn't have to beg for votes. But where was the Old Man of City Hall? Was he on some kind of maneuvers in the countryside? Sammy would never leave town. Boys and girls from Dennis Mangen's office began to scuttle in and out of the Mayor's rooms. They didn't have a blemish on them. They arrived fresh from law school with pigskin briefcases and theories on the ways and means of smothering crime in the City of New York. The girl prosecutors were harsher than the boys. Mangen's girls wouldn't even smile at a deputy mayor.

They emerged from Sammy's rooms one morning, with the Old Man himself. He loked like a Mayor who was walking in his sleep. His eyes would focus on the ceiling and nothing else. He wore slippers rather than shoes. The slyness had gone out of him. Why was he captive to Mangen's girls, meek in their presence? The girls drew reporters out of their closet, and the Old Man held a news conference on the steps of City Hall. "Misery," he said. "Lads, I'm in poor health. The Mayor can't have red meat. They give me grass to chew. I'll strangle on it if I have to run this City."

The reporters looked at Sam and rocked on their toes, trying to fathom his gibberish about grass and red meat. "Your Honor, does this mean you're pulling out of the race?"

"That's the rotten truth."

The reporters shoved a bit closer to Sam. "What will happen to the Democrats?"

"Ah," the Mayor said, "they'll survive."

The Democrats caucused on the same afternoon. Party chiefs spent an hour praising the Old Man. "Wonderful Mayor. The very best. We'll miss him dearly. We will." Then they went scratching for a new candidate. They didn't have to caucus very hard. The candidate had come to them like a thunderbolt. It was Rebecca of the Rockaways.

She arrived at the old Police Headquarters and hugged Isaac the Brave. Isaac was chagrined. "Rebecca, I'll get out soon as I can clear my desk."

"Stay," she said. "The Cultural Committee can spare one little room . . . Isaac, we have to talk. I'll need a good cop. I want you to stick with the Police."

Isaac grew more and more depressed. What Mayor renounces his candidacy a few weeks before November? Only Sam. The Board of Elections had to strike Sammy off the lists and print Rebecca's name. The Board was an old hippopotamus. It couldn't have roused itself. The Board must have known for a month that Rebecca would be on the ballot. That hippopotamus took its instructions from Sam.

Isaac dialed City Hall. It was a worthless occupation. You couldn't get Sammy on the phone. "What's your name, sir? Sidel, sir? We'll tell him that the First Deputy called." Isaac understood that most of this malarkey wasn't Sam's. The great god Dennis was behind it all. Mangen had gotten Sam to close his shop. They must have been bargaining while the hippo went to the printer with its ballots. Whom had the Mayor offered up to Dennis? It had to be Tiger John.

But the Tiger was still issuing memos out of 1 Police Plaza. The memos could have been for the cops of Peoria, Illinois. The Tiger mentioned riot batons, gas masks, all-weather shoes. Isaac grabbed at the memos in disgust. Cops were dying, and the Tiger wanted gas masks and a certain kind of shoe.

It encouraged a madness in yourself to interpret every line. John was hysterical over something. Isaac didn't have to guess why: Mangen's grand jury was in harness again. Twice a month Dennis would imprison twenty-three ladies and gentlemen in a secret room at the World Trade Center. He wouldn't let them out until they produced bills of indictment for him. When the jury doors opened, a twitch would spread from judges to lawyers and cops. You couldn't be sure where Dennis would strike.

The man had no shame. He walked into 1 Police Plaza with those girl prosecutors of his and a pair of City marshals. They went up to the fourteenth floor and arrested Tiger John. The PC had to wear handcuffs in front of his lieutenants and clerks.

He was booked at the precinct on Ericson Place. Officers had to search through his pockets and fingerprint the PC! They photographed him with his gray support hose dragging around his calves. He wasn't put in a separate holding bin. He sat with all the thieves. They were trundled over to Manhattan Supreme Court in a little truck, and he was arraigned before a judge who stared at the Commissioner with a crooked mouth. Tiger John was charged with extorting money from prostitutes and lending "his office, his title, and his good name" to help pimps and other vermin of the City. Bail was denied. The judge wouldn't set a vulture out in the street. John had to go to Riker's Island.

His Honor, Sammy Dunne, would permit no confusion among the Police. He stood before television cameras inside the rotunda of City Hall. The Mayor wore a dark green suit. His cuff links shimmered against the cameras and the lamps in powerful hues. He seemed recovered from his recent spell of witlessness. "I won't talk about Johnny Rathgar," he said. "If he's clean, we'll find out . . . and if he's guilty, we'll send him to the dogs!"

"Your Honor, who's the next Commish?"

"Only one lad could take on that job . . . with so much corruption smacking us in the face. Isaac Sidel."

The reporters were eager to know where Isaac was.

"Ah, he'll be here soon enough."

Isaac couldn't escape Sammy's call to become the next "Commish." Old shots of Sam and him, bumbling from synagogue to synagogue last June, appeared in the *Times*, the *Post,* and the *Daily News.* Television interviewers began to converge on Centre Street. The Mayor's office was phoning the boy every fifteen minutes. New York was still without a Police Commissioner. The Mayor had to swear Isaac in. Sammy's aides purred at Isaac on the phone. "Commish, His Honor needs you in the Blue Room."

The "Commish" had to run to Rivington Street for a tie, a shirt, and a handkerchief. The worm tugged at him while he changed his underwear. Isaac crossed the Bowery, cut through Chinatown, and showed at City Hall. The worm ate pieces of him. He might have swooned if the press hadn't come out of its closet to catch him in time. He blamed it on a lunch of bananas and cream. It was a big lie. Isaac hated bananas and cream.

The Mayor was in the Blue Room, near the portrait of Martin Van Buren. Isaac whispered into Sam's lapel. "You're a cocksucker in your heart, Sammy Dunne."

"Later," Sammy growled under his breath. "Laddie, why are you sweating so much?"

"Because I have a worm in me that says I shouldn't be your Commissioner."

"Wipe your forehead. You can't always listen to a worm."

Isaac took his oath of allegiance, muttering after Sam. The little Mayor had Tiger John's old badge, with its blue enameled face, and an eagle crouching on five gold stars. He pinned the badge on Isaac, and invested him as Police Commissioner. The press corps stood around Commissioner Isaac.

"Commish, what happens when Becky takes over from Sam? Will you be out of a job?"

"Probably," Isaac said with a moan. He could feel the worm gorging under his heart. "She has to win the election first. His mouth tightened. "Then we'll know. I serve at the Mayor's convenience."

"Are you going to help prosecute Tiger John?"

"Speak to Dennis. He hasn't asked me to cooperate yet."

"Commish, will you shut down Whores' Row?"

"I'm only a cop," Isaac said. "I don't make the laws."

Isaac nodded once or twice and walked out of the Blue Room with Sammy Dunne. His Honor was quiet in the halls. Isaac shook Sammy's arm. "You made a deal with Mangen, didn't you?"

"You've got bats in your ear."

He followed the little Mayor into his private office. "Pretty work," Isaac said. "Pretty work. You fed Tiger John to Mangen, just like that. What did you promise the idiot boy? That he could hold on to his precious bankbooks in a jail? They'll tear his eyes out at Riker's, don't you know? They've got lads over there that aren't too enchanted with Police Commissioners. Sam, couldn't you have fixed a better bail hearing for little Johnny? Or did you conspire with Dennis and the judge to get him out of the way? Prick, I campaigned for you. I told lies in the shuls . . . and Becky gets it all."

"Ah, shit," Sam said. "A Mayor has to live . . . did you want me to go waltzing with John under the judge's bench?"

"No," Isaac said. "You're too dignified for that. But how did you get involved with Dermott Bride?"

"That crow with the black hair? He ain't even an Irishman. I wouldn't touch Dermott Bride."

"But you took his whore money."

"Not from him. You saw the press I had a year ago. My own Party was anxious to throw me in the river. Get rid of the old guy. He has a bad smell. I had to take care of myself. I don't have me a wife. I wasn't going to crawl on my knees with a pension from the City."

"So you went to Coote McNeill. The grand old tyrant of the Force. And he unleashed Dermott's money . . . nickel-and-dime shit. You're the Mayor. Why didn't you fiddle with the budget?"

"Jesus, man. I'm not a thief."

"Oh, you're too smart to grab with your own two fists. You found yourself a buffer, a go-between, Tiger John. He was your bagman, your messenger, your boy Friday. Then Mangen came along, and you got scared. McNeill had to dismantle his operation. He sent the king into exile. He killed Arthur Greer."

The Mayor had an ugly notch around his eye. "Don't talk murder to me. I never met this Arthur Greer."

"Of course," Isaac said. "His Honor doesn't mingle with nigger pimps. You're the good Irishman. But why didn't Mangen arrest Coote McNeill? It won't be much fun bringing Tiger John to trial."

"McNeill's gone," the Mayor said.

Isaac looked into that notch over Sammy's eye.

"Coote retired last week. He bought himself a house in the Old Country."

"The Old Country," Isaac muttered. "Everybody lands in the Old Country. But it doesn't make sense. Dennis could reach into Ireland if he wants . . . He'd rather have the idiot boy. He'll go the easy way and carve Tiger John."

Isaac developed a leer that dug into his chin. "Don't take me for granted. I'm not your suck. I don't exist to cradle City Hall. You cornered me into this job. You blabbed to the papers that I was your man . . . but you might get a little sorry."

Isaac walked out of City Hall. Clerks and typists stared at him. The new "Commish" didn't have a slouch like Tiger John. You could listen to the crunch of his body. He didn't patter away from the Mayor's office, as if he were a man without shoes. He went across the road to Police Headquarters. The cops had a plaza to themselves, a hub of concrete with terraces and rails, and a huge shithouse on top of it, a mausoleum of red brick.

They swarmed over Isaac soon as he entered the building. "Commish, Commish." No one had seen his hide for months. Now they had a Commissioner, all right. Not that pussyface, Tiger John, who had screaming fits in the halls, and would punish a borough commander for looking at him the wrong way. (What was the right way to look at Tiger John?) The State Prosecutor caught him with his pants down. They handcuffed the pussyface in front of a thousand cops. Disgraced the Department he did. Mangen made a home for him on Riker's Island. There he'll sit, without a postcard from the boyos at 1 Police Plaza. The pussyface can write his memoirs, describe how he stuck his fingers in a whore's pocket. But let Mangen come for Isaac the Brave! You couldn't drive the new "Commish" out of Headquarters. Never in your life.

He didn't go in to claim the territories of a Commissioner. He went to the First Dep's office on the thirteenth floor. The hair crawled on Isaac's head. Something was horribly wrong. He had an office choked with strangers. He walked from room to room; captains and clerks looked away from Isaac and stared at the walls. Who

210

were these miserable people? "Where's Havisham? Where's Brodsky? Where's Marvin Winch?" The captains heard that roar out of Isaac. He picked on one of them. "What's your name?"

"Smiley. Captain Smiley."

"Who put you here?"

Isaac burrowed into the captain with his eyes. "Are you deaf, man? Who put you here?"

"The Chief Inspector."

"You worked for Coote, you prick and a half?"

Smiley must have seen the devil in Isaac's face. His jaw dropped out from under his chin.

"And what did you lads do when I called this office?"

"We took the message upstairs. To the McNeill."

Isaac flailed the air with both arms. "Out," he said. "All of you. Get the hell out of here."

Captains and clerks ran from him. They didn't know how to please the new "Commish." They stood in the hall, with their pencils, holsters, and gum erasers. Coote had smuggled a whole team into the First Dep's office. McNeill got rid of Isaac's men a bundle at a time. They were probably licking dust off fingerprint cards in five boroughs.

One flight up and he was in the Chief Inspector's office. Coote's people hunched behind their desks. Isaac studied the walls. Then he cursed himself. He was stupid as a cow. McNeill had fishing paraphernalia tacked up all over the place: thin, beautiful rods that could whip into a perfect fisherman's arc, trophies with such tiny lettering, it would burn your eyes to read, fishhooks, maps of a hidden trout stream, photos of amazing salmon catches, pieces off an ancient lucky boot. Isaac had seen the bloody things before. McNeill had the same paraphernalia up in his old rooms at Centre Street. Isaac had to look at this shit on the wall to give his head a little shake. *Coote* was the Fisherman Annie had told him about. Coote, Coote the Fisherman. God, he might have saved that girl, if he could have remembered those hooks, salmon, and trout.

Isaac pointed to a fat clerk. "Take that junk off the wall and ship it to your old chief with the compliments of Isaac Sidel. No . . . tell him, Love from the Commissioner. He'll understand."

Cops were gathering outside the Chief Inspector's office.

Stories had spread like a crazy fire in the building: the "Commish" would march into a room, breathing hell on his captains. You couldn't avoid the scrutiny of Isaac. He had a menace sitting on his brows. One wrinkle of his eye, and a man was doomed. Isaac snatched a lowly sergeant from the hall and brought him into the Commissioner's office, made him a master clerk. "Sergeant, I want you to take every cunt in the First Dep's office, every creature who worked for McNeill and Tiger John, and threw them to the Badlands. Give them precincts in the South Bronx."

That's how Isaac began his reign at 1 Police Plaza.

TWENTY-NINE

THEY drifted into Headquarters, blue-eyed boys rescued from the provinces. Their boss had come home. The boss seemed gloomy in his Commissioner's coat. His eyes had shrunk since they last saw him, months and months ago, when he sank into the ground and disappeared, in order to destroy the pimps of New York City. They understood part of his gloom. He missed his old sweetheart, Manfred Coen.

They talked about the worm in his belly. "It's eating him up. Soon there'll be nothing left of Isaac." But Isaac survived. He was teaching again at the College of Criminal Justice.

It was just before election time. People in the class were wearing buttons that Becky Karp produced in less than a week: VOTE MS. REBECCA. It was her war cry to women and men.

The buttons enraged Isaac. He built his lecture around them. "Flotsam," he said. "Politics. Ms. Rebecca Karp." The Commissioner had developed a machine-gun language. He shunned sentences, threw words and particles out at the class. He pounced in front of the room in a coat that hung on his body. He could have been a scarecrow, or any ragged man, with coal-black eyes.

"Buttonface. Whorehearts . . . lovely hour to vote."

He snickered on his feet. Then he turned articulate, muttered a complete sentence to the class. "They know how to fuck us, the lords and ladies who manage our lives."

His stalking near the blackboard had begun to mesmerize the student firemen and cops. It didn't matter what the Commissioner said. The class would have gone to hell with Isaac. "Those darlings have picked a beauty for us. Rejoice. The people's candidate, strong as apple cider. Our Lady of the Buttons, Ms. Rebecca Karp. How do you become a Mayor in such times? You step on an old man's back, that's how. You rise up on his shoulders and watch him sink. Then you manufacture a million buttons. You distribute them to the faithful. And you promise a lot. A white borough for the Irish, the Italians, and the Jews. Dental clinics for the Latinos and the blacks. A paradise in Far Rockaway for the over-sixty-fives. Boys, girls, it don't mean shit. The planet is running low. The subways are having a heart attack. You can't tell the difference between garbage and pennies in the street. But go on, pin Rebecca to your blouse. Who knows? It might do you some good."

There he was, insulting the next Mayor of New York. How many Police Commissioners are prophets and fools in one gulp? The worm drove through him with its many tails. There had to be a spy in the class.

Isaac hovered close to the door. He couldn't escape the green eyes of Jennifer Pears. He looked for signs of growth in her belly. Isaac wanted evidence of *his* child. He found nothing but natural curves.

"What month is it?"

Jennifer stared at him. "November."

"No, no," Isaac said. "For the child." He couldn't recall the pregnancy of his own wife. What was Kathleen when she was carrying Marilyn the Wild? Did she have a gargantuan waist by the second month? Blast an old cop's memory! He'd have to go before the Medical Board and prove he was a sane "Commish." He'd curtsy for the bastards and count the fingers on his left hand.

"It's the third month," she said. "You can see a little bulge if you pull my skirt apart."

She took Isaac by the elbow and led him out of John Jay.

"Have you decided to marry me?"

"Shut up," she said.

"We can't go to my hotel. The pimps would cut our throats. They're not fond of Police Commissioners and their girlfriends."

She brought him home in a taxi cab. Isaac could feel the doorman smirk at him. He never liked the East Side.

"Where's Mel?"

"He's working, you idiot."

"And the little boy . . . Alexander?"

"He's at school. Isaac, what's wrong with you?"

He was a lost, anxious child under his Commissioner's coat. He shivered in his socks. Jennifer had to unlace his shoes while Isaac growled at her. "Woman, I won't sleep with you until the husband goes . . ."

He crept into the coverlets, a frightened dog-boy with hair on his arms and a wild fur over the rest of his body. Nothing could sooth a "Commish." He had a foulness in his heart. The dead seemed to follow Isaac. They wouldn't lie still. He'd buried Coen, he buried Annie Powell. He brought rabbis in for them. What more could he do?

He made love to Melvin's naked wife. He touched that thickening in her belly. The fur smoothed on him as he pushed into Jennifer Pears.

He couldn't stay very long. Jennifer's digital clock blinked twenty to three. Alexander was coming from the Little Red Schoolhouse. Jennifer didn't wear any clothes to the door.

"Can I see you tomorrow?" Isaac said.

"Tomorrow's Election Day."

"So what?"

"Mel will be here."

"I thought the husband'll be out capturing votes for Ms. Rebecca."

"Isaac, don't be a prick. Rebecca doesn't need votes from Mel."

She went out naked into the hall and kissed Isaac on the wrinkle over one eye. "Come Thursday. For lunch."

He scowled in the elevator. Doormen couldn't intimidate him. He had the monkey at the plugboard dial Headquarters and ask for the Commissioner's car. A surly boy named Christianson, who'd chauffeured Tiger John, arrived in a black Mercury. Isaac could have changed drivers. But he liked the boy's silences, his contempt for every other vehicle on the road. Christianson swept around fire trucks, pushed buses out of their lanes, challenged any police car that dared crawl in front of the "Commish." The boy had a telegram for Isaac. It wasn't in its usual cellophane jacket.

"Who opened this?"

Christianson shrugged his boyish shoulders. "Dunno, boss. I found it on your desk that way."

"You," Isaac said. "Look at my face. I'm not Tiger John. You tamper with my mail again, and you'll have to drive without your kneecaps."

"Yes, boss."

Isaac unfolded the telegram.

POLICE COMMISSIONER
N.Y. CITY-N.Y.

SIDEL MEET ME ST. STEPHENS WED
10 AM URGENT

THE KING

"Christianson, what does this say to you?"

"Sounds like crazy talk."

"Do you know where St. Stephen's is?"

"Could be a church somewhere."

John must have taught his chauffeur never to commit himself. He'd have to sack the boy very soon.

"Christianson, take me to Aer Lingus. Right now."

Isaac left for Ireland on Election Day. He wasn't curious about the results of Rebecca's little pilgrimage to glory. She'd become Mayor-elect soon as the polls shut down, and the City would have a broken duck, His Honor, Samuel Dunne. Sammy deserved whatever crippling he got. He shouldn't have grabbed at whores from City Hall. But the Party wouldn't forsake its Old Man. Who can tell? Ms. Rebecca might give him the gatekeeper's job at Gracie Mansion.

Isaac had his own problems. The "Commish" was rocking over the water (in an Irish plane) on the strength of a miserable telegram. He didn't trust the words. Little Dermott wouldn't have begged for Isaac in such a bald way. He wasn't a showy man. He had too much breeding to sign a telegram with his pet name. *The King.* Someone else had signed it for him, and written the goddamn message. Whatever it was, Isaac couldn't avoid it. *Urgent*, it said. *St. Stephens. Wed. 10 AM.*

He was at Dublin airport on Wednesday morning, around half-past eight. He wasn't Moses Herzog on this trip. Isaac had little use for camouflage. He didn't come over to kill a man. He was only the "Commish." He hadn't booked a room at the Shelbourne. He was returning to New York on the afternoon flight.

A cab brought him into Dublin. He hadn't bothered to convert his dollars into Irish pounds. The driver took his money without any qualms and let him off at the northwest gate of St. Stephen's Green. It could have been August. Isaac had the same chill about the ears. He strolled along the rim of the park. Men and women churned by him in their November clothes. It was a school day. You couldn't find laddies hunching in the grass. The white and brown ducks were gone. Isaac didn't see a bird in the old pond. He passed the stone bridge. A man was sitting inside the gazebo. His head was upright, under an eight-piece woolen cap.

Isaac could recognize a king by his ears. Aristocratic they were. Without points, or hanging lobes. But that dark Irish-gypsy face had a strange, unbending manner. A live man don't sit with a perfectly cocked head. Dermott's eyes were open. He had a Crotona Park grin. His neck was wired to the gazebo wall. His throat had been slit. The blood congealed under a napkin that had been thrust into the collar of his shirt. Isaac didn't have to guess. The king's bodyguards must have murdered him. They'd done a terrific patching job. His ankles and wrists were wired up, and you'd have to look down his collar to peek at the blood. "Ah, you poor son of a bitch, you shouldn't have come here. Dublin ain't for you . . ."

What was the use of unwiring him? His neck might drop off. The blood began to soak through that bib inside his collar. Isaac left the king undisturbed. A park warden would discover the dead man in the gazebo and call the Irish gardai. The cops would shrug it off. They'd hold the corpse at Dublin Castle for twenty hours and declare it a "painful case," altogether unsolvable, like any gangland killing, American style.

It was a fine touch to put that eight-piece cap on his head. The king's scalp of black, black hair might have

217

brought attention to itself. You can't be much of a killer without a love for detail. Isaac strolled back to the northwest gate. The king's bodyguards were there, four old men in identical eight-piece caps. Isaac nodded to Tim Snell, that old sergeant from the Chief Inspector's office.

"Morning, Tim . . . lovely work, that . . . wire a man by his neck."

Timothy smiled. "We thought you'd appreciate it, Isaac."

"Did you cut him with his own knife?"

"Yes, we did."

"Then that telegram came from you."

"Naturally," Tim said. "I composed it with the king's fountain pen. Took me half the day. To find the right wording, you see . . . we wanted to celebrate your new job. Congratulations, Isaac. It's not every old bugger of a cop who can stand in Stephen's Green and talk to the Commish."

"Don't let the title fool you, Tim. I'm the same lad you drove through the quays three months ago. It's a bit crude to murder your boss."

"Him? He was nothing to us. Dirt under your thumb, that's all. Mr. Dermott Bride. A stoolpigeon he was that licked his feathers and walked out of the Bronx . . . we work for a real king."

"The Fisherman . . . you slit throats for Coote McNeill."

"Shhh," Tim said, with that smile of his. "It's not nice to mention names in a public park. Why don't you come with us, love? We have the automobile across the road. We can continue this conversation with cushions under your ass . . . and don't you scream for cops. They're good boys, the gardai. But dumb. They won't be much help to you."

It was instinct that preserved Isaac the Brave. He caught Timothy with an elbow and shoved him into the other old men. The teeth clattered in their heads, and their caps fell to the ground as they gave a little sigh. Isaac bolted out of the park like a rabbit in city pants and shoes. The old men recovered their hats and chased after the "Commish." You could hear them huff along on Grafton Street. Isaac ran with his elbows wide. He could outwit four old murderers who had a hard time breathing.

He took to the alleys, chose a crooked trail from Grafton to Dame Street. He crossed the Liffey at Temple Bar and Wellington Quay. The river had lost its dirty color. It wasn't frog-green, like a piss-pond or a spittoon. It was almost purple under the bridge. November had cleared all the mud.

Isaac didn't keep to the south wall. He crept up to Mary's Lane and found a car-for-hire agency on Constitution Hill. He wouldn't get out of Ireland this afternoon. That corpse in the gazebo had interrupted Isaac's plans. He was going to pay a visit to Coote McNeill.

The "Commish" had done a bit of homework before he got on the plane to meet Dermott in an Irish park. His blue-eyed boys tore the Chief Inspector's files apart until they unearthed an address for Coote. The Fisherman's place was next to Screeb in County Galway. Screeb was where Isaac had the mind to go. The man from the agency lent him a map. Isaac bumped down Constitution Hill into the lower regions of Church Street. He was driving a little French car. The "Commish" was used to having his body chauffeured around. He had trouble with the steering column. It wasn't where it ought to be. It had moved from the left side to the right. Damn the French and the little cars they brought into Ireland. Didn't the Irish have their own make of wagon? A Phoenix Spark? A Donnybrook? A Cromwell Cadet? A Grand Drummartin? Holy Mother! He was on the wrong half of the road. The Irish were a mad people. They invented their own traffic laws to confound a man and tire him to death. Left is right, me boy, and right is left. The "Commish" had to reeducate himself on King Street North. *Isaac, stay left, left, left.*

He had a baby's crawl. He crossed the Liffey by mistake and got stranded in Dolphin's Barn. It took him three hours to break out of Dublin and find the road to Mullingar.

He drove thirty miles, then it grew dark on him. He stayed in a cottage that night, with an ironmonger's widow and her seven kids, near the town of Kinnegad. The children's whining came through the walls. It was a relief to Isaac. It kept him occupied. He didn't dare fall asleep. Coote's old men might be at the window. He had his bed and breakfast and crept back on the road early in the morning.

He wasn't dispirited on his second day in the Irish countryside. Teaching himself how to maneuver a wicked car on a wicked road had done remarkable things to Isaac. Pushed like a heavy thumb through the matting in his brain. Dermott didn't belong in an eight-piece cap. The king had to die before Isaac could remember him as a boy. Isaac's chief, First Deputy O'Roarke, had sent him out to tame a wild gang, the Devils of Clay Avenue. He traveled to the Bronx, a young inspector growing bald behind the ears. He couldn't understand where the gang got its reputation from. The Devils were a bunch of shivering boys. These were the lads who had conquered a borough? Their single property was a shack in Claremont Park. Who was it that led those raids into every corner of the Bronx? Not their president, Arthur Greer. Sweet Arthur always stayed at home. Isaac had to poke behind their idiotic grins. Only one other boy appealed to him. Little Dermott McBride. Short and dark he was. A cop's intuition told him *this* was the leader of the raids. He had a sadness around the eyes that reminded Isaac of his "angel," Manfred Coen, whom he'd pulled right out of the Police Academy. Isaac happened to need a sad-looking boy to infiltrate a gang of Polish thieves that was causing mayhem in the garment district. Coen was on special assignment to him. Isaac wouldn't give him back to the Academy. He liked having Blue Eyes around.

Twenty miles out of Kinnegad it struck Isaac that Coen and Little Dermott began to mix in his head. Isaac's batteries had crossed somewhere. It was his sorrow over Manfred, his own fucking guilt, and not that worm in his gut, that had eaten into Isaac's memory. He must have had a wish at the time that Manfred could enter into Dermott and steal away some of Dermott's intelligence. Then Isaac would have had an "angel" who was more than beautiful and dumb. It would have meant a reshuffling of brains, a lessening of the king to puff out Manfred Coen. But Isaac wasn't a ghoul. He wouldn't harm one boy to glorify another, just because they had the same sad eyes . . .

He got to Screeb. It was nothing but a fork in a road. He'd been traveling a good eight hours. He got lost in Galway City until a baker's boy led him out of that trapping of streets. He went along the coast. Isaac had the

Atlantic under him. He had to stop for cows and sheep. He left the car and began to walk. Stones and trees weren't a proper landmark. You could have blindfolded him outside Centre Street and dropped him anywhere in Manhattan. Isaac would have felt his way. He had the gift. He could nose out the contours of a neighborhood. *Boys, I'm in the Heights. Around Audubon Avenue, I'd say. West of Highbridge.*

But a country road mystified him. Isaac walked with his teeth near the ground. God knows why he was traveling with a curl in his spine, like a hunchback. Was it to make himself less of a target for Coote's men? He looked up once and saw the corrugated roof of a house. He'd stumbled upon a castle in Screeb. *Castledermott.* That's what Annie Powell had said.

The castle had a yellow lake. Isaac heard a plop in the water. A man was fishing the lake, a small man with boots up to his arse. He would stare into that yellowness and grunt. "Come on up, me beauties." He was a fisherman without a fishing rod. He worked with a net and a plain billy club. He smacked at the water from time to time. But the net wouldn't fill. It was a senseless occupation. The man hadn't struggled with one lousy fish.

He stood near the rim of the lake. He was deaf, deaf to anything that didn't come from the water. Isaac could have plucked hairs off the man's head.

"Afternoon to you, McNeill."

An eyebrow knit for a moment. Then the face relaxed. "Ah, sonny, I was expecting you . . ."

"Am I talking too loud? I wouldn't want to disturb the fish."

"But that's the point," Coote said, swinging his billy club. "I'd like to disturb them with this." He had a look of total menace as he bit into his jaw.

"Are you murdering salmon these days, Mr. Coote McNeill?"

The Fisherman eyed Isaac with disgust. "Not the salmon . . . I'm going after carp. They destroy a lake, sucking in the mud. Vermin is what they are, filthy animal fish. They can grow fat and live to fifty. So I club them in the head."

"You've been banging at the water, but I don't see many carp in your net."

"That's because they're tricky bastards. They keep to

221

the bottom. They dirty the lake and drive out all my valuable fish."

"Why don't you hire Tim Snell to club the water with you? . . . you might get a few more hits."

"Sonny, I don't need Tim to clear a lake. He has other business."

"I know," Isaac said. "He had to write a telegram and wire up the king . . ."

The Fisherman continued to slap water with the billy club. The lake turned brown near his boots; no fifty-year-old carp came up from the mud.

"Was Tim going to wire me up too?"

"You're daft," the Fisherman said. "Sonny, I could have had you killed ages ago."

"What about those shotguns you delivered to Centre Street?"

"That was nothin' but a tease . . . you're too precious to put underground. Jesus, the chances I had to get at you . . . the great Isaac roosting in Times Square with charcoal on his face. It's Mangen that kept you alive. Dennis' baby is what you are . . . and don't you get bright ideas about catching me alone in the water. I have lads in the house. If I whistle to them, sonny boy, they'll shovel out a grave for you . . . you'll rest with all the carp."

"Why did you summon me to Ireland, Coote?"

"To talk . . . Mangen was up on his haunches, so I had to get out."

"You didn't even have time to pack your fishing rods. It's a pity, but I had your office boys pick the rods off the wall. Have they arrived?"

"Not yet. You owe me something, sonny. Don't get comical with me." He thumped his chest with the billy club. "This old man made you Police Commissioner."

"Sure, you and Sammy fucked Tiger John and pinned his badge on me. It was a good cover for all of you. I come in and you ass off to your castle in Screeb and rid your lake of carp. A charming life. You gambled that I had enough affection for an old Mayor not to harm him. I couldn't prosecute Sammy if I wanted to. He's made his pact with Dennis. He won't starve when the money runs out. Rebecca will provide for him. That leaves you. Now what is it you need from me? You have your yellow lake . . ."

"I don't want my picture in the newspapers. I'm in seclusion here. I'll have me an angler's club. I'll start up a bit of a hotel. Lease my salmon rights to worthy fishermen . . . Isaac, the whore shit is dead. Why rake it up? Mangen has Tiger John. He's satisfied."

"Oh, I wouldn't disturb you, Chief. You're safe. You butchered everyone around that could do you harm. You were like a pope in New York City. The Mayor kissed your hand. And you took every boy from my office and farmed them out. They had to ride the ferry to work. You were smart. You left me a boy or two until the very end, so Isaac wouldn't know."

"Sonny, it ain't my fault you didn't come to Headquarters. I couldn't have done a thing with John if you'd been there. But we could count on you. If you weren't sleeping with the Guzmanns, you'd be in some other filthy pile. You could never sit on your ass. And don't accuse me of butchering people. You butchered when you had to . . . like the rest of us. You killed your own boy, Blue Eyes, because that daughter of yours was crazy about him, and you couldn't stand the idea."

"The Guzmanns killed Coen," Isaac muttered into the lake.

"Indeed. Nasty souls they were . . . they made chocolate bars in the Bronx . . . and you had to declare war on them, Papa Guzmann and his five idiot boys."

"Papa gave me a worm."

"You deserved it," McNeill said. "Don't play Isaac the Pure with me."

Isaac watched the billy club slap water again. The net dropped down and rose up empty.

"There ain't that much difference between us," the Fisherman said. "I took for myself, and you used the Department for your own imbecile cause. You killed, you maimed, you gouged out eyes, sonny boy."

"But I didn't wire a man to a bench, just to show off."

"I had to dispose of him, and one way's as good as another. He was getting to be a nuisance, you know. He falls in love with a shopgirl and we have to suffer for it. What kind of king is that? He was a gutter boy before I picked him up. The Department put him through college."

"I got him into Columbia . . . not you, or the Department."

"Piss on your brains," the Fisherman said. "You were

223

always a little slow behind all that cleverness. Dermott belonged to me and Ned O'Roarke."

Isaac stood an inch out of the water, his toes collecting mud. He'd inherited his job from O'Roarke, the old First Deputy Commissioner. He was Ned's protégé, an apostate Jew among the Irish. Did O'Roarke hide Dermott under one knee without telling Isaac?

Coote grinned at that slump in Isaac's shoulders. "Ned made a Yalie out of him. It was a bit too close having him in town. So we groomed the lad in New Haven. A little gentleman he was. We let him steal. We let him have his books. We let him run the nigger whores with Arthur Greer."

"And when O'Roarke died, you stuck your hand in the pot . . . and pulled out a pretty penny."

"Would you have me chewing gumballs for the rest of my life? The king was my creation. Tell me why I shouldn't benefit from it? Him and the nigger got to be millionaires. Boys of thirty carrying hundreds of thousands in their pockets. Then he gets shopgirl Annie for a mistress and a wife. I sit him in Dublin because Mangen is coming on to us, and he neglects our business over Annie Powell. Imagine, going itchy for a stupid cunt that's nothin' but a whore, when he can have any woman on this earth. Him with education, money, and a gypsy's eye."

"*Annie*," Isaac said, "what did you do about Annie Powell?"

"Jesus, the girl saw my face . . . I couldn't let her whore in the street with Mangen's shooflies running everywhere. I paid a boy in a taxi cab to climb up on her back . . ."

Isaac's toes fell into the water. Coote wasn't an idiot. He could sense the rage that was coming over Isaac. The "Commish"'s forehead swelled out like a diseased melon with tiny bumps on it. "Mother Mary," the Fisherman said, "you didn't go and fall in love with that whore, did you now?"

He raised his billy club. It was a warning to Isaac. *Keep out of me lake.* But Isaac rushed at him. The billy club landed at the base of Isaac's neck. He felt a crunching in his scapula. His head tumbled down. But he shook off that motherfucking blow. The billy club whistled behind Isaac's ear. The old man had been too eager. He missed his chance to brain the "Commish." Isaac slapped the billy club away. He grabbed the old man by the roots of his scalp and shoved that head into the yellow lake. He kept it there without a touch of mercy, using his elbow as a fulcrum to dig between Coote's shoulder blades. Bubbles rose around Isaac's fist. Coote's arms jerked under the water. Then the old man went still. Isaac gave Coote's body to the salmon and the carp. He didn't see any signs of movement from the house. The chimneys revealed one lousy tail of smoke.

Isaac stepped out of the water. His shoulder humped up on him. Coote's old men could have ripped the nose off his face. But nobody ran after Isaac. He beat the ground with his shoes until he arrived at his little French car. He mumbled a benediction to the Irish. *God bless all little cars with the steering wheels on the right*. Then he drove out of Screeb.

THIRTY

HE got past the customs booth at Kennedy. Where were the guys with handcuffs and the warrant for his arrest? No one touched the "Commish." It was a good year for murder. They let you strangle old men in the water these days.

The "Commish" got his chauffeur on the line. "Christianson, it's me. Turn on your sirens. I'll expect you outside Aer Lingus in eighteen minutes."

Christianson wouldn't disappoint his boss. Isaac was tucked away in his rooms at 1 Police Plaza before his hands could turn cold. A button lit up on his telephone console. It was the Mayor's "hot line" to Police Headquarters. Isaac could have let that button glow day and night. He banged on the console and growled into the phone. "Sidel here."

"Laddie, how are you?"

"Grand," Isaac said.

"Have you heard the news? . . . McNeill expired. The poor sod drowned in his own fishing pool."

"Did you say drowned? That's a terrible pity."

"Well, the Sons of Dingle are paying to have the corpse fly home. He wanted to be buried here, you know. We'll be having a service for him, Isaac. At St. Pat's." Isaac had been rubbed in Kelly green. He knew all the rituals of Manhattan Irish politicians and cops. They always sing their prayers for the dead at St. Patrick's Cathedral.

"Ain't he entitled to an Inspector's Funeral?"

Only Isaac could call out the color guard to honor a dead cop. The PC plucked his chin. He wasn't sorry that he'd pushed McNeill's face into the water. *I'd murder him again and again.* But why should he forgo the honor guard for Coote? Thieves had to be laid to rest like any other man.

Isaac said goodbye to the Mayor and rang up Jennifer Pears. He excused himself for missing lunch with her. "I was out of the country. Swear to Moses . . . had to make a short trip."

"Trip?" she said.

"To Mother Ireland."

"Isaac, is that where your people are from?"

"They might as well . . . I'm Irish to the bone."

Jennifer laughed at him. "Come for lunch . . . right now."

Isaac screamed for Christianson, but he couldn't escape from Headquarters so fast. His mentor, Marshall Berkowitz, was in the vestibule. The PC wouldn't run out on Marsh. An aide brought him in to Isaac. Marsh stared at the furnishings of a Commissioner's office: the flags, trophies, pictures, drapes, the huge desk of burled oak that had belonged to Teddy Roosevelt when he was Commissioner of Police.

"Marsh, you'll have to forgive the décor. It's Tiger John's. I haven't had time to move in." Isaac looked at the dean's broken shoes. "Is it the wife? . . . Marsh, has she disappeared again?"

The dean nodded to Isaac. He had bubbles on his lips.

"Why didn't you let Mangen know? His shooflies kidnapped her out of my living room . . . don't you remember that?"

"Mangen says he can't help me now that you're the Commish."

Isaac put the keys to his apartment on Teddy Roosevelt's desk. "Go to Rivington Street, Marsh. She's probably there. I can lend you a few boys and a squad car. I'm as good as Dennis when it comes to kidnapping people."

He didn't like betraying Sylvia, but he had to give her

227

over to Marsh. *That fucking dean is the father of us all.*
He taught Isaac, Mangen, and little Dermott the tyranny
of moocows coming down the road. Marsh was a different man when he had his nose in a text. He could tear
your lungs out with a few words on Mr. Joyce. *Did I ever
tell you about Joyce's eyepatch? Don't believe his biog-
raphers. That was a perfectly good eye under the piece of
cloth. He wore it to impress the beggars of Paris. So he
could squeeze pennies out of them. Joyce was the biggest
sponge in the world.*

He was late for Jennifer. They had to rush through
nibblings of hollandaise sauce. Jenny's boy would be
home from school in half an hour. It was curious business. In and out of bed, like a squirrel in the trees. Do
squirrels have mistresses too? What did it mean when
you could feel a child in your *mistress'* belly? And how
come the worm was lying so still? It hadn't stirred since
Isaac touched ground in New York City. Did the
motherfucker pick up some Irish disease that was shrinking its head and tails? That little purring monster used to
adore Jennifer Pears. Now the monster wouldn't purr.

Isaac could hunger for Jennifer without the participa-
tion of a worm. She kissed the bruise on his shoulder, but
the Commissioner couldn't come. He stayed hard inside
Jenny until the doorbell rang. "It's Alex," she said. She
got into her panties and a blue robe to greet her little boy.
Isaac dressed and walked into the parlor. Alexander
peered at him from the long prow of a rain hat.

"Remember me?" Isaac said. "I'm Dick Tracy."

Jennifer laughed and unzippered the rain hat. "He's a
liar. Call him Isaac. He's the Police Commissioner."

Alexander pulled on his nose. "Do you have a gun?"

"Not today," Isaac said. "Commissioners don't have
to wear a gun."

Isaac seemed to diminish for the boy. He went into his
room to play, while his mother was stranded in the parlor
with Isaac the Pure. The robe dropped to Jennifer's belly.
Isaac sucked on one nipple with a mad concentration.
His pants were suddenly on the floor. He lost his inhi-
bitions with that boy a room away. He clung to Jennifer
and was able to come.

"How did you hurt your shoulder?"

228

"It's a gift from Ireland," Isaac said. "I had to kill a man. He was a thief and a son of a bitch."

"Do you often go on business trips like that? . . . I suppose it's all right. They'll have to forgive you. We can't have *two* Commissioners sitting in jail. The City would fall apart . . . who are you going to murder next?"

"I'm not sure." He kissed Jennifer on the mouth, and it was like that first kiss they'd had near the elevator, with his tongue down her throat. A girl could hardly breathe.

"What's going to happen to our kid?"

"Nothing. I'll have it, and it'll stay with me and Mel."

"Can't I be one tiny portion of its father, boy or girl?"

"No."

Isaac left with a scowl on his face that could have eaten through a wall. Jenny grabbed him by his good shoulder. "Weekends are out," she said. "But you can come on Monday . . . and the day after that."

Isaac crept into the elevator with Monday fixed in his head. Jennifer locked the door. She gathered the ends of her robe and pulled them close to her until she was ready for her boy. She strolled in and out of mirrors, catching the little puffs under her eyes. A lady of thirty-three. She had a husband who lusted after fifty-year-old mayoresses. Would he move into Gracie Mansion after Ms. Rebecca got rid of Sam and rolled her carpets in? They could have their politics on a Persian rug. Jenny walked into the toy room to be with Alex. He was almost five, her little man. He had a set of Lionel trains that wound across the room like the territories of an unfathomable world. Tracks snaked into one another. Tunnels bloomed. Alex presided over every switch. He could make bridges collapse, have engines explode and spit out their parts, and torture a caboose with his system of flags and lights. You didn't need a mother when you had Lionel trains.

She stooped over Alex with Isaac's seed dripping out of her. She mussed his hair. "Want an Oreo sandwich, little guy?" Alex was too busy attending all his different tracks to think about food.

Isaac was on the steps of St. Pat's, surrounded by his own Police. Fifty captains had come out in uniform to honor the great McNeill. The Shamrock Society had black handkerchiefs and mourning bands. The Irish would never disappoint their dead. Isaac could hear a murderous gnawing behind him, a gnawing of many throats. The Sons of Dingle stood in their eight-piece caps. They were with Timothy Snell and the Retired Sergeants Association. Old Tim mashed his throat as hard as any Dingle Bay boy. His eyes were shot with blood. "Timmy," Isaac said, "did you fly in with the corpse? It's a pity he went and drowned himself."

"Murderer," Tim pronounced under his breath. "The best Chief we ever had. He meant no harm to you . . . Isaac, you better not stand in the open too long. You might twist your leg and fall. You'd have a lovely time bumping down St. Pat's."

"Quiet, you prick. This ain't a castle in Screeb. I rule here. The Irish sit under me. You know, Tim, I keep having this dream. It's about little Dermott. He's still wired up in the park, just the way you left him. He says, 'Isaac, do me a favor. If you catch Tim Snell, wire him to Delancey Street' . . . go on back to your funeral party before I shut down the Dingle Bay and steal your fucking sauna. You won't have a room to piss in. Move, I said."

Old Tim shrugged at Isaac and joined his fellow mourners. He marched up the stairs and went into the big church with the Shamrocks, the Sons of Dingle, and the Retired Sergeants Association. Earlier Isaac's honor guard had raised the bier out of the funeral truck, struggling with it on their shoulders until they got it into St. Pat's. Isaac didn't go inside. He'd lend his honor guard, but he wouldn't join the Requiem for Coote. He remained on the steps with his hands in his pockets.

He whistled to himself. The melody cracked on him. Isaac couldn't blow air. His cheeks contorted and his mouth turned grim. He had the shakes. Something was diving near his groin. His guts twisted in and out. The "Commish" had a corkscrew in his belly. Mother Moses, that worm had been lying in wait. The monster picked its moment to get at Isaac. What did it mean? Was Isaac in some kind of heavy labor? The worm was going to give him twins. A gypsy and a blond Jew. Baby Dermott and baby Coen.

Ooooooo! His knees waltzed out. Isaac had to sit on his bum. Celebrants ran up the stairs to be with Coote McNeill. Cops were arriving a little late. They saluted their Commissioner, paused, and went in. It was funny seeing Isaac with his knees in his face.

Another lad arrived. It was Tiger John, handcuffed to a "screw." Isaac had bullied the Corrections Department into letting John out of Riker's for an hour so he could come to the funeral.

"Morning to you, Isaac."

Isaac's mouth puffed like a dying fish.

"That man needs a glass of water," John told the screw.

The screw wasn't concerned with Isaac. He shook the handcuffs. But John refused to walk. "Isaac, should I get one of the priests for you? They must have a glass of water somewhere in St. Pat's."

Isaac pushed on his ribcage like a bellows and brought up bits of air. He belched out a few words to Tiger John. "You can go in, Johnny . . . I'll be fine. How are they treating you over there?"

"So-so," the Tiger said. "I get the Commissioner's grub. Piss and black pudding . . . They let me teach the fundamentals of banking to all my little brothers."

The screw yoked on the handcuffs with one fist, and John had to crawl. Jesus, they were a funny pair, that Corrections officer and the old "Commish," with their rumps climbing together. Isaac was going to tell the screw to ease up on poor John, but the worm gathered under Isaac's ribs and uncoiled itself with a squeeze of its tails. Isaac tore his collar away. His windpipe rattled. His fingers turned blue. The little bastard was out to choke Isaac the Brave.

He couldn't rise up from the stairs. Isaac had to lull that creature to rest. He started to hum.

> There was once a Commish
> Who lost his mind
> On the steps of St. Pat's.
> He'd killed one lad too many.
> He went to Ireland
> To cure himself
> But he couldn't break that habit
> Of getting people killed.
> Isaac the Commish
> He brings carnage
> Wherever he goes.

The worm must have liked the humming it got. It began to let go. The tails disappeared from Isaac's ribs. He was still too weak to get off his ass. He sat with his ruined collar, while the Fisherman had his Mass.

Two bodies came out of the church. Mangen and his shoofly, Captain Mort.

"Boyos," Isaac muttered. "Are they finished in there? Why are you hurrying the dead?"

Mangen continued down the stairs.

Isaac held out his hands. "Arrest me, you son of a bitch."

Mangen stopped and turned to look at Isaac. "Do you have to make a spectacle of yourself outside an Irish church?"

Isaac appealed to Captain Mort. "You're my witness, Cap. I killed a man."

The shoofly wouldn't speak. Mangen crept closer to Isaac. He sat on the steps with him. He was wearing gorgeous red-and-brown socks. He motioned to Schapiro, and the Captain went to the bottom of the stairs.

"Isaac, what sort of killing have you done?"

"*Him.* The guy in the coffin. I made him drink his yellow water . . . well, are you going to arrest me or not?"

"Isaac, I'm no magician. I can't arrest you for a crime that didn't take place . . ."

The "Commish" had a violence in the chips of his forehead. "What the hell do you mean?"

"McNeill drowned, may that old man rest in peace . . . his own boys saw it. He was in the lake, slapping for fish. And he fell. They ran out of the house, but they couldn't revive him."

Isaac slid with his bum to a lower step. "Are you happy now? The Tiger's in jail, McNeill's dead, and Sammy's over the hill . . . you even have me working for you. I sent out two cops to steal Sylvia Berkowitz from my own apartment."

"The woman's a little nuts. She can't make it alone. She has her flair of independence, and then she falls apart."

"Dennis, if you're going to play the wise man who brings together husbands and wives, what about old John? Will you furnish a wife for him at Riker's?"

Mangen stood up. "John doesn't need a wife."

232

The Special Prosecutor abandoned Isaac on the stairs. He jumped across Fifth Avenue with Captain Mort. Isaac wasn't done. He'd sit until the funeral was over. Then he'd ride down to Headquarters with his honor guard and those captains of his who were in mourning for Coote McNeill.

THIRTY-ONE

IT was a house of ragamuffins, cell block 5, where inmates wore jogging suits, fedoras, Navy fatigues, cashmere sweaters with holes under the arms, silk scarves with mousy rents in the lining, odd pieces of prison clothes. No two men had trousers that matched. It could have been a training camp for clowns. But the clowns never smiled.

There had been two attempted hangings last month. The block had its own suicide squad, volunteers who would go from cell to cell and reassure brooding inmates. The suicide squad was the only touch of sanity on Riker's Island. The screws were crazy here. They would rush through block 5 with gas masks and billy clubs and shout "Geronimo." God forbid if you got in their way. More than one prisoner had been trampled upon and left in a gallery to moan and bleed, until the suicide squad appeared with an improvised medical kit.

When Tiger John Rathgar heard "Geronimo," he would hide in a corner of his cell and wait for the gas masks to finish prancing through the block. He began to talk like everybody else, Rastafarians, Latinos, blacks from Bushwick Avenue. "Cocksuckers. Motherfucking screws." But John was the former PC, and that gave him a certain cleverness over the prisoners of his block. He understood the reason for gas masks and billy clubs. The screws would have been eaten alive if they'd come unarmed. They were frightened to death of John's block. There were cannibals among the population, according to them.

John was shown all the amenities that were proper for a "Commish." The screws sneered at him, but the Rastis, the Latinos, and the blacks would nod quietly and leave John alone. They wouldn't break into his cell and harangue him for contributing to their destruction. Only the white prisoners were uncivil to John. These men would stick out their tongues and cry like lunatic apes. "Tiger, Tiger, we're gonna burn your ass."

They didn't lay a finger on the old man. But the threat was always there. John had to chew his carrots in the mess hall with his ass off the edge of the chair and his eyes searching for hostile spoons and forks. You couldn't tell where an attack would begin. John stayed out of the recreation room. He didn't have to weave baskets and look at a ping-pong ball. He sat on his bunk most of the time. He pulled a blanket over him so you couldn't see what he was doing. Then he would take the bankbooks out of his pocket and remove the worn rubber band. John wasn't greedy. He didn't hunger for the amount registered in each book. What he liked best was to leaf through the different names. *Simon Dedalus. Gabriel Conroy. Leopold Bloom. Gertrude MacDowell. Anna Livia Plurabelle. Nosey Flynn . . .*

A screw was knocking on the bars of John's cell. The nose valve of his gas mask was open, and he was able to shout at John. "Are you deaf?" John gathered the bankbooks under his knee. Then he came out of the blanket to acknowledge the screw.

"You have a visitor, Mr. John."

Tiger John shrugged. It was after dark. Riker's didn't let visitors in at such an hour.

"Come on, you. Out of that fucking corner."

John stuffed the bankbooks into his pocket and climbed off his bunk. He followed the screw into the gallery and across block 5. A few of the prisoners winked at him and made friendly grabs at his shirt. "Freedom, man . . . you blowing out of here."

John grew into a frenzy. A pulse started to beat in his neck. His mouth was dry. It had to be an important

235

guest. They wouldn't open Riker's for an ordinary stooge. The Mayor had come for him. The Man himself. The Honorable Sammy Dunne. Who else? Ah, they'd show these lads what a Mayor could do. Him and Sam, they'd be in the sweatbox at the Dingle before midnight.

He entered the visiting room and found nothing but dumb gray walls. He was put into a grimy cubicle. He stared out at the spook on the other side of the Plexiglas. It was only Isaac the Brave.

John frowned. "Jesus, I was hoping for Mayor Sam."

"Forget it," Isaac said. "Sammy couldn't even show up at St. Pat's. He's as much of Mangen's prisoner as you are . . . only Sam gets to sleep outside. Do you have a lawyer, John?"

"The best. He screams at me on the telephone twice a day."

Isaac saw the bulge in Tiger John's pocket. Bankbooks. They couldn't have been worth a penny to John. Mangen must have frozen the accounts. He'd use them as evidence at John's trial, if a trial ever took place. Who could tell what was in the great god Dennis' mind? He could quash the indictment in another six months and let John slip out of jail with a pack of foolish bankbooks. Hadn't he shamed the Police? He'd gone into Headquarters and arrested the PC. Mangen forced the Department to clean house. He could advertise this when he ran for Governor next year on the Republican ticket. But Dennis had other means to turn John into a ghost. He could push back the trial and have Tiger John sit like the Count of Monte Cristo, until his sideburns covered his nose and he became the invisible man of Riker's. Who could say how many poor, shrunken devils schlepped through these galleries at the House of Detention?

"Can I get you anything, John?"

Isaac's lips seemed to swell through the Plexiglas. "No," John said. It was a ludicrous sight. Laughable. The old "Commish" and the new with a glass wall between them. "You should have taken better care of me, Isaac. You were my First Dep . . . now go away. You bring a man bad luck."

John walked out of the cubicle. The screws would remember that Isaac the Brave had summoned him from block 5, and they'd torment John for it. He wouldn't be able to flip through his bankbooks in peace.

236

He heard a strange, soft pluck from the roof over block 5. It couldn't be anything like a drizzle. The house gang would have gone ape by now, cursing, mopping floors with the blankets they swiped from the cells, measuring the leakage, so they could put garbage cans under the worst holes. White puffs trickled down from the roof. You could catch them with a finger. Mother Mary, it was the first snow of autumn. John touched the white puffs to his face. November snow was godly snow. The flakes could heal. *Simon Dedalus. Leopold Bloom.* What more could a man need? John patted the little books in his pocket. Then he winked at the screw behind him and waltzed back into his cell.

JEROME CHARYN'S

**"BRILLIANTLY CONCEIVED
CRIME-AND-PUNISHMENT TRILOGY"**
Time

MARILYN THE WILD

**"One of the best tough detective novels . . . brilliant and
engrossing, true to the madness of the times, and absolute
fun to read."**

Los Angeles Times

 AVON/32409/$1.75

BLUE EYES

**"Packed with manic energy, peopled with bizarre characters
and outrageous situations, written with a sense of humor."**
Chicago Sun-Times

 AVON/31500/$1.75

THE EDUCATION OF
PATRICK SILVER

"A lead-in-yer-liver cop story."
Boston Globe

 AVON/53603/$2.75

In these three novels, Jerome Charyn masterfully evokes a
cityscape of depravity and retribution on both sides of the
law and creates characters that Herbert Gold, writing in the
Los Angeles Times, described as ". . . larger than life and
full of life, totally incredible and totally believable. . . .
A special, important and precious novelist . . . these books
constitute the highest kind of novelist's art."

JC 11-80

GREAT READING
FROM AVON 🔺 BOOKS

**"AN AMAZEMENT . . . ENCHANTING
. . . ELECTRIFYING."**
The New York Times

**"MAY BE A CLASSIC FOR READERS
NOT YET BORN."**
Philadelphia Inquirer

"TO READ IT IS TO FLY"
People Magazine

**THE NATIONALLY ACCLAIMED NOVEL BY
WILLIAM WHARTON**

NOW AN AVON ◆ PAPERBACK 47282 $2.50